I0550414

Cornerstone:
The Sazh

Book Four of the Cornerstone Series

by

K.A. Krisko

TULK
TALES

Publisher

First Edition
ISBN-13: 978-1-7320213-6-5

Cover art and design by

Viper Cider
Graphics

VC

Viper Cider

Visit my web page at:
Kakrisko.com

Table of Contents

CHAPTER ONE

"Just call me Jason," Jason Japert said, extending a hand. His invitation to familiarity was accompanied by what Lorcas took to be a smug smile.

Lorcas grimaced internally, but he shook hands. Jason settled himself behind the table on the opposite side of the booth. The meeting was taking place in a quiet cafe on the very edge of Rook's territory, where Lorcas felt relatively safe but also where he was unapt to be recognized by any of the Fell Ken. It was enough of a neutral zone for Japert to feel safe as well, if he had checked with anyone beforehand about its location.

"Detective Japert," Lorcas replied formally, ignoring Jason's request. He wasn't interested in being friendly. "Understand that I'm taking a risk."

Jason sobered. "I appreciate that, I appreciate that." He clasped both hands in front of him on top of the table. "I came alone, as you requested. I am armed, but I'll keep my hands where you can see them. I have no reason to harm you. I'm not a Knight or any other enemy of yours; I'm a law enforcement officer. I'm neutral. My integrity is important to me."

Lorcas leaned back a little and glanced around the cafe. The main reason he disliked Japert was because through diligent investigation the detective had gotten a little too close to the truth. But now he needed that skill.

A waitress approached, and Japert ordered a coffee and a lunch special. Lorcas skipped the coffee in favor of water, but he ordered the special as well. He didn't know enough about the restaurant to have a favorite or usual meal.

When the coffee arrived Jason stirred it slowly, although he hadn't added any milk or sugar. "You're going to have to fill me in and give me some solid background on your organization," he said. "That's part of the deal. Plus, I don't know exactly what you need from me and I won't be able to help you if I don't have the truth."

"I'm sure you know a lot of it by now," Lorcas said. "You were with Terry Bell when we picked up the books for Jack, so I know you've been hanging around her. I'm sure she's told you most of it."

Jason sat back and quit stirring the coffee. "Let's get one thing out of the way. I'm not hanging around with Terry Bell, not in the way you mean. I'm a married man with two kids, and like I said, my integrity is important to me. Granted, we're separated right now, because my wife thinks I'm nuts after what I think I saw a year ago, but I'm hoping to correct that at some point in the future. It's just that Terry is one of the only people I can talk to about what I saw. Jack Bright and his group aren't any more open to me than you are. I'm nobody's friend. But Terry isn't one of your Fell Ken people and she's not really one of the Knights either, and I don't suspect her of being the perpetrator of any particular heinous crime. That's what we've got in common. But she doesn't know enough about what's going on between the two families, or groups, or whatever they are, to give me a solid background, so I'm going to have to hear it from you."

Lorcas considered Jason for a minute. He knew from experience that the detective could seem to be friendly and gullible, but then come to a shrewd conclusion. But Jason sounded sincere, and he'd already made the decision to trust him.

The waitress set down their plates, and there was a minute of silence as they both prepared their food. Lorcas took a bite and watched while Jason doused his fries completely in ketchup.

"It's a long story, but I'll try to be as brief as I can," he began. "It's going to sound ridiculous, but you don't have to believe anything I'm going to say. All you need to accept is that the Fell Ken and the Knights believe it."

Jason nodded. "I'm glad you realize that. I did see something that I can't explain, but I'm not willing to abandon everything I know about the earth and life and science and jump into your belief system whole-hog." He paused for a bite. "Why don't you start with the history of this feud between you and Jack Bright? When did this all begin?"

"Between me and Jack? Three years ago, but that's only the personal part. The feud, as you put it, goes back a lot longer than the lives of the two of us," Lorcas said. "It started hundreds, if not thousands, of years ago. We don't know when Rook, the entity you saw, arrived here, or where he came from, or whether perhaps he evolved here on earth. Jack's people think he's an alien, but a friend of mine says he came from the 'deep, dark foundations of the world', whatever that means. But the most important part for us started about 600 years ago, with his previous incarnation."

"Incarnation?" Jason scoffed. "You make it sound like it gets reincarnated every once in a while."

"Not exactly, but kind of. Anyway, about 600 years ago, there was this guy named Zumar. His family had moved to somewhere on the northeastern Adriatic coast, into what would be Croatia, coming down from the north from what was Bohemia, now in the Czech Republic."

"Wait, is this supposedly the same Zumar who lives up at Cliffview now?" Jason interrupted. "Terry's told me about him."

"Yes. Remember, I told you that you don't have to believe it. Just understand that this is our history and it's where we're coming from. His father was a merchant catering to what was the very beginning of the middle class, other merchants and similar people who were beginning to want what the rich people had and who had enough money to buy a few things now and then. He sent Zumar back up north to set up some new trade routes and rekindle some connections. But Zumar is kind of a smart-ass, and he apparently pulled a shady deal or otherwise crossed the people he was supposed to be dealing with."

Jason laughed. "Guess there were smart-asses 600 years ago too, huh?"

"Yeah, not so funny, though, is that these guys caught Zumar and beat him to death. They were craftsmen who were employed by some local lord to help build a fortified residence, so they dumped his body in a hole that had been dug for the foundation and the next day they covered it over with a big rock that had been cut as the cornerstone. That cornerstone happened to contain the spirit, or soul, or whatever you want to call it, of the entity we call Rook."

4

"Okay, Zumar's body was dumped under a magic medieval rock. How does this relate to your two families?"

"I'm getting there. Rook was trapped in the rock and needed help to be able to move out and grow stronger. He managed to salvage Zumar's spirit, and for the next hundred-plus years, Rook's spirit and Zumar's spirit just kind of hung out in the rock, while families came and went and the construction got added to and built into a real castle. At some point it was abandoned and partially fell down. But then about 450 years ago, a new lord obtained the property and went about rebuilding it. And when he moved his extended family in, they brought along an adviser, an alchemist whose name was Paracel."

"Parra..." Jason repeated.

"PAHR-atz-el," Lorcas said, putting the emphasis on the first syllable. "Others have made him out to be kind of stupid, but I think that's a mistaken impression, and Rook thought he was an appropriate ally. Zumar went out and introduced himself to Paracel in the form of a ghost, not much more than a shadow. Paracel was willing to believe he was having important, divinely-inspired visions, especially as time went by and Zumar passed on requests from Rook that resulted in increases in Paracel's power when they were accomplished. Rook's strength began to grow and he began to be able to move around through the stones of the castle, inhabiting them, if you will, and Paracel began to rise in his family's esteem because of the things he seemed to be able to do. He obtained a number of items with special powers he used to impress people, and he seemed to have conversations with spirits who would do his bidding."

"Uh-huh," Jason said. "So this alchemist basically became a wizard in the eyes of this noble family, kind of a Merlin. Or maybe a Rasputin."

Lorcas nodded. "This family believed in an old kind of nature-based religion and it didn't seem strange to them that a demi-god or spirit would favor them. Paracel seemed to be ageless, and several generations of this family grew up with him. But somewhere along the way part of the family converted to Christianity, which was happening in that area at the time, and they began to view Rook as a demon or as a familiar to Paracel's witchcraft. Eventually things came to a head and the Christian part of the family sacked the castle and killed most of the other side in a kind of Crusade. A few of them escaped, and those people became the Fell Ken, so-called by the rest of the family as an insult. It's a translation into English that basically means the 'ones who know the bad side'. And the Christian group became the Knights, or Koen as we call them, the Knights of Earth Natural. Implying that Rook is unnatural."

"Ah-ha," Jason said with a grin. "So there's the origin of the family feud, and your name, incidentally. And that's continued to this day? Jack's on one side and you're on the other. You and Jack Bright are distantly related, then. How did you all end up here?"

"The few remaining Fell Ken hid after the castle was sacked. Rook and Zumar's spirits retreated back into the Cornerstone. The Knights thought they'd killed the demon, but the Fell Ken knew better, although Paracel had been murdered, or died of old age when Rook withdrew. The survivors had a continuing low-level connection to Rook and his powers. Eventually their descendants rescued the Cornerstone and hid it, and about 150 years ago they brought it to this country for safe-keeping, along with a bunch of other items

6

they'd located and regained over the years. Once they were here, the Fell Ken increased quietly, but the Knights were always looking for them to re-appear somewhere. I think some of them suspected Rook wasn't completely gone. The Knights obtained items that had belonged to Paracel, as well as parts of the castle when they could, so they'd be alerted if any Fell Ken came looking for them. Everything just kind of went along that way until my family came along. And for some reason Rook decided I was the one to start rebuilding, and Zumar contacted me."

Jason ate a few fries thoughtfully. "The 'Chosen One'."

"Not so much," Lorcas said wryly. "Perry said I'm just in the right place at the right time and that I have a specific role to fulfill." Lorcas remembered Perry scolding him about that specific idea, cautioning him not to think he was special. "Whatever the reason, I started the rebuilding with the help of the local Fell Ken who'd been guarding the Cornerstone for generations. Jack Bright and the local Knights figured it out, partly because I fell into their trap of seeking Fell Ken items that they owned. They were in this area because my father had made an attempt to awaken Rook before me and his activities drew their attention, although they didn't know specifically where the Cornerstone was. Once they realized what was happening and where, they went about trying to stop us. They made the first move against us three years ago. That was the explosion that brought down what we'd built up to that point and killed a bunch of the Fell Ken, including my advisers Perry and Delva and incidentally my mother. Since then, we've been stumbling along without the knowledge of the previous generations, much of which hadn't yet been passed along, and the feud with Jack Bright and the Koen has become more serious."

"Okay," Japert said. He paused thoughtfully. "You know, I think you're basically a good guy. You've got yourself wrapped up in something that's not totally your own doing, a thing you inherited through no fault of your own. I've told you this before. Now I've got a little more understanding of how this thing goes way back. Jack Bright was personally responsible for a bunch of deaths, or at least he ordered the hits. Now you, I think you might've been peripherally involved with the disappearances of Korrin Bright and Robert Dover, but I don't think you did it yourself. And Kyle Bright, well, that was some sort of weird accident."

Lorcas didn't answer. He was a bit more responsible for Korrin's death than Jason suspected, but he wasn't going to try to explain that whole incident. Bob Dover's death had been an accident, though he'd helped cover it up.

"But I still don't understand what you need me for," Jason said, pushing his plate to the side, "or why this is so secret-squirrel from your own people."

"You were here during the rising event," Lorcas said. "What did you think was going on there?"

Jason looked uncomfortable. "I don't know. I don't have a very complete memory of that whole thing. I was attacked and drugged, and when I came to, all I remember is chaos. I remember seeing Terry and running that way. It seemed like there was an earthquake or some kind of volcanic event. I remember that the whole castle seemed to have gotten a lot bigger all at once. And I saw something up near the top, but I don't know what it was. The further in the past it gets, the less it seems like most of what I saw was real. It was drug-induced hallucination."

Of course, that was the most logical way to look at things, Lorcas thought. Japert had indeed been drugged to keep him out of the way, and given Marek's history with such attempts, he was lucky he'd survived.

"We call that event the Rising," Lorcas explained. "You don't need to know the details, but there's a lot of confusion about what was supposed to happen, a lot of conflicting information in various books and tracts, and nobody's really sure who deceived whom about the procedure. Recently I've found out that Paracel was likely trying to create a device to reduce Rook's power. He wrote about the procedure in a book that the Knights had and that Jack managed to decode. Jack sent Terry to try and activate the device, but what happened instead was the sudden leap forward in development. Rook told me it was all a ruse that he and Paracel created to fool the Knights, but that doesn't actually seem likely. It's more likely that when we built this castle, Rook changed the mechanism for his own needs."

"Interesting. Why would Paracel want to do that? I thought they were good buddies."

"So did I. It seems that Paracel saw something in Rook he didn't like. He changed his mind and tried to figure out how to get rid of Rook. I still don't know exactly why, but I'm beginning to feel like I need to find out. And Rook is none too pleased that I've made contact with this friend I mentioned earlier, a woman called Mira. In fact, Rook pretty much destroyed the road up to Cliffview and accused me of betraying him."

"I was wondering about that," Jason said. "News said it was seismic activity, but given the area, I had my suspicions that it had something to do with you and Jack Bright."

They both paused as the waitress came by to refill coffee and water. Jason stirred his slowly again. "Who is this Mira to you?" he asked casually.

Lorcas hesitated. Jason didn't need to know all the details. "She's one of what Paracel referred to as the Allies. There are four of them. She's the Water Ally, also called the Wellspring."

"Allies of what?" Jason asked in a puzzled tone.

"Specifically of the Fell Ken and not Rook. They are entities or powers Paracel called upon or used as part of his earth-magic. There's an item associated with each of them as well, an Object of Power. I don't know much about any of them except Mira, and I don't think you need to know much more than that, either. It's not relevant."

"You never know," Jason said, "but I'll accept that for now. You can fill me in later if it turns out I do need that info."

"Now we're getting to what I need you for," Lorcas said. "To be brief, Rook partnered with a twelve-year-old boy to try to overthrow the Entourage, which includes me, possibly because he felt betrayed and wanted someone he could mold himself. This boy's parents are missing, but they apparently went along with the plan. We can't figure out how this happened so quickly or what exactly could have convinced them to do this, since it's a betrayal of the Fell Ken's chosen system of organization, not just me but also Tondra, Tomash, and the community. The boy's been, shall we say, temporarily removed from the picture - don't worry, he's alive - but we can't even find his parents to figure out what happened. And now Zumar - the one who's 600 years old - has apparently decided to die for real. It seems like a strange time for him to do that. Some of us suspect there might be someone inside the Fell Ken, maybe someone with ties to the other side of the family, who is trying to separate me from Rook and remove or cast suspicion on members of the Entourage."

10

Jason leaned forward, resting his elbows on the table. "And you can't trust anyone now. Whoever is doing this, they have to be pretty well-respected and well-placed in the Fell Ken or nobody would listen to them. You think they convinced this boy's parents that their kid should replace Rook's chosen buddies. And then the parents conveniently go missing so you can't ask them about it. Then the other person who has the closest ties to Rook suddenly ups and kills himself. Also convenient."

"Yes. So is this all a coincidence or is something going on? I'm not an investigator and we don't have anyone who is. There are a few Fell Ken on the Seaside Heights police force, but they're not really detectives. And even if I did have enough time to do an investigation on my own, it's doubtful the guilty party, if there is one, would admit anything to me."

"Also, it can be helpful to have outside eyes," Jason agreed. He tapped his fingers on the table, thinking. "You know I've been on medical leave off and on during the last year."

"I may be able to find out what kind of drugs were used on you if you're still suffering the effects and see if there's an antidote. And I may have some influence over what happens as Rook moves south and east towards your area. You've seen what he can do."

"You're saying you'll protect my family," Jason said. He sat back with a slight sneer. "That's approaching blackmail: you do this for us or we'll let Rook destroy your house."

"I didn't mean it that way," Lorcas said. "It was just an offer."

"Huh." Japert grabbed a toothpick from a dispenser on the table and chewed on it for a minute. "Here's the other question: you say you want to find out who, or if, there's some person inside the Fell Ken who's trying to take out the Entourage and separate you from Rook. But I also read between the lines when you mentioned Paracel. You're having second thoughts about being associated with this thing, which I think is admirable. Maybe your 'friend' Mira believes something along those lines, too, which is why Rook thinks you're betraying him. So do you really want to re-connect with Rook?"

The waitress came with the check, and Lorcas waited until she left to continue. It gave him a minute to collect his thoughts.

"I don't know," he said honestly. "There are some questions I need to answer for myself. I'm not asking you to have anything to do with that. I'm not asking you to believe what I believe. All I'm asking is for you to investigate the human beings with an outside eye, as you put it, and see if you can give us some likely suspects."

""Us?"" Jason asked. "Is there an "us"?"

"Right now, there's just me," Lorcas admitted. "Tondra made the suggestion to contact you in a kind of off-hand manner a while ago, but I haven't brought it up since."

"Good," Jason said. "If you can't trust anybody, then you can't trust anybody. Are you willing to accept what I find?"

"I can't guarantee that I'll act on anything that you find," Lorcas said, "at least, not in a way you'd understand."

There was a long pause, but finally Jason nodded. "I'm interested. I like this kind of stuff, I'm bored, and I'm curious about what's going on up there. And I'd appreciate you looking into an antidote for me. But we'll have to come up with some story to get the cooperation of the rest of the Fell Ken."

"I've got some ideas," Lorcas said. "After seeing what you saw at the Rising and thinking it over for a while, you've decided to believe in Rook and you've also decided that the Fell Ken are the side to be on. There's precedent for that: Alan, Tondra's husband, is not Fell Ken or Knight, but he's risen into a powerful position in the organization. And I can say that with Zumar gone we need someone who can act as a bodyguard for me and Tomash, and with your background you'll make a good fit."

"Isn't your rock dragon going to have an issue with me? Not that I believe in it."

Lorcas smiled for the first time. "He's not a dragon, despite what you may think you saw. I think your mind just filled in the gaps with something familiar. But I'm pretty sure Rook won't do anything to you without my request. We still have a strong relationship and I'm still important to his development."

"Just don't get on your wrong side, huh?" Jason replied.

"I'm not going to feed you to Rook," Lorcas said. "Not on purpose, anyway."

"Okay," Jason said with a grimace. "Anybody who might suspect what I'm there for? Anybody who could be an issue?"

Lorcas thought for a moment. "Tondra. She's the one who mentioned it in the first place, and she's not going to have forgotten that. She's smart and suspicious. But if she does guess, we can bring her in on it. I'm ninety-nine-percent sure it isn't her who's the bad guy. I'm sure it's no one in the Entourage, but we still shouldn't tell anyone except Tondra and maybe Alan. There are some issues with the others."

"Like what? Tell me what you know," Jason said.

"Well, Zumar's dead, or at least maybe dead. Raine has made some questionable decisions in the past, and while I don't think she's the one, she might not be totally trustworthy. In fact, she cooperated with Jack Bright recently in order to accomplish something for herself. And Tomash has another issue, one that has to do with the kid I told you about earlier, Dirk. Some of Dirk's energy was used to heal Tomash from the poison he received when he was stabbed, and we don't know what effect that will have on him yet."

"Stabbed by Don Bright, who's now a fugitive," Jason mused. "I didn't realize he'd been poisoned."

"No, we've kept a few things quiet," Lorcas said. "We prefer to deal with our business between ourselves."

"The Hatfields and McCoys, taking a life for a life through the generations, going back 450 years." Jason shook his head. "I have to think about this. I know I'll be stepping into some sort of danger, and I'm not that much of an adrenalin junkie. But I'm curious. Give me a few days. Don't contact me; I don't want it to be easy for people to figure out we've been in touch. If I decide to do this thing, I'll show up at your house and we'll go from there."

"All right," Lorcas agreed. "I'll get your lunch."

They shook hands again. Jason slid out of the booth and left the cafe. Lorcas paid the tab and loitered for a few minutes, waiting until he was sure Jason was well out of the area. Then he walked quickly to his car, on alert because of how close he was to the edge of Rook's influence. He rarely went anywhere by himself anymore, and he hadn't been outside Rook's sphere in several years.

Safe in his car, he wavered. The freedom was appealing. He had been watched, guarded, and mentally encroached upon for a long time. Now he was making a questionable move, one that might not meet the approval of the Fell Ken. He could just drive off, leave the area completely, leave Rook and Cliffview Estates behind. He considered for a minute, but it wasn't a realistic idea. He didn't have any means of support and he knew he'd suffer if he left Rook's influence completely. He'd experienced that before, and the grief, guilt, and horror of his situation had been almost more than he could bear. Besides, he had obligations, and he didn't want to betray his friends and colleagues.

But it couldn't hurt to take the long way home. He put the car in gear and headed west and south. Past the town's limits, the countryside turned to green agricultural and grazing lots, similar to the landscape around Lafayette. The road wound gently, rising through the fields and scattered farm communities toward the more heavily-treed coast.

At a 'T' intersection past the fields in the forest, Lorcas chose to turn south. There were glimpses of open sky through the trees to his right and he knew he was close to the oceanside cliffs. The road here was narrow, shadowed by firs and spruces. The land to his left rose into sharp hills and occasional cliffs.

He tuned into his own mind from time to time, checking to see if he was experiencing any issues from his separation from Rook, but to his surprise he didn't feel different. He began to really enjoy his drive. The area was isolated, probably inhospitable to farming or ranching and without fresh water sources to encourage settlement. It might have been logged in the past, he thought, as he occasionally passed openings in the forest. He had never been through there before or even heard anything about the stretch of road. The GPS on his dashboard didn't show it, nor did it classify the surrounding property as 'park' or 'forest', so he assumed it must be privately owned, though he saw no signs.

Eventually he figured he should turn around. He began to look for a turn-off or pullout, but there weren't any, and despite the infrequent cars coming the other way, he was hesitant to try to pull a U-turn in the middle of the narrow road where no one could see him well from around the corners.

Finally, he noticed a dirt track leading off to the left. He slowed to take a look at it; it didn't seem to be too muddy and appeared well-maintained. There was no 'No Trespassing' sign or other designation. It appeared to rise gently, and Lorcas considered that it might take him to a viewpoint as well as a good turn-around.

He followed the track up through the woods, feeling suddenly slightly on alert. He passed a low stone wall on either side, but still no sign.

A few hundred yards further, the road left the heavy forest and crested an open hill. Lorcas slowed quickly. Beyond were copses and groves laid out over a series of rolling hills, basking in bright sun. Ahead of him and just to the side was what appeared to be a small stone church or chapel. And, he noted, there was something else.

He pulled over in front of the chapel and stepped out cautiously. Everything was silent except for a buzzing in his ears, or perhaps in his mind. Between him and the building was a rock.

He walked slowly over to it and stood before it. It looked almost exactly like the Cornerstone. It was the same size, shape, and color. Carefully he bent and placed a hand on it. He felt an almost electric buzz.

He stood quickly, an unaccounted dread creeping into his mind. He walked slowly towards the chapel. He paused in front of the heavy wooden door, then laid a hand on the iron lever.

It did not move, but as Lorcas looked at the iron plate upon which the lever was mounted, he noticed a familiar shape. He pulled the Key on its chain off from around his neck. It fit into the odd-shaped keyhole and turned easily, with a well-oiled 'thunk'. He draped the chain over his neck again and tried the lever once more. It moved with a metallic clank, and the door swung open inward.

He stepped into the cool, shadowed interior. It was not completely dark; there were windows all around the upper walls, covered with rippling clear glass rather than stained-glass. To his immediate right was a small table with a white cloth, a candelabra, and a guest book on it. Other than that, it was empty, except that directly ahead at the far end was a stone stage. It was clean and well-kept.

Lorcas moved forward slowly. The dimensions were eerily familiar. He knew the number of steps it took to traverse the chapel in the castle, and this one matched foot-for-foot.

He could see no designation or icon telling him what denomination of church it might be. There were empty niches around the sides, nothing behind the stage but an off-center door that would lead, he knew, to the steeple. He stepped carefully up onto the stage, and then stopped cold.

Directly in front of the dais was a hollow in the stone of the stage. He went down on one knee, his heart beating, and ran his fingers around it. It was in the shape of a thick, chunky cross, and he was sure it was the same size as the depression in the Keep that accepted one of the four stones they had found in Perry's basement.

His neck prickling, he stood quickly and strode to one of the sides. There was another depression there, the correct size and shape to accept another stone. The third one was also there, in the center of the opposite side. Lorcas hurried to the door he'd come in. At first, he didn't see a hollow there; the door was in the center of that wall. But then he found it, out of the way under the table where no one would twist an ankle stepping in it. All four of them were there, the correct sizes, shapes, and depth.

"What is this place?" Lorcas muttered to himself. He backed quickly out the door and slammed it shut behind him. Outside he hurried past the stone, trying not to look at it, and threw himself into his car. He jammed it in gear, made a hasty circle, and headed back down the dirt track. All sorts of possibilities flowed through his mind, and he didn't like any of them.

CHAPTER TWO

Lorcas parked the Subaru in his driveway and retrieved a bag with a few groceries, his excuse for going out, from the passenger-side seat. Inside he threw the bag on the kitchen counter and paced in the living room. He needed to talk to someone about what he'd found. In the past he would've gone directly to Zumar, put up with some jibes and roundabout hints, and eventually extracted any information that might be relevant. Even if Zumar didn't know the specific answers to his questions, he could often guess at a direction to go or make a nebulous connection that Lorcas hadn't thought about. But that was no longer an option.

Raine was perhaps the next most logical, given that she had the education in Fell Ken history that many of the rest of them were lacking, as well as access to Delva's books and papers. But he was wary of contacting her; besides her questionable decision regarding Jack, Rook had been unhappy with her interference and many in the Fell Ken felt they'd been used without their knowledge or permission in the unauthorized 'Turning' ritual Raine had led at Zumar's memorial service. She occasionally lurked around the castle, checking to see if the spell had worked, but usually only dared appear for a brief period. The rest of the time she spent in Seaside Heights, where, Tondra had told him, she was attempting to resurrect Delva's coven. But people were hesitant to become involved with her, and Lorcas dismissed the idea of contacting her until he'd exhausted other options.

His best bet, then, was Tondra. He threw himself down on the couch and grabbed his laptop to gather as much information as he could before going to her. She would expect him to have done some research. A quick look at online maps showed him what his GPS unit had shown: an area of the coast with no settlements, not designated as park, forest, or open space. At least the road showed up, but he could find no official road number or name. He checked the satellite view and found the little church, but the zoom-in was limited and there was no street-level view. The only other constructions in the area were a few buildings not far from the church but up a different road and further inland. They were gathered in a group in a shallow valley with a large building occupying the central point. Once again, Lorcas could find no designation or address there.

He tried a few searches on terms such as 'local churches' and 'historic church buildings' but got nothing that seemed relevant. Finally, he set the laptop aside and walked down past Tomash's house to Tondra and Alan's.

The house was silent and no one answered his knock. Frustrated, he turned to the castle. He didn't go there much anymore, for more than one reason. But he had left a number of books up in his top-floor office, ones he had obtained and collected outside of his father's library and hadn't collated yet, and he wanted to retrieve a couple of them to see if they referenced other cornerstones or similar rocks besides the ones he had found to build the original chapel.

He trudged over the bridge where Dirk had challenged him, up to the door into the Banquet Hall, and from there began the long journey to the top.

"We really ought to add elevators, Rook," he grumbled. "At least escalators. I'm sure you could do it." Rook, of course, did not answer him, although he felt a distant twitch in his mind. Rook had not been in evidence lately, and Lorcas didn't know what he was doing or where he was spending his time.

When he reached the upper floors, he paused. He told himself it was to catch his breath after the multiple flights of stairs, but deep within he knew he was dreading the last part of the trek. Finally, he took a deep breath and walked quietly through the Keep to the door that opened onto the King's Garden.

He crossed the garden, still green and growing despite now being confined to the rooftop. He detoured to arrive at the eastern end of the chapel rather than the northern side, gently pressed the latch, and pushed the door open slowly.

Tomash looked up at him as he stepped inside. Tomash was sitting on a folding chair, his elbows on his thighs, some twenty feet from Zumar's crypt. The crypt lid had been pushed back so a sliver of dark interior was visible. Late afternoon sun filtered down the western stairwell through the water-themed stained-glass windows in shades of blue and gray, diluted by the southern windows' yellows and reds. A shaft illuminated Tomash's blond hair, imbuing it with a ruddy hue that reminded Lorcas unnervingly of Dirk as he stood on the bridge above the roiling fires of the crevasse.

Tomash spent every day sitting on that chair staring at Zumar's crypt. He had been there since shortly after the memorial, when Raine had suggested that the crypt be moved from the old Keep to the chapel to take advantage of the 'concentration of power' she felt was there. He only left to eat and sleep. Lorcas had not seen him read, use a phone or computer, or do anything else. He simply sat and stared. So far, there had been no indication that Raine's attempt to 'turn the wheel' and reposition Zumar on the circle of life and death had worked. Zumar still lay within, quiet and still, although there was at least no indication that he was beginning to decay.

"Hey, Tomash," Lorcas said as casually as he could muster. He hugged the southern wall of the chapel, away from Zumar's open crypt and behind Tomash's chair. He did not really want to get a glimpse of Zumar's pallid face. "Just going to grab a couple of books. Any change?"

"No," Tomash said. He returned to his watchful posture.

"You don't happen to know where Tondra is, do you?"

Tomash shook his head, and Lorcas trotted up the stairs to his office and grabbed the books. He paused for a moment to look out over the sea. It was misty as usual at Cliffview, but clear enough for him to just barely make out the top of the tower between swells. He wanted to talk to Mira, but he was fairly sure she wouldn't be able to give him any insight into the new stone. He was more interested in getting her take on Raine's ceremony and the possibility of actually raising Zumar. He felt as though his grieving for Zumar was on hold until he knew for sure that the Messenger wasn't coming back.

As he made his way back through the chapel, Tomash sat up straighter and turned his gaze slowly from Zumar's crypt. "You know, I wasn't that sorry when I thought Dirk might take my place. I never really wanted to be anything but a normal person. Now I'm sitting here, alive because I was taken into the Fairy realm and healed with the energy of a twelve-year-old sorcerer's apprentice who's doomed to wander in some alternate reality, staring at a dead six-hundred-year-old man who was formerly alive because a rock wraith decided to reincarnate him, waiting for him to be revived by the time-turning spell of a suicidal teenage ghost."

Lorcas struggled to find a reply, but failed. Instead, he stood awkwardly, balancing the ancient books on one arm.

"Don't you ever just want to be a normal person?" Tomash continued. "Don't you ever wish none of the last three years happened? All the death, the stress, the uncertainty, not really understanding where we're heading or what we're doing, or why it's us that are doing it. Sometimes I wish Rook had never appeared. Though of course that would mean Zumar wouldn't have appeared, either." Tomash shrugged and looked down. "I guess that's basically blasphemy around here. The rest of the Fell Ken would have a fit if they heard the person who's supposed to be their King saying this."

"I don't know, I'm sure others have doubts as well," Lorcas said carefully. "Besides, maybe you're still feeling the effects of the poison Don stuck into you. Who knows, maybe one of the things it does is create doubt. That's not your fault."

Tomash shook his head. "I don't think so. I just keep thinking back over the last few years and what's happened. I'm not a leader. Tondra's better at it than I am, always has been. I feel like a fake, like people think I'm going to be able to do something in the future that I won't ever be able to do."

Lorcas balanced the books on the edge of Zumar's crypt without looking down into it. He'd never heard Tomash express doubt before. The two of them had been friends for several years now, hunting through the depths of Rook's tunnels together, but they'd never really talked about the future or about their roles in the Fell Ken organization. In fact, this was the most Lorcas had heard Tomash talk at all since his recovery.

"I get it. I mean, I've been just kind of stumbling forward for the last three years. I never know what I'm supposed to be doing. It all just happens and then I have to deal with it. I wish Perry and Delva were still here all the time. I know a lot more than I did, but it's not enough. There are still big gaps in my knowledge, and I know that Rook has misled me a bunch of times. For that matter, so did Zumar, maybe even more than Rook. What does the end-point of what we're doing look like? I have to admit I don't know. And I'm supposed to be the guide, the main conduit between the Fell Ken and Rook."

Tomash smiled slightly, the first time Lorcas had seen him smile since before he'd been stabbed. "I'm glad to know I'm not the only one with a little Impostor Syndrome. I suppose we shouldn't be talking this way right in the middle of Rook's castle."

"No, probably not. You could come hang at my house any time, you know. It's a lot warmer and more comfortable than sitting here."

Tomash turned to the crypt. "I know. I just feel like I need to be here if Zumar does come back. I won't sit here forever. Maybe just a few more days. Just to be sure."

Lorcas sighed. It had already been too long. Raine's ritual should have worked within a day or two. But he didn't know what to do about it. Tomash had to work through whatever was going on in his brain. Hopefully eventually he would give up and come down from the castle, and they could shut the lid of the crypt and go on, as Alan had urged before.

"Okay, Tomash. I gotta go take a look at these books. I'll see you later."

Tomash sank back into his usual position on the folding chair and lapsed into silence. Lorcas pushed open the door next to the crypt and headed across the King's Garden.

As he exited the castle at the bottom, he saw Tondra's SUV pull up in front of her house. Alan didn't seem to be with her.

"Hello, Lorcas," Tondra greeted him as he walked up, then frowned a bit. "You weren't up in the castle, were you?"

"Just getting a couple of books," Lorcas replied, showing her the volumes.

"Is Tomash up there?"

"Of course."

"Ugh." Tondra slumped. "He needs to stop this."

"I think he needs to work through whatever's going on in his head," Lorcas said. "I know he feels bad about Zumar and Dirk and remember, he's still recovering. But I think he'll come around." For the first time, he actually felt like that might be true.

"He at least needs to come down and eat dinner," Tondra said. "I'll run up there and get him."

"Hang on a minute," Lorcas said. "I need to talk to you about something."

Tondra raised her eyebrows. "Come on in while I put the groceries away."

Lorcas followed her into the house. "Is Alan here? I can explain to both of you at once."

"No," Tondra said shortly. "Just tell me. I'll decide whether to tell Alan later."

Lorcas shrugged. He'd noticed what seemed to be some awkwardness between Tondra and Alan lately, since Zumar's memorial, but he figured it really wasn't any of his business.

"You know that today I decided to take a run into town to pick up a few things," he began.

"Yes," Tondra said. "I could have picked them up for you."

"I know, but I wanted to get out of here for a change," Lorcas said.

"I don't blame you. I know you've been stuck here a lot."

"So after I picked up my stuff, I decided to take a drive. It was a real nice sunny day down there, and I thought I would be pretty safe in my car."

"Probably," Tondra agreed. "I don't think the Knights have been lurking around waiting for a chance to assassinate you lately. There's kind of a lull in the hostilities."

"Yeah. I drove out to the coast and down through the forest south of Copsberg and Foreston. I got on this little two-lane road. The area doesn't show up as park or forest land or anything like that on GPS, but there aren't any 'private property' signs either. You grew up around there, so I was hoping you might know something about it."

Tondra, who had been shelving the groceries, turned to face him. "Not much. I know approximately where you're talking about. There's nothing out there, no summerhouses or camps or coastal access. Cliffs on

26

one side, forest on the other. Why? Is something weird going on?"

Lorcas smiled tightly. "Not sure. When I decided I needed to start back I turned off on this dirt road to the east. It took me up to this little stone church on a hill. Still no signs of any kind, but it looks like it's been taken care of and may still be in use."

"Interesting. Did you try looking it up on a map?" Tondra asked.

"Yeah, I checked when I got home. The church shows on satellite view, but you can't zoom in on it and there's no address or label. The only other thing around there is a little collection of buildings a bit further down the road, all centered around one big stone structure, but I can't tell what that is, either."

Tondra narrowed her eyes. "I'm pretty sure there used to be a little monastery of some type down there. That might be what you're seeing. It would explain the church, although why it wouldn't be with the rest of the buildings, I don't know."

"I might," Lorcas said. "There's something else there, at the church. There's a cornerstone."

"What do you mean?" Tondra demanded, her voice alarmed.

"I mean a cornerstone," Lorcas repeated. "It looks pretty much exactly like our Cornerstone. It's sitting there right outside the church. It's not one of our building stones; we found all of those."

"Does it, you know, feel like anything?"

"Oh, yeah, when I put my hand on it, it was almost buzzing. But I didn't necessarily feel like I was in better contact with Rook. It was more just … Rook-like."

Tondra put her hands on her hips. "That is very strange. What was the church like? Did it seem connected to the stone or did it seem to be there by coincidence?"

"Very connected." Lorcas told her about his Key fitting the door and about finding the impressions in the stone floor. "There weren't any goblets or stained-glass or anything, but there were niches around the room and the window openings seemed to me to be the correct size to accept windows like ours."

"Is it some kind of copy?" Tondra mused. "Is someone trying to attract Rook's power by building what they imagine is a knock-off of our chapel?"

"Could be, but that doesn't explain how my Key fit exactly or the feeling I got from the cornerstone," Lorcas said. "What do you know about the monastery?"

"Not much," Tondra said. "I only vaguely remember that there was one in the area. We need to find out more about this."

"That's why I got these books," Lorcas said, gesturing to the volumes he'd balanced on the back of the couch. "If I recall correctly, these two talk about expansion plans. I stuck them up in the office because I never found them interesting. They just seemed to be discussing establishing offshoots in other countries 400 years ago. But now I'm wondering if there might be some clue in them to what's going on."

"That's as good a place to start as any," Tondra said. "I'm sorry I don't know anything more about that area off the top of my head. I never paid it much attention."

"I suppose I could ask Rook about it directly," Lorcas mused. "If he doesn't know about it, he might appreciate the information, and it he does know about it, it might serve to show him that I'm still in tune with what's going on in the area."

"I wouldn't, not right now," Tondra said quickly. "Let's try to figure things out on our own. It could be nothing, no need to bother Rook. Take a look at those books, and you might be able to access land records and figure out ownership of the monastery. I have some Fell Ken business I have to attend to or I'd help, but once I get a break, I might be able to pitch in and see what I can find, too."

Lorcas paused. "Let's not tell anyone else about this right now, okay, Tondra? I mean, besides Alan, if you want. I don't want the word getting around and maybe getting back to the Knights. We need the freedom to be able to explore a little bit without worrying about them popping up behind our backs."

"I get it," Tondra said grimly. "I'm glad you still feel like you can trust me. At least you and I know that it's not one or the other of us two. And I'll decide when to tell Alan, but not right now."

Although she didn't say it outright, Lorcas knew she was talking about the possibility of a spy or saboteur in the Fell Ken at Cliffview. As she closed the cabinets and he picked up his books to leave, he realized that she hadn't eliminated anybody else at all: not Raine, not Tomash, and not even Alan. And she obviously didn't want him to talk to Rook.

The news about the monastery brought a few new possibilities to light for Lorcas. Of course, there was the mystery of the Key, one of the Fell Ken Objects of Power, and where it had come from. Mira had hinted that it might be connected to a member of the Knights who had loyalties to the Fell Ken, possibly a monk. That would, of course, have been hundreds of years in the past, but perhaps stories or documentation might be maintained in a monastery connected to that person.

Lorcas set the books down on his coffee table and immediately realized that there were a couple more he should have picked up. Had he known about the monastery before going up there, he would have grabbed them. Now he would have to make another awkward trip past Tomash and Zumar's crypt.

He sighed. He wasn't going to trek back up there right away. Maybe he could time it for when Tomash was down for a meal or sleeping. In the meantime, he could read through the two books he'd brought down.

Since it was still a nice afternoon despite the ever-present Cliffview mist, he took a seat in the screened-in porch. He didn't use it much, but he kept it set up with a few chairs and a table. From there he could glance up at the castle every once in a while and keep track of comings and goings. He could only read a paragraph or two at a time anyway, since the books were in archaic hand-written script that taxed his brainpower.

Eventually he saw Tondra hike up the hill, and a few minutes later she and Tomash emerged. He snapped the book closed and tossed it on the side table. He paused just long enough outside the front door to be sure the two of them had entered Tondra's place, and to allow Alan, who had just arrived, to make his way from his truck to the door.

Then he hurried up the hill, over the bridge, and through the castle. This time he strode through the garden quickly and into the chapel's north door, then up the stairs. He threw a few books from the bookshelf onto the desk, looking for the ones he wanted. He selected a few, taking one he wasn't sure about so he wouldn't have to return a third time. Then he tucked them all into the crook of his arm in a stack and trotted back down the stairs.

He paused at the bottom of the flight despite himself. At this time of year, the lowering sun streamed through the western and southern windows, including the 'control panel', suffusing the interior of the chapel with gold and red. The gears in the control panel turned languidly, throwing spiraling shadows. The light played over the very edge of Zumar's crypt like waves on the ocean, twisting and flowing as though the beams were alive, tendrils of light worming their way into the interior of the crypt itself. Although he could not see inside, he imagined that the stained-glass-altered sun fell through the narrow slot between the lid and the side, maybe warming Zumar's body as he lay.

"Psst!"

Lorcas jumped and looked around. He was sure he'd heard someone whisper. But Tomash was not in the chapel, nor was anyone else.

"Over here!"

This time there was no denying it. Lorcas put the books down on the chair and moved toward the crypt. He leaned over hesitantly and looked inside.

Zumar still lay in the same position, arms crossed over his chest, full length upon his back. Lorcas stared at him, his heart thumping.

Zumar opened his eyes.

"Zumar! You're awake!" Lorcas exclaimed.

"I've BEEN awake," Zumar replied in exasperation, but he still didn't move. "Every time that window light hits me, I've been awake. Damn, it's hard to get you alone!"

"You've been waiting to get me alone? Just lying there? For how long?"

"A while. It doesn't matter. Remember, I did this for hundreds of years. We need to talk."

"Do you need help? Let's get you out of there," Lorcas said. He put a hand against the lid to give it a shove to make more room.

"No! No! I have to stay here. Where's Rook?"

"I don't know, not anywhere close," Lorcas said, "but I can call him!"

"No," Zumar repeated forcefully. "He can't know I'm awake. Neither can anyone else. You cannot tell anyone."

"Okay," Lorcas replied, puzzled. He turned suddenly as a distant sound alerted him to the door of the Keep closing. "Tomash is coming. What do we do?"

"Nothing," Zumar whispered. "I lie here for now. Come back when you're absolutely sure no one else will know, including Rook and Tomash, too. If anyone else is around, don't come. I'll wait. I'm good at waiting. At least I'm good at something," he added ruefully.

"I'll come back tonight when Tomash is in bed," Lorcas said hurriedly.

"That might not work, but if you do come, bring a candle or something with a flame," Zumar answered. "If you've got some Smokeweed, you can add that, too." Then he closed his eyes, and Lorcas backed quickly away from the crypt as Tomash walked into the chapel, holding most of a sandwich in one hand.

"Evening," Lorcas said, gathering his books from the chair. "Just picking up a few more books. You're not planning on staying up here all night, are you?"

"Maybe," Tomash said, arranging the folding chair a bit, "but probably not. Tondra will come kick me out if I stay too late."

"I'm sure she will," Lorcas said casually. "If you decide to come down earlier, stop by and grab a beer. I'll be there."

He headed for the Keep and the stairs down, taking them so fast that he almost missed his footing a few times. Zumar was alive, but he had to keep it a secret. What was going on? And what did Zumar need him, and only him, to know?

He waited impatiently for it to get dark, pacing first in his house and then in the screened-in porch. From time to time he paused, surveying the neighborhood, watching as the lights flicked off one by one. He saw Tomash make his way down the hill to his own house in mid-evening. The sounds of people talking on an evening walk, children's voices, car engines, garage doors, faded away until finally Cliffview was silent and asleep.

Lorcas made his way up to the castle in the dark, relying on his own knowledge of the route, the ambient light from a sliver of moon, and the porch lights of the homes below him. Inside the structure it was much darker and he used his pocket flashlight, keeping the beam pointed at the floor and away from windows and casements.

When he entered the chapel, he closed the door firmly behind him. He stood at the end of the crypt to light the candle he'd brought, as well as a pipe full of Smokeweed. When the flame steadied, he slipped the flashlight and lighter back in his pocket, sucked on the pipe, and approached the casket anxiously.

It was too dark for him to see inside through the sliver of space between the edge of the casket and the lid, which had been pushed aside at an angle. Using a drop of wax, he stuck the candle to the rim and gave the lid a few hard shoves. It ground back a few inches at a time.

Then he pulled the candle off and lowered it into the casket. The smoke from the pipe, which he had laid on the rim, flowed into the dark interior. The wavering flame lit Zumar's face from below the chin in unnerving relief. There was no movement, and Zumar's eyes remained closed. Lorcas began to wonder if he had somehow imagined the conversation that afternoon.

Zumar's eyes snapped open. For a brief moment they reflected the red and orange of the candle flame as though he burned with an internal fire. Then the flame flicked out, or rather, it seemed to Lorcas, it was sucked forward and extinguished.

Lorcas stood in the dark for a moment, then fumbled in his pocket for the lighter and re-lit the candle. As the light illuminated the casket again, Zumar sat up abruptly. He glanced around hurriedly before focusing on Lorcas.

"What did you do?" he demanded, slurring his words.

"Uh, I brought a candle, like you asked," Lorcas replied, confused.

"No," Zumar said, readjusting himself in the casket. He spoke a bit more clearly. "I mean, what did you do to revive me?"

"Oh. Nothing. I didn't do it, Raine did."

"Raine. Of course." Zumar ran a shaky hand across his brow.

"So what she did actually worked?" Lorcas asked. He found himself somewhat surprised, although things Raine had done had at least partially worked before.

"Yes, but no," Zumar said cryptically. "Do you know what she did?"

"I was there," Lorcas said. "I didn't know what she was planning. It was supposed to be a memorial ceremony, but she did some sort of ritual that involved fire and turning the wheel of time."

"Fire," Zumar repeated. "You invoked the Sazh."

"I didn't do it," Lorcas repeated, "and what the hell is the Sazh?"

"It's the Fire Ally," Zumar said. "Help me out of this thing."

34

Lorcas slid an arm around Zumar's back and part lifted, part dragged him out of the casket. Zumar's legs didn't seem to be working very well, so Lorcas sat him on the folding chair and crouched next to him, steadying him with a hand on his shoulder.

"I thought you didn't know anything about the Allies," Lorcas remarked.

Zumar stretched and rotated his neck. "I certainly know about this one now. You, or Raine anyway, probably thought the Fire Ally would be like Mira, a person or a being that exists on its own, that has its own body and mind. But it's not. It can only exist by inhabiting someone, and that someone is currently me."

Lorcas raised his eyebrows. "You're telling me that you're inhabited by some other entity, this Sazh?"

"Don't worry," Zumar said wryly. "I'm still me. But the Sazh gives me some other qualities, you might say. Unfortunately."

"Like what?" Lorcas asked, eying Zumar suspiciously. He now wasn't sure what he was talking to, or whether he was talking to more than one being.

"Do you remember the qualities of fire?" Zumar asked. "The ones we traditionally associate with it?"

Lorcas considered for a moment. "Fire is associated with candles, of course, with the smoke from the Smokeweed, and with red and orange. It's considered a masculine force, its direction is south, its season is summer. It's also associated with the Sword, with both curing and harming and with creating and destroying. That's why Raine used it in the ceremony."

"Think about some of the more obscure associations," Zumar urged.

Lorcas hesitated. "Truth and purity, as in burning clean, I guess."

"Yeah, that's the one." Zumar rubbed his eyes. "Truth. I've been inhabited by truth."

"Well, that shouldn't be a problem," Lorcas said with a combination of amusement and irritation, tempered only by his relief at seeing Zumar alive, "unless you mean you haven't been truthful in the past? Why would you have lied?"

Zumar glanced at him. "As for that, my loyalties lie with Rook, or at least they did. And I've told you a whole lot of the truth. There are a few things that I might've held back for my own reasons and my own safety. But now you've got to know what I know. For one thing, like it or not, I have to tell the truth. And the Sazh won't be satisfied and leave me alone until I tell it all."

"And if it does leave you alone?" Lorcas asked. "What will happen then?"

"Frankly, I don't know. You must know that I made the choice to go to my rest myself. I'm sure Rook told you that. He agreed to allow me to go, to release me. But my spirit didn't leave, because, well, we can discuss that when we have more time. And then Raine did this stupid ceremony and infected me with the Sazh. So yes, her ritual worked to invoke the Fire Ally. As far as reviving me, I never actually left. I tried, but it didn't work. And now I know, and now I don't necessarily feel like dying permanently anyway."

Lorcas sobered. "All right. Tell me more. I'm listening."

But Zumar stopped suddenly. "Rook absolutely can't know I'm awake," he hissed. "He will know I've got the Sazh, and he'll know that I know I didn't die. He'll know that I understand why."

"I won't tell him," Lorcas assured him. "I'm pretty sure I can keep him out of at least parts of my mind."

"But he's moving now!" Zumar said. He lurched to his feet, took a couple of steps, and grabbed the side of the casket. "I'm awake, so he can feel me, released or not. We've been together for too long. That's the thing. We'll only be able to talk a bit at a time."

"What are you going to do?" Lorcas asked as he helped Zumar clamber back in.

"I'll lie here and go into a kind of trance, deeper than I was this time. It's close enough to death that Rook won't pay me any attention. You can wake me again with flames. Pull the lid back so Tomash won't see that it's been disturbed."

He lay back and crossed his arms over his chest.

"But there are some things I need to know!" Lorcas protested. "I found a little church south of here, and there's a cornerstone there. I can feel something in it; it's got to be connected to Rook. I need to know what you know about that or at least anything you can guess about it."

"I figured as much. I hope we're not too late," Zumar said, settling his head.

"What the hell is it?"

"I guess I'd call it … an egg," Zumar replied.

"What? An egg of what?" Lorcas exclaimed.

But Zumar's eyes were closed, and he did not answer. Lorcas stared into the dark casket for a moment more, but he could hear, at the very edge of his senses, the grinding of rock that signified Rook's movement. He hurried around to the other side of the casket and braced his back on the wall for a better shove. Then he returned the lid to its previous position and pinched the wick of the candle.

He purposefully turned his mind to other things, inane thoughts Rook wouldn't be interested in, as he hurried back to his house. But what he desperately wanted to think about was what Zumar had said about the Sazh, and what the hell he meant about the new cornerstone.

CHAPTER THREE

Lorcas waited impatiently for several days for Rook to go away. Rook seemed to be lurking around the place, generally quiet but sending out a few low-level vibrations and grinding sounds whenever Lorcas walked through the neighborhood. At least Tomash appeared to be slowly cutting back on his hours at the crypt. That would make it easier to visit Zumar when, and if, Rook finally took himself off to attend to other business. Of course, it also meant that Tomash was probably accepting Zumar's death, while Zumar was not in fact dead. Not telling Tomash the truth was so difficult that Lorcas just avoided running into him as much as possible.

He was beginning to feel that if he had to deal with any more secrets, he'd mess up and tell the wrong person something. He was keeping his contact with Jason a secret from everyone. He was keeping the existence of the chapel secret from everyone except

Tondra, who was keeping it from Alan. He was keeping Zumar's awakening from everyone. He was keeping Tomash's doubts from everyone else, as well as his own doubts and Tondra's doubts about the trustworthiness of the rest of the Entourage. He was keeping it all from Rook. He could feel the build-up of stress, made worse by the waiting.

After a while he couldn't stand it anymore. His investigation into the church and the monastery had stalled, partly because he didn't want to waste his time on tangents if Zumar could point him in the right direction. And besides his desire to find out what Zumar knew about the new cornerstone and whatever else he hadn't been telling the Fell Ken, Lorcas felt bad knowing that Zumar was simply lying there in the dark, waiting, probably bored out of his skull. So one afternoon Lorcas hiked up to the castle.

He paused in the Banquet Hall and allowed his mind to turn to Rook's whereabouts. Usually, anymore, he tried to block out that part of his mind. He wasn't sure exactly when he had begun to prefer blocking Rook to communicating with him. It seemed to have been a gradual thing over the last year or so, but however it had come about, it was his preference now, and Rook seemed to have accepted it. But it was easy enough to wake it up. Rook had permeated his being, insinuated himself into Lorcas's subconscious mind, and despite their recent disagreements and his bonding with Mira, the connection remained in one form or another.

He quickly discovered that Rook was somewhere deep below. He accessed the basement catacombs through the door in the Banquet Hall's wall and started down in the semi-dark. Rook was far down in the depths beneath the castle, past where any semblance of finished rooms ended, through a series of rough-hewn rock-walled burrows and warrens. It was damp and musty down there, not to mention dark, and Lorcas was less than comfortable with the distant drip of water, occasional fiery chasms, and the scuttle of claws on stone. He did not have the Sword, since he had formally turned it over to Tomash as the rightful owner, but he took the Staff, partly to help feel his way along the uneven tunnel floors, and pulled the Key on its chain to the outside of his shirt as a kind of protective talisman.

Finally, he reached a vast, dim chamber that appeared to be a dead end. The twilight faded away to pitch darkness around the edges. There was a pile of rocks in the middle and Rook was there, part of the boulders and part separate, curled around, on top of, and through them. He seemed asleep, but Lorcas could feel that he was not.

"Hello Rook," Lorcas said conversationally. In a way, he realized, he missed his interactions with Rook. There was a kind of familiarity to it, with a not-unpleasant undercurrent of excitement and intrigue.

"Hello there," Rook replied, partially unfurling an eyelid but keeping the light within the eye dim.

"What are you doing?" Lorcas asked. There was no point in beating around the bush, even though Rook was often obscure in his own answers and questions.

"Napping," Rook said.

"Ah. I didn't know you needed to nap." Lorcas moved further into the room and chose a boulder to sit on. It was cold and a bit damp. He pocketed his small flashlight, relying on the dim ambient light in the chamber.

"All things need rest," Rook said, "especially if they're not eating well."

Lorcas recognized that statement as a subtle dig at him. "I'm not trying to starve you," he said, "but your diet is a bit unorthodox."

He sat quietly for a moment, trying to decide where he wanted to go in this conversation.

"Do you miss the Messenger?" he finally asked.

Rook readjusted himself a bit as though uncomfortable or perhaps a bit miffed, but Lorcas kept his seat, despite a few displaced pebbles that fell from the ceiling.

"Perhaps," Rook said. "He was with me for many of your years. Enough time to count even to me. It was he who drew me forth, after all."

"Can you still feel any part of his spirit?"

"Perhaps a little bit," Rook admitted. "Your deaths are usually quick, but in one who has been permeated with the spirit of life for so long, it may be a more drawn-out process."

"I suppose," Lorcas said. "Are you not working now, then? I thought you were going to enter a period of expansion and move to the south."

"That period has begun," Rook said, "but I must wait for certain processes to be complete."

"Like what?" Lorcas asked.

Rook readjusted himself again. "You would not understand. Your kind is petty and cannot see what the future could hold. That is why you need me."

Petty, Lorcas thought. Was Rook worried that he would be jealous of something? He still didn't have all the pieces he needed.

"Well, I just thought I'd check in with you," Lorcas answered. "You missed our last Sunday meeting. I was wondering if there was anything you wanted to tell me."

"I had nothing to tell. It would have been a waste of time. Besides, I see you have disregarded our agreement in that respect and come to me outside of our appointed consultation."

"Only because I was worried about you," Lorcas said, "and it wouldn't have been a waste of your time if all you're doing is napping anyway. It's never a waste of my time."

"Hmmph!" Rook snorted in what Lorcas had come to interpret as a laugh. "You want something, but I cannot decipher what it might be. Perhaps because I am tired."

"No, nothing," Lorcas said. "Only curious about you and your plans. I'll leave you to nap, then. Far be it from me to disturb your beauty sleep. Call me if you need me." He slid off the boulder and turned to the tunnel he'd come through.

"I certainly hope your curiosity is satisfied, although I doubt it," Rook replied. "I, too, am curious about many things, but not so curious that they will keep me awake." Rook exhaled deeply and settled into the pile of stones as though they were memory foam, the eye slowly closing.

Lorcas did not return to the surface. Rooks' sudden insistence on sleeping was odd, but he had at least gotten one piece of information: as far as he could tell, Rook had no intention of leaving the castle any time soon. He'd be down there snoozing for an unknown period of time, waiting for whatever else had to happen before moving off. That meant Zumar was trapped for the moment, but at least Rook couldn't seem to feel him strongly enough to be suspicious. And without Zumar's help, Lorcas needed to look elsewhere for the answers he needed.

He followed the tunnels up for a while, but turned off before reaching the developed levels and made his way to the slot that led into Mira's passageway. He hadn't summoned her in quite a while, since before Raine's attempt to turn the wheel. He wasn't sure what he needed from her, but the desire to visit was compelling and he'd been holding off, just looking for some excuse, for some time. Now he felt like he at least had a reason, a few questions she might be able to answer. And he really had no one else to talk to; Tondra knew about the church and the cornerstone, but not about Zumar or Jason Japert, Alan knew even less, Raine was persona non-grata among the Fell Ken, and Tomash couldn't be told what Lorcas wanted to tell him. Mira would be safe.

He passed the ocean tower and felt the muffling green light begin to press on his ears. The sound of his Staff as it thumped on the floor seemed louder and as if it might attract too much attention, and he picked it up and carried it horizontally. He made it to the clearing and the shore of the lake without incident, and stepped up onto his favorite rock.

He stuck the end of his Staff in the water and agitated it a couple of times. He wasn't sure how long it might take for Mira to arrive when he was summoning her unexpectedly and without having done so for some time, but he had only been sitting on the rock for a few minutes when he saw the prow of the little boat break through the fog. He stood up and offered Mira a hand to help her out onto the shore as the boat came to a halt, but she ignored him and leapt out lightly.

"Hello, Mira. Been a while," Lorcas said.

"Has it?" she asked. "I don't keep track of your time."

"I suppose it hasn't been all that long," Lorcas admitted. "A few weeks. A lot has happened, though. I need someone to talk to, and I can't tell the rest of the Fell Ken what's going on." He sighed. "The only one who knows part of it is Tondra, and even she doesn't know what's going on with Zumar."

44

"Ah. But of course, I am safe to complain to, as I am unlikely to spread rumors amongst your people. And I am happy to see you, as well, and I'm fine, thank you."

Lorcas caught the rebuke. "I'm sorry. I did skip the niceties. It seems a bit ridiculous to stand on ceremony with you. I mean, you don't care about human formalities, do you?"

"Perhaps not," Mira said, "but it is sometimes nice to believe that I've been summoned for my company, rather than only for my skills. Of which, it is true, I have many. Shall we walk?"

Lorcas raised his eyebrows. "After you," he said. He laid the Staff carefully on the rock.

Mira strolled across the soft green vegetation around the lake in the opposite direction from the trail to Rook's tunnel. Lorcas followed, trying to keep his mind on what he wanted to ask her. It was difficult; her clothing seemed to float around her, almost as though it was made of water rather than fabric, and it shimmered with the suggestion of color which disappeared as soon as he tried to focus on it. Mira's realm, or these borderlands that abutted it, always made him feel slightly disoriented.

At the edge of the woods there was another pathway, wider, almost a narrow road, with a firm surface. The trees were not as close here, although everything was still pervaded with green and Lorcas could see no sky or ceiling through the leaves above. They were able to wander along side-by-side.

Lorcas began by filling Mira in on the memorial for Zumar and Raine's surprise ritual, when she had enlisted the entirety of the Fell Ken congregation in an attempt to re-position Zumar on the wheel of time and invoked the Fire Ally. Then he explained how he had found the monastery, how he had discovered that

Zumar was awake, and what Zumar had said about his possession by the Sazh and the fire of truth.

Mira laughed lightly at that. "I did not realize the Sazh was what you refer to as the Fire Ally," she said. "It is not an entity in and of itself, as your Zumar has discovered, but a kind of spirit that can only live in others. Most humans do not enjoy contact with it, as the burden of truth burns them; it is not in their nature to be truthful. Only the very strong can withstand it for long." She sobered, and a frown flickered across her features for a moment.

"Is Zumar in danger, then?" Lorcas asked worriedly.

"If you are referring to possession by the Sazh, I suspect he might be best equipped to deal with it of any of you. I have had little to do with him and no physical contact, but his spirit seems to me different from yours, and I doubt the Sazh can consume it quickly," she said, although she looked thoughtful, and Lorcas wasn't sure she was telling him everything.

"I've honored his wish to leave him in a trance while Rook is in the area, and I haven't told anyone else, except you, now." Lorcas paused and rubbed his temples with the heels of his hands. "It's driving me crazy! I need to know what he has to tell me and I need to know what's going on with the chapel, but Rook just keeps hanging around! I even went to see him just before I came here, and he just says he's 'napping', curled up under the castle in the dark. Who knows how long he'll be there? He doesn't experience time the way we do either, like you. It could be a long time."

"And Zumar thinks that if you wake him, Rook will know he is awake. And he does not want to deal with Rook."

"Correct. He's afraid of Rook now for some reason. It has to do with this truth thing, I think. Maybe it's what Paracel knew, and Rook will know he's telling me and betraying him. Rook was definitely upset with Raine when she completed the turning ritual and invoked the Fire Ally. He told me he didn't need Zumar anymore and allowed Zumar to die, even moved the lid of the crypt over him, and I think he assumed that was it, that Zumar, being now a useless inconvenience, was gone and out of the way, along with any knowledge Rook might not want the Fell Ken to know. I think he just removed his support from Zumar and assumed that would do the trick. I don't yet know why Zumar made that decision. But obviously Zumar's soul, or essence, or whatever it is, didn't leave completely. Either Raine restored it or it never went away. Now Zumar is not only awake, he's apparently alive without Rook supporting him, and he doesn't want Rook to know."

"That is very interesting. I wonder, myself, about the reasons behind his failure to die appropriately. You suspect that Rook won't like it," Mira said. "Rook wants Zumar dead, and if the first attempt didn't do the job, you're afraid he might try again, and be more successful."

"Yes," Lorcas said. "I don't know if it's only the Fire Ally supporting him, if he still has some support from Rook, or if he can actually survive on his own. If it's the Fire Ally, the Sazh, I don't know if it has a boundary, a place it has to remain within, or if taking Zumar into the normal world would be possible. Otherwise, I might try to just take him away somewhere."

Mira did not answer for a moment. They were standing in a small opening in the trees along the path, and in the silence Lorcas thought he could hear trickling water.

Mira cocked her head as though listening as well. "He could come here," she said.

"He could?" Lorcas asked.

"Of course. He has been here before," Mira pointed out.

Of course, he had been, Lorcas realized, with no apparent ill effects. "Would he be safe here?"

Mira sniffed. "Your Rook has little power here. This is not his realm, although it may be adjacent in some way. You bring some inkling of him with you, but it is faint and does not bother me or the other inhabitants here. It is not enough to form a conduit for him. I do not think Rook could come to this borderland without a strong trail to guide him, much less over the water to my home."

"Then Zumar could stay here?" Lorcas gestured around. "He could live here, and I could come meet with him and talk to him?"

"I would take him over the water with me. It would not be a problem for him, since he passes back and forth between the worlds already. He is a sprite, you might say, a minor being of both lands. This I perceived during my short interaction with him before. It's likely he was so in life, even before his association with Rook."

Lorcas raised his eyebrows. "That's news to me. I thought Rook made him what he is."

"I assumed so as well, but your information has changed my mind. If I am correct, my world will not harm him, nor will it affect his ability to return to yours. He might find it interesting, and I am at least marginally interested in knowing more about him. He is, I think, similar to many other minor beings who inhabit the edges of things. Often, they are mischievous and deceitful, tricksters who make their way by manipulating things to their advantage. It is their nature. I am used to them."

"But now he's inhabited by this fire spirit, this Sazh," Lorcas reminded her. "Is that something you could deal with?"

"Of course," Mira said. "Remember, I was the one who provided your kind with the Sword, an object of fire, given me years ago by another who was possessed by the fire spirit, a powerful king who was able to keep it within him without burning. His truth made him great among you. My waters here will soothe and cool the burning, as I soothed the king before. Eventually the Sazh will leave him and find a new host." She laughed lightly. "But that host will not be me!"

"All right," Lorcas agreed. He turned and paced, thinking. "Now my task will be waking Zumar and getting him here before Rook notices. How am I going to do that?"

"I would suggest not attempting to come here through Rook's tunnels," Mira said.

"No," Lorcas agreed. "The absolute worst thing would be to bring him right down next to where Rook is sleeping and to try to make it through the tunnels before Rook wakes up."

"Then you'll have to bring him to the tower," Mira said. "That is the only other convenient access for you. Can you carry him?"

"You mean fly as my raven form?" Lorcas asked. He shook his head. "I believe sustaining my shadow form relies on taking power from Rook. He would know, and if he saw or felt what I was doing, he could cut my power and drop us both right into the ocean."

Mira looked thoughtful again. "I am not so sure of that," she said. "However, if you are not confident in that power, it would be best to avoid it."

"The best option, then, would be to wake Zumar and get him outside the castle itself as quickly as possible, onto a boat, and out into the ocean," Lorcas continued. "But I would need help for that."

"Perhaps the King of the Knights, your Jack, could help you," Mira suggested. "He does have a vessel."

Lorcas glanced at her. "Maybe." He grimaced. "I don't really want to involve him, though. We are still sworn enemies, even if we've cooperated in the past."

He mused for a minute. "I know someone else who might have access to a boat and who might be willing to help. If I could get that part taken care of, I might only need to involve one other person, perhaps Tondra, to help me get Zumar out of the castle. I'll need someone watching the neighborhood and someone ready to provide a distraction if necessary. Tondra doesn't know that Zumar's awake at this point, but she's the one I trust the most, and she's got the skills and guts to do what needs to be done. Once he's here safe, the others could know."

"It does not sound so difficult," Mira said.

"Doesn't it? But Rook is likely to feel it as soon as Zumar is fully awake. Despite his willingness to let Zumar die and the removal of his support, I'm sure they're still bonded to some extent, and Rook knows pretty much everything that happens within the boundaries of the castle anyway. I'd guess he's hanging around now because he suspects something. He admitted he could feel some part of Zumar still, and of course he can feel what I am doing in many cases. He could cover the distance between us much faster than we could get out of the castle and down to the boat, and knowing he was being betrayed, he would probably be very angry." Lorcas shuddered, remembering facing off with Rook outside the castle when Rook had accused him of betrayal once before. "And I don't want to make Rook mad!"

"Then don't," Mira said.

"Don't bring Zumar?" Lorcas asked, surprised.

"No, don't make him mad."

"How would I avoid it? If he wakes and figures out what we're up to, that Zumar is alive and being removed without his express permission, he will be mad no matter what I say."

Mira sighed. "Rook belongs to you. You do not belong to him. He is your manifestation, yours personally, but also that of Zumar and that of the Fell Ken. You are in control of him, not the other way around. So do not allow him to be mad."

"I don't think you understand," Lorcas replied.

"I don't think you understand," Mira snapped. "Take your life back. You have given it away, created this manifestation as a physical representation of your peoples' ills, imbued it with your hopes for a better future, and abdicated your own responsibility for creation of that future. Its shape is yours, however odd that you have chosen this particular shape."

She turned and began walking purposefully along the path again, and Lorcas scrambled to follow.

"Start small," Mira continued more gently. "Do not allow Rook to become mad. Hold him within you like an emotion over which you have control. Do not allow him to dictate your actions or your fears. Take a bit of your spirit back from him. You will only need to exercise this control for a few minutes while you remove Zumar from the castle and bring him to the boat. Then you can consider how to continue."

Mira turned abruptly off the path. Not far into the woods they came to a small stream tumbling down dark rocks. Mira stopped there. She pulled a small vial from some hidden pocket in her clothing, leaned over the cascade, and filled it. Then she stoppered it firmly and handed it to Lorcas.

"What's this?" Lorcas asked.

"A gift for your friend, the Japert," she said. "It was his misfortune that he experienced an interface with Rook's world without preparation or predisposition. In addition, your alchemist poisoned him. This will clear any remaining poison from his system and help his mind accept what he saw. It will give him clarity and relieve his burden. I am not without sympathy for those ordinary humans who accidentally encounter worlds outside their knowledge and control. Rook is an interloper, albeit one brought forth by you and your kin. Humans have a right to their own world, and a right to be able to predict what will happen within it."

"I'm sure he'll appreciate it," Lorcas said. "That is, if he trusts me enough to take it."

"That will be up to you to accomplish," Mira said. "Remember that I gave you my waters to heal you and provide you a choice in your dealings with Rook. Perhaps your shared experience will persuade him." She returned to the path and turned towards the clearing and her lake.

At the shoreline she stepped directly into the boat and turned to face Lorcas.

"I will be waiting for Zumar's arrival," she said. "Summon me when you are here." The boat moved backwards smoothly and rapidly disappeared into the fog.

Lorcas was left standing on the shore watching her disappear. As usual, his interaction with her was both instructive and frustrating. He felt as though there was some difficulty in communication, some poor translation, when it came to discussing Rook and how much control he was able to exercise over what Rook did. On the other hand, she was correct: Rook had been brought forth this time by the express wishes of the Fell Ken, facilitated by him. It seemed like he should be able to impose more of the desires of the Entourage onto Rook's development, rather than simply obediently following Rook's whim. Was that a matter of poor translation as well, or purposeful obfuscation? The responsibility for much of that communication had fallen to Zumar, and Zumar obviously had a few things he needed to get off his chest.

Eventually he roused himself and made his way back. Along the way he began to put together a plan.

As he stepped out of the Banquet Hall, he could see a car parked outside the wall near his house. Someone was leaning on the side, arms crossed, as though waiting for him.

"Jason Japert," Lorcas muttered to himself. "Just who I was looking for."

Jason caught sight of him as he descended the hill and raised a hand. As Lorcas reached his property, he waved Jason in through the gate.

"Come on in. There's something we need to discuss," Lorcas said, holding the door, "and I have something for you."

Jason scanned the place quickly as he entered the living room, then chose a seat on the couch.

"You want a soda or anything?" Lorcas offered. It occurred to him that he might just be able to slip Mira's gift into a drink, without explaining it.

"Nah, I'm good," Jason said. "You look a little … green."

Lorcas glanced down at himself. There was, perhaps, a bit of Mira's aura left around him, but it was faint. "Never mind that." He grabbed a drink and sat in the armchair across from the couch near the library door. "I've got something I need you to do. First of all, do you have access to a boat?"

"Sure," Jason said. "I co-own one. A bunch of the guys from the department all went in on it together. It's not as nice as Jack's, but it'll do for an afternoon of fishing."

"Not fishing," Lorcas said. "Can you navigate in the dark?"

"Uh…" Jason paused. "Maybe. I mean, if it's not something too hairy. I could get up and down the coast and into a marina."

Lorcas thought for a minute. "I have a task for you. If it works out, you'll be a hero to the Fell Ken and they'll probably answer any questions you have for any of them."

"That sounds good," Jason said. "When do you need me and the boat and where?"

"I'll need you to be ready to go in that little cove just south of the slump. I don't know when yet. Why don't you find out when you can get the boat first and we'll plan from there?"

"Okay. How many passengers would I be expecting? It's not that big of a boat."

"Just three, possibly four," Lorcas said. "Me, Tondra, possibly Alan, and Zumar. And two of us will disembark pretty quick. Do you have a GPS?"

"Yes, there's on-board GPS."

"Good. I'll need you to go out in the daylight, find the site, and get the coordinates for it and for the cove. That way you'll be able to find both of them in the dark."

"Other than the cove, what site would I be finding?"

"A tower off the coast of the castle," Lorcas said. "Work on getting the boat and I'll tell you the rest of the plan when we've gotten that far. And don't mention it to anyone. Tondra doesn't know she's going to be involved with this yet."

Jason raised his eyebrows. "I'll keep it under wraps. Are you going to give me any clue?"

"Not right now." Lorcas shook his head. "I have to talk to Tondra and get the plan down."

"Looking forward to it," Jason said. "Let's get this show on the road!"

Lorcas took a drink and swirled the can around for a minute. "I have to warn you," he said, "this could be scary."

"Scary, huh? How scary? Like what I saw last year during the Rising?"

"Something like that," Lorcas admitted, "but possibly closer. And angrier."

"Huh." Jason considered for a minute, then took a deep breath and blew it out. "Well, that's not my favorite thought."

"And after Zumar and I get off, it might be up to you and Tondra and Alan to create a distraction," Lorcas continued. "I hope that boat can move."

"I hope so too," Jason said.

"Then are you on board with this, pardon the pun?" Lorcas asked.

Jason smiled briefly. "Yep. I've told you before, I'm not an adrenalin junky like some cops. But I do like to solve problems, and I have a dangerous case of curiosity. Plus, I'm bored."

"Good," Lorcas said. "Let me know when you've got the boat. Just call me, don't come back up here."

"Will do." Jason stood to go.

"Wait." Lorcas got up and returned to the kitchen, where he'd laid the little vial on the counter. He picked it up and brought it back to the living room.

"This is for you," Lorcas said, holding it out to him. "I told you I'd look into an antidote for the poison."

Jason took the vial gingerly. "This is it, huh?"

"That's it."

"And I'm supposed to do what with it? Drink it? And trust you that this won't do anything bizarre to me?"

"Drink it and trust me," Lorcas repeated. "I myself have taken this same cure. It helped my back and also gave me some clarity about my relationship with Rook, gave me back a little power. And I don't have any reason to harm you. I need your help right now." As far as it doing something bizarre, he could not, of course, guarantee that, so he didn't address that part of Jason's question at all.

Jason stared at the vial for a long moment, then suddenly popped the stopper out and upended the vial over his mouth. "Too late to back out now," he said with a grin. "Tastes like moldy water." He handed the vial back to Lorcas.

"Let me know if it works," Lorcas said.

"Sure thing," Jason said. "I'll let you know if my wife says it works, too."

"Good luck with that," Lorcas replied. He checked outside before letting Jason head for his car; the fewer who saw him there the better. He watched the detective's vehicle leave before going back inside. His next move would be to get Tondra alone and work up a plan with her. After that, he would only be able to hope that Zumar could cooperate quickly when he was awakened, and that what Mira said was true.

CHAPTER FOUR

Lorcas made no attempt to visit Zumar over the next few days. He didn't talk to Tondra about his plans, either; the less time she had to worry about what was going to happen, the better. He had plenty of time to wonder why he was trusting Zumar implicitly on this instead of Rook. He was a failure as a Lorecaster, that was for sure. But somehow, he did trust Zumar. He had a strong feeling that Zumar was suddenly on their side; and that meant, he realized, that he felt that Rook was on some other side.

It seemed to him that Tondra was drawing away from Rook as well, given her response to the discovery of the chapel. He wasn't sure about Alan's thoughts, but Tomash had certainly expressed concern about what they'd been doing and where they were going, so he wasn't alone in his doubts. He knew through Tondra that some of the Fell Ken congregation had cooled a bit on both Rook and the Entourage, especially Raine, after having been used unwittingly in the time-turning ritual. Then there was Mira, insisting that he, himself, had 'manifested' Rook, and that he could therefore control him. He'd never felt in control of Rook, but if she was right, then he wasn't actually betraying Rook, he was just changing the direction of his own manifestation. But then he would circle back to his relationship with Rook over the past several years, to how everything had always seemed out of his control, to how strange it was that he had somehow created the whole situation when it seemed so unfamiliar and unknowable.

There was no answer he could arrive at, no complete solution. Something was missing, some bit of knowledge, and he could only rely on his own instinct for now. That instinct told him to get Zumar out of Rook's control. Once that was done, he could work on getting the answers he now had to have. It was time to know the truth, the complete truth. Without it, he could not make the decisions necessary to move the Fell Ken forward, whatever direction 'forward' ended up being, and he knew it was his responsibility to do so to the best of his ability.

He turned to working out the logistics of Zumar's escape. It would be dark; he had decided to make the move at night, when he knew he could wake Zumar with candlelight and when Tomash would not be there to deal with. He had an idea of what the community looked like after sunset, how many lights were usually on and such, and he could probably risk walking the path once to reconnoiter, but the routes inside would have to wait until they were actually underway. He wasn't sure his memory of the internal arrangement was complete, but there would be no chance to double-check.

With the plans as complete as they could be, Lorcas could not avoid turning his mind to his own preparation. Unless things went more smoothly than he anticipated, he was going to have to stand up to Rook. It was doubtful Rook, seeing that the Messenger was alive and awake and possessed by the Sazh, would happily allow him to go about his business without any kind of confrontation. Rook's agreement with Zumar had been that Zumar die, not that he live on while possessed by one of the Fell Ken's 'allies'. And Zumar had expressly requested that Rook not know he was awake.

Lorcas had stood up to Rook before, but never in such an obvious act of defiance. He put together a number of lies in his head that might stall Rook for the short term, but he knew his mental connection to Rook was such that those lies would be easily discoverable should Rook choose to push his way in. Mira's suggestion that he simply not allow Rook to become angry seemed out of the question, as he had no idea how to go about it.

He pondered how he could increase his mental resolve and strength. All his power seemed to come through and from Rook, or at least through Rook's creations. He paused in his living room, where he had been pacing, as that idea circulated in his mind. Through Rook's creations, he thought. But some, or most, of the objects and rituals he'd drawn some sort of power from before were actually Fell Ken creations, and he had used them even in the absence of Rook himself.

Of the designated 'Objects of Power', he no longer had either the Sword or the Ring. The Sword, he had learned through Mira, rightfully belonged to the King and was to be wielded by him, and the Ring, which had been used in the time-turning ritual, was also in Tomash's possession. He did have his Staff and the Key. The Staff had supposedly been created by Paracel, but although light, it was a bit unwieldy and might get in the way when he was trying to hurry and support Zumar. The internal wand in the Staff was smaller, but would still require one hand to hold. He might be able to stick it in his belt, but then he risked it falling out or poking him.

That left the Key and the goblets, or subsidiary items like the robe. The Key was probably the most powerful of those, as well as the most portable. He knew it was considered a symbol of the center, the soul or beginning of things. It was traditionally held by the Lorecaster himself, along with the Staff. It had been Rook's first gift to him, appearing in a niche in the wall of the incomplete chapel. At Zumar's suggestion he had swallowed it and it had become part of him, lodging in his chest. He had used it on several occasions and he kept it with him at all times, although he no longer went through the pain and inconvenience of replacing it in his chest each time. But he really knew very little about the Key, he thought, running his fingers over it as it hung from its chain. And there likely wasn't time to find out much about it before he needed to act.

There was one other possibility. He recalled how, at the very beginning of his connection with Rook, he had channeled what Raine referred to as 'passage power' in order to defeat the Knight, Korrin Bright, who was attempting to chop him up with the Sword. He knew now that he had unwittingly performed a power-gathering ritual that was associated with the chapel, with the old earth-magic, and with going through doorways, symbolizing moving from one state to another. He might be able to recreate that pattern, especially since he was sure he had seen some sort of drawing of it in one of his books. But that would require going to the chapel and moving around and through it repeatedly, where Tomash and Rook at the very least would be apt to notice what he was doing. And while the back door and one side door were accessible, the southern door now opened to a multi-story drop.

There was, of course, another chapel. It seemed to be the same size and configuration. It certainly seemed to be connected to Rook and the Fell Ken. And this very Key opened the door there. Would a ritual performed there increase his power and give him the advantage he needed?

There was only one way to find out, of course. But he was hesitant to return to the chapel alone, with its odd cornerstone knock-off and its possible connection to the monastery. It felt dangerous in the way unknown pieces of the Rook and Fell Ken story often did, something that needed to be managed with information he didn't have and didn't know where to find. Zumar's description of the rock as an 'egg' did nothing to ease that discomfort. He didn't like the image of something suddenly hatching, especially if he was busy with a ritual.

After a moment of indecision, Lorcas pulled out his cell phone. He scrolled through his contacts and made a call.

"Hey, Lorcas!" the slightly over-enthusiastic voice on the other end answered after a couple of rings.

"Hey, Jason," Lorcas replied, grudgingly switching to the informal. "How are you feeling?"

"Good! Good! I think your potion worked! No bad side effects that I can tell."

"Glad to hear it. How are you coming with the boat?"

"I've got a couple days that would work, and I can get it pretty much any night. No one will even notice. Was gonna call and see if you wanted to show me where this location is I'm supposed to GPS. I mean,

I know where the cove is, but you'll have to take me to the other spot."

"It might be safer for you to do it yourself and not draw any attention to me. I can probably describe it well enough for you to find on your own. But that's not why I was calling. I have another task for you, if you're not too busy."

"Busy, ha. I only wish. I've got more time on my hands than I know what to do with. Whattaya need?"

"There's a piece of property I need to get some information about. I tried to figure out the online property records, but I need plat numbers and such and I can't get those for the property in question, at least not as far as I can figure out. It just doesn't show on any of the public county records."

"Okay, I have an idea how that system works, so I might be able to extrapolate if you can show me where it is on an overhead photo or something."

"I can do that. In fact, I was planning on going out that way in person. I could use some protection. It's on the edge of Fell Ken territory and could be associated with the Knights. It might be dangerous, at least for me. You want to come along?"

"Sure. Might as well get those bodyguard credentials beefed up."

After they set up a meeting place and time, Lorcas hung up and stuck the phone back in his pocket. He wasn't sure what Japert could do about Rook-style forces, but he could certainly act as a bodyguard against flesh-and-blood humans. And if Jason could figure out the formal location of the chapel and monastery, he might have better luck finding the ownership records than Lorcas had. Besides, Lorcas wanted the company. He could be fairly open with Jason, even if Jason disbelieved much of what he was saying.

Lorcas found the book he'd remembered with the passage-power pattern in it in the library and took a picture of the page that described it on his phone. He also grabbed a goblet, a bottle of wine, a candlestick, a random rock, and his Staff and threw them in the back seat of his car.

The meeting place was a defunct gas station not far from the 'T' intersection outside Copsberg, and he had plenty of time to reconsider as he drove, which he did several times. However, eventually he pulled up at the old, out-of-service pumps. Japert was already there, leaning on his car in the sun, his mirrored sunglasses reflecting sky and trees.

"Your car or mine?" Jason asked as Lorcas rolled down the window.

"Mine," Lorcas said. "The road's dirt and rocky and I'm not sure your sedan will make it. Besides, I know where I'm going."

Jason got in and Lorcas waited for him to fasten his seat belt. Then he headed for the intersection and turned left.

"So what is this place you're looking at that doesn't show up on the county plats?" Jason asked.

"A couple pieces of property we think might have been associated with either the Fell Ken or the Knights in the past," Lorcas replied. No need to give Jason details; he probably wouldn't believe them anyway. "You'll see one of them when we get there. The other one's further south and I haven't actually driven in to that one. I think you'll find them interesting."

"No doubt," Jason replied. "'Interesting' is the name of the game." He fell silent, but Lorcas saw that he looked out the window at the dark trees crowding the road and glanced at the GPS from time to time.

Eventually Lorcas turned off on the dirt access road, and a couple of minutes later he parked near the new cornerstone. He got out cautiously, but once again it seemed deserted. Jason climbed out as well and looked around.

"Nice view," Jason said. "I don't know anything about this area. Looks like a little church. Kind of out-of-the-way for services, though."

"Purposefully, I'm sure," Lorcas said. "I think it's associated with a small monastery just down the road, maybe exclusively for their use. Last time I was here I didn't know about the monastery, though. Now I want to take another look with that in mind and do a couple of things that'll help me figure out if this is Fell Ken property or not. If it is, what I do may work. If it doesn't work, that may mean it's not Fell Ken property. Or it might not mean anything."

Jason raised his eyebrows, but his eyes remained hidden behind his sunglasses, and Lorcas couldn't really tell what he thought.

After another minute of observation, Lorcas walked toward the chapel. He paused just for a moment at the stone, laying a hand upon it. The familiar buzz was still there. He glanced at Jason, who crossed his arms over his windbreaker as he watched, but said nothing.

Lorcas used the Key to open the main door in the narrow end of the chapel closest to him and pushed it back as far as it would go. He paused to make sure it would stand open by itself. Then he went to each of the smaller doors in the long sides. Both of them opened from the inside without being unlocked. With those two ajar, he opened the steeple door, realizing as he did so that the chapel was set up exactly opposite to the one at Cliffview, with the steeple to the east rather than the west.

His curiosity drove him to mount the narrow stone steps to the steeple itself. Looking out from the highest window on the third floor, he could see rolling hills to the east, dark fir forests, and, just to the south and almost out of view, the buildings he knew must be the monastery he had seen on the overhead photos. They were barely visible in a long, shallow valley nearly a mile away, by his estimation.

Jason had followed him up into the steeple. "That's the other property you're talking about, huh?" he asked. He leaned forward cautiously and looked down out of the open casement.

"Yes," Lorcas said. "There's quite a bit of land in between the two, so I'm not positive they're associated."

Jason squinted. "Looks like maybe a road or trail crossing that hill over there," he said. "Disappears behind that other rise."

Lorcas saw it once it was pointed out. "It might connect the two properties. Hard to tell. Will you be able to figure out the plat numbers, do you think?"

"Sure," Jason said. "I could probably have done that from the overhead shots, but this is more interesting. The monastery's a pretty substantial property, looks like. I'm surprised it's not on the county plats. It's got to show up in some records somewhere."

Lorcas put a foot up on the sill so he could lean out a bit and get a better view of the surrounding countryside. As he put a hand on the outside of the casement, he felt the sharpness of the edge of the stones there. He examined the construction more closely. The stones used to build this chapel appeared fresh-cut, not old and weathered like the ones in his chapel. In addition, he could see mortar in a thin line between blocks. The original didn't have mortar; it was held together by some unknown force, as though the pieces were magnetically attracted to one another. This one, while obviously connected to the new cornerstone outside, was human-made.

That, of course, might affect the ability of the building to help him channel any power, he considered. Nevertheless, they were there now, and he might as well try. Jason followed him down the stairs and out to the car, where he unloaded the objects he'd brought. He handed a couple of them to Jason to carry. Back inside, he poured a little wine into the goblet and set it on the small table inside the entry on the western wall. The candlestick went along the southern wall, the rock along the northern wall, and he leaned his Staff against the eastern wall.

He brought up the picture of the ritual on his phone. "Just stand there and watch," he told Jason. "Let me know if anything happens that I should know about."

"Like what?" Jason asked.

"I don't know. Whatever. Take a look outside from time to time, too."

Jason crossed his arms and leaned against the wall inside the southern doorway. Lorcas began the pattern slowly. He departed the room through the southern door, then rounded the outside to the east, entering again through the northern door. He reversed it, rounding to the west, then left and re-entered through each of the side doors. After completing it he did it again faster, and then a third time from memory at a trot, his footsteps echoing on the stone floor.

He paused in the middle of the room after the third time, and it occurred to him that since the chapel was backwards from the Cliffview one, perhaps he needed to do the whole ritual backwards. Or would that undo it? The cardinal directions were still the same, after all. He couldn't remember how many times he'd run in and out during the chase with Korrin Bright, but three times seemed to him to be enough. He wasn't even sure how he'd use this passage power in a confrontation with Rook, and he couldn't tell if anything had actually happened anyway. A few tendrils of mist seemed to hang in the doorways, but that might be a function of sun on cold, damp stone.

"Well?" Jason demanded.

"Can't tell," Lorcas said. He was starting to feel silly. "I was hoping it would be more obvious. I'm not sure. Could be Fell Ken, could be Knights, could be I just didn't do things right. Help me take this crap back to the car."

"What should I do with the wine?" Japert asked with a grin.

"Don't drink it," Lorcas said quickly, but then he reconsidered. Maybe drinking it would give Jason a better connection to the Fell Ken. "Or do drink it if you want. I don't think it'll hurt you. It's a nice European red from the Lindens' wine shop."

"Marek Linden? I'll pass," Japert said wryly. "I've already had one encounter with substances of his. I'm still recovering from that." He carefully poured it out of the goblet and back into the bottle, spilling only a few drops on the stone floor, where it disappeared almost immediately.

They collected the rest of the objects from around the perimeter and stowed them in the car. Back inside, Lorcas closed the steeple door and the two side doors, jiggling them to make sure they latched.

"Hey," Japert said softly, "we've got company."

A dark shadow crossed the floor, and Lorcas turned quickly. A figure loomed in the western doorway, blocking out the light. It was covered entirely, from head to foot, in a heavy dark robe with a hood, the border of which dipped down and obscured its face.

The robe was fastened loosely around the waist with a rope. The figure's arms were held in front across the body with the hands completely hidden by long, loose sleeves.

The figure paused for a long moment as Lorcas stared. Jason moved a few paces closer to him protectively, one hand inside his windbreaker. Then the figure took several slow steps forward. Its movement was smooth and soundless, as though it wore felt slippers rather than hard-soled shoes.

"Uh, we didn't mean to trespass," Lorcas said. "The door was open, and we just stepped inside to…"

"The door was not open. Only the holder of the Key could have opened it," the figure hissed. "Our Key." From the tone of its voice, Lorcas guessed it was male, although he still could not see any features.

"Don't know what you're talking about," Lorcas replied as lightly as he could muster. The figure took another couple of steps towards him, and Lorcas glanced around, trying to decide which of the two side doors to make a break for. Jason followed his gaze unobtrusively with his eyes.

"It does not matter. I have been expecting you. You summoned me," the figure continued. "I have arrived, and I am now at your service. Perhaps."

"I didn't summon you, or at least I didn't intend to," Lorcas replied "I don't know what you mean."

"You have opened the way to the other lands, passing through doorways. Such a thing is no accident," the figure continued. "You have come, as I knew you would eventually. You have spilled the wine here and opened doors. You have the Key. You will have the other Objects of Power as well, undoubtedly. But give me our Key now, and we can discuss things further." One of the arms twitched beneath the robe, as if he was stifling an urge to reach out.

"I don't think so," Lorcas replied. He clutched the Key in one hand, intending to drop it down under his shirt collar, and was surprised to find it buzzing like an electrified bee. He quickly let go. He moved slowly towards the north door, keeping his eyes on the monk, if indeed it was one.

"You have nothing to fear," the monk whispered hoarsely. Somehow that pronouncement made the hair stand up on Lorcas's neck rather than reassuring him. The monk stopped in the center of the chapel. "Nothing to fear from me, at least. There are many worse things than I. And I am open to negotiation. I only ask that you give me the Key, so that you will not be tempted to use it again."

Lorcas laid a hand on the door latch of the northern door.

"Yeah, well, I'll keep that in mind, thank you. Right now, though, I'm going to take off, if you'll pardon us."

The monk made no move towards him, and Lorcas opened the door. He stepped out and Jason crowded quickly out after him. Lorcas shut the door firmly and they retreated to the car, Jason trotting sideways, hurrying Lorcas along in front of him. The monk did not follow, although a glance back showed Lorcas that he stood in the open western doorway through which he had entered.

They jumped into the car and Lorcas pulled it around and headed back down the entrance road immediately, while Jason re-holstered the firearm he'd been holding beneath his jacket into an underarm holster.

"So, that was creepy," Jason said as they paused at the bottom of the road.

"I didn't expect anyone to show up," Lorcas said, "but he did confirm that this chapel has something to do with the Fell Ken. That part about the Key and going through the doorways, that's Fell Ken stuff. Though he kept referring to it as 'our Key'."

"I doubt he just felt you there and showed up because of it," Jason said. "There's probably some security system, a sensor on the door or the roadway. Or maybe he just happened to be around."

"Maybe," Lorcas said. He thought about the monk's mention of spilling the wine. There was no way the monk could have known that, even if he'd been lurking about watching the passage power ritual, unless he somehow could feel what was going on in the chapel.

"What was he talking about, that stuff about the other lands?"

"I'm not sure about the 'opening other lands' stuff, but he was talking about this Key," Lorcas said, indicating the chain that hung around his neck.

"Yeah, I figured that out," Japert said, "I just wasn't sure why he wanted it so much. It's an interesting one, though. It looks old."

Lorcas glanced down, then cautiously felt the Key again. It wasn't vibrating anymore.

"I don't know why he wants it, either," Lorcas said. "It's one of the Objects of Power, an historical piece passed down through the Fell Ken. I've used it for a number of things over the years, but I don't know a lot about it."

"Maybe you should find out," Jason suggested.

"I've tried. A lot of information has gone missing over the years."

"Sounds like that monk knows something about it. Maybe you should ask him."

Lorcas glanced at Jason. "Right now, that doesn't seem like something I want to do."

"You said the place is associated with the Fell Ken," Jason pointed out. "Guy's creepy, all right, but he didn't threaten you. He let us leave. He knew why you were there. And he contacted us alone with no obvious weapons, unless there was something hidden in that robe. In fact, it sure seemed like he knew you. Seems like he's your kin, or some buddy of them. Creepy doesn't necessarily equal dangerous, unless you know something I don't."

Lorcas considered. Maybe Jason was right. He could have asked a few more questions.

They reached the pavement, and Lorcas turned the wheel to the right.

"Wait!" Jason said. "I thought we were going to check out the monastery."

"After that little episode? I'm not sure it's safe," Lorcas protested.

"Why wouldn't it be safe? I'm not afraid of a few creepy monks, myself, though I would prefer to see their faces. And hands," he added.

Reluctantly, Lorcas turned the wheel left and the Subaru bumped off the dirt track onto the pavement. He drove slowly so they wouldn't miss an entrance road.

"It'll have to be past this hill," Japert said. "It looked like those buildings were in a pretty good valley, it should be fairly obvious."

Sure enough, about a mile down the road the forest opened up around a more substantial, gravel-reinforced roadway. But this time there was a rock wall a hundred feet or so along with a metal gate and a 'No Trespassing' sign. On the right side was a smaller sign that said simply 'Order of the Key'.

"That pretty much confirms that the chapel and the monastery are connected," Lorcas said. He was secretly relieved that they couldn't access the main monastery. He felt like Jason didn't understand the

71

seriousness of the situation, and the gate made an easy excuse.

Jason sat forward with his elbows on his knees, staring at the sign and the gate. "Huh. Now I'm curious. "Order of the Key", huh? I ought to be able to figure out who owns this, one way or another."

He sat back and looked at Lorcas. "What now? You got what you wanted at the chapel. I could probably grab the boat for an hour or so and get that GPS location. I've got time. You could come along if you want to."

Lorcas put the car in reverse and backed out onto the road.

"I don't want to draw attention to myself. I don't think anyone will care if they see a boat out there. Boats go by all the time. Most of the time they don't stop, or if they do, they're just taking a look at the castle. It's not like it would be unusual. But there are certain people who might notice if I was on that boat. They might be able to notice even if they couldn't see me."

"Okay," Jason said with a shrug, "tell me where it is, then, and I'll get it myself this afternoon. You said you wanted to get this thing done. We have to get that location first."

Lorcas described the location of the tower top to Jason verbally and then drew him a quick sketch when they got back to the abandoned gas station.

"You'll see a disturbance in the water. Head that way, but don't let the swells bring you over the top. Just get close. We have to be able to get there in the dark, but once we're fairly close we'll be able to see it."

"Got it," Jason said.

"You'll need to bring us right up to it the night we do this," Lorcas told him. "Zumar and I are going to have to disembark. Will you be able to do that?"

Jason shrugged. "Remind me and we'll throw the bumpers out before we get there."

"I don't care if you bump into it," Lorcas said. "I think it'll be the least of my worries at the time."

"Well, I don't want to damage the boat," Jason said. "It has to get us back safely, and besides, I don't have enough money to repair it right now."

"Fair enough," Lorcas said.

"What are you going to disembark onto?" Jason asked suspiciously. "It sounds like it's just a pointy spire."

"Don't worry about that. I have a method. I've done it before."

"Ten-four," Jason said with a grin. He slid into his sedan, taking the paper sketch with him.

Lorcas waited a few minutes, then headed home himself. Once he'd parked, he grabbed a soda and walked casually out to the wall along the cliff. He sat down, hoping it just looked like he was enjoying the afternoon sun and a drink. After a while he saw a boat, smaller than Jack's, run up along the coast. He watched as the boat slowed near the tower area and bobbed in the swells.

Lorcas looked around casually. There were a few children playing near the wall, but he didn't see any adults or any sign that the children had noticed the boat. Except, perhaps, one. One child seemed to be sitting off to the side by herself. It was hard to tell for sure, but he thought it could be Kara, Dirk's younger sister. She and her brother, Saber, were the only two remaining members of the Katzbalger family, being raised by other members of the Fell Ken.

The boat made a tight loop around the top of the tower and he heard the distant growl as the engines engaged and brought it up on plane. Now, Lorcas thought, he had everything he might need to go through

73

with his plan to rescue Zumar. There was no reason to put it off any longer. He needed to do it soon.

CHAPTER FIVE

The rescue attempt, Lorcas realized, now had to occur quickly. Not only did he need to act while he had whatever power he might have gleaned from the chapel, but he was also concerned that the monk, whoever and whatever he was, might somehow alert Rook or even the Knights about Lorcas's visit. Rook might be able to feel it himself, if he was somehow directly connected to the new cornerstone.

Jason Japert was available the night of the day following their visit. Lorcas wanted to go in the dead of night; he didn't want to risk anyone in the neighborhood being awake and about. He also felt that Rook often paid less attention when he knew the Entourage and the rest of the Fell Ken were usually asleep. Rook didn't expect people to be doing things then. On the other hand, Lorcas wanted it near enough to when people might be up and stirring for them to be able to call for help on the way back and get it quickly, should they need it.

They set the time for 4:00 a.m. Jason assured Lorcas that he'd be there a few minutes early. He told Lorcas he had timed how long it took him to get from the cove back to his boat slip on the way home from gathering the GPS information, and he'd also recorded the route so he could follow a GPS track instead of trying to navigate off the coast in the dark.

Lorcas finally settled on briefing Tondra beforehand rather than trying to rouse her in the middle of the night. He wanted to contact her alone, but also give her a say in who else was involved. He stationed himself on his screened-in porch in early evening and began a vigil on her house, part of which he could see past the corner of Tomash's house. He was hoping for a time when Alan was out for a few minutes or Tondra was otherwise alone.

His chance came when Tondra headed up the hill to fetch Tomash down for dinner. Lorcas quickly sent her a text before she entered the castle, where cell phones didn't work.

"I need to speak to you alone. Don't tell anyone else," he typed.

He saw Tondra pause near the bridge and pull her phone out. She glanced towards his house, and he watched as she concentrated on the phone. Lorcas avoided talk-to-text since he not only didn't want to be overheard most of the time, he also felt that speaking aloud created more of a conduit to Rook than typing. It appeared that Tondra was doing the same.

"I'll text you after I get T fed," her reply read.

Lorcas bided his time. He watched her and Tomash come down the hill. They'd be occupied with dinner for at least a few minutes, so he grabbed himself something to eat, even though his nerves were affecting his stomach. Finally, Tondra texted him again.

"About the new chapel? Should I come to your house?"

"No," Lorcas replied. "I don't want you to be seen here." He stepped out onto his porch. He could see Tondra leaning up against the corner of her house.

"Okay, go ahead," she texted.

"First thing you need to know is that Zumar is alive," Lorcas wrote. He watched for her reaction and saw her straighten.

"That's awesome!" she sent back in a minute. "Where is he?"

"Still in his crypt, in a trance. We have to get him out of the castle without Rook's knowledge. He is in danger. That is about all I know so far. We have to act fast. I trust Zumar on this."

He quickly outlined his plan, including Jason's role. "I'm sorry I couldn't tell you earlier," he finished. "Please trust me on this. I can give you more details at another time."

"I do and I can't wait to hear. What time do we meet?"

"About 3:45. Jason will be at the cove by 4:00. What do you think about involving Alan or Tomash? I wanted to give you that choice."

There was a pause before Tondra texted back.

"I would prefer not to. There are several reasons for that. Of course, the fewer people involved the less apt Rook is to notice. That's one of them."

Lorcas considered the text. Tondra was obviously leaving something unsaid, but they could discuss that some other time if it was important. He had given her the choice, and she had opted against it. He would honor that. Besides, she was certainly right about Rook.

"Will you be able to get out without Alan knowing?"

"Yes, and I'll keep Tomash at home tonight as well."

"You'll be able to do that for sure?"

"I have my methods," Tondra replied. "Both of them will be getting a good night's sleep."

Lorcas raised his eyebrows. "One other thing," he texted. "After I take Zumar to Mira's, you'll be alone outside with Jason if you don't bring someone else. You may need to deal with Rook. I'll be back as quickly as I can, but there may be some time when it's just you."

"I understand," Tondra said. "I'll be ready."

Lorcas ended his text and sat back. His choice of Tondra had been a good one, he knew. Once she made up her mind about a course of action, she wasn't likely to waver. He had never seen her sidelined by fear and he knew she could think on her feet. Of all the people in the Entourage and the Fell Ken, he trusted her the most thoroughly. She had accepted his explanation without question, and he accepted her decision not to involve Alan. That kind of trust was vital now.

It was very dark at 3:45 a.m., with only a sliver of moon ducking in and out of the clouds. Lorcas fiddled with the Key impatiently as he waited just past the corner of Tomash's house. He had come out a few minutes early, having nothing better to do. Exactly at 3:45, he saw Tondra slip out of her door. He noticed a brief metallic shine as she stepped into the porch light.

She joined him a moment later.

"You brought the Sword," he whispered.

"Yes. I realize it belongs to the King, but technically, I was chosen to co-lead along with him. I don't see any reason I shouldn't wield it. I am good with a sword, better than Tomash. And Tomash won't miss it tonight."

Lorcas nodded. It was a good idea; Rook might hesitate to challenge the one who held the Sword, a symbol of the will of the Fell Ken.

"You're sure Tomash won't appear suddenly? And Alan won't notice you missing?"

"I'm sure. Long ago I had Marek provide me with a little kit. I wasn't sure what I might need to use it for, but it seemed to me to be a good idea. I'll deal with the consequences of that later, I'm sure." She laughed tensely and weighed the Sword in her hand. "Of course, the Sword takes up one hand. I don't have a scabbard. I can leave it behind if it's more important that I have both hands free to help."

"No!" Lorcas replied. "I can carry or drag Zumar myself if I have to. He's smaller than me by a good bit and he should be able to stagger along. I like the idea of having the Sword."

They both stood silently for a moment longer, looking up at the castle. In the distance, Lorcas thought he heard a boat motor whine, then drop in pitch. He took a deep breath.

"I guess we'd better get to it."

Tondra nodded. Lorcas moved away from the corner of the house carefully and took a look around. Of course, no one was up. The hill before them seemed steeper in the dark, the castle loomed as though it leaned over them. He allowed his mind to search briefly for Rook, but he heard and felt no movement.

He walked carefully, feeling for anything that could trip him up. The path to the bridge was worn smooth by the many feet that had gone along it at this point, but there were occasional rocks and roots. Tondra followed close behind. The bridge across the chasm glowed ruddy in the fiery red light from below, the source of which Lorcas did not know. They crossed quickly and made their way to the Banquet Hall door as usual.

Inside it was pitch black. Lorcas lit the way with his pocket flashlight. He had decided to take the most direct way there and the easiest way back. Occasionally they passed windows and casements which let in a small amount of light from outside. There, Lorcas lowered his light to avoid alerting anyone.

Finally, they arrived at the Keep and made their way across the King's Garden to the chapel. Lorcas went to the crypt immediately. Now that they were underway, he wanted to get everything done as quickly as possible.

"Help me push back the lid," he whispered to Tondra.

Tondra leaned the Sword against the crypt and together they shoved the lid as far back as they could, until one corner hit the wall. The grinding of stone on stone seemed loud in the silent room. Tondra stepped back and picked up the Sword again, and Lorcas noticed that she shuddered involuntarily. After all, she had not seen Zumar alive again, and could only imagine his corpse there in the murk of the crypt.

Lorcas had worn a windbreaker to guard against the nighttime damp as well as to provide himself with some extra pockets. He pulled out a candle and lighter and lit the wick. Then he leaned over the stone rim and held the light over Zumar's chest, below his chin. His mouth felt dry and he could feel his heart beating as he pressed against the sarcophagus. Tondra craned over his shoulder. The flickering candlelight created weird patterns across Zumar's pallid face and the interior of the crypt.

The candle wax began to drip, and Lorcas caught it with his other hand. There was no motion from Zumar, no indication that he was beginning to awake. Lorcas searched his mind, trying to remember if there was anything else he had done before or anything Zumar had indicated he had to bring. Zumar had mentioned the Smokeweed off-handedly, so he hadn't thought it important. But perhaps it was? He changed position restlessly; his arm was getting tired from the awkward position.

He glanced over his shoulder at Tondra. "It's not working. Last time I lit some Smokeweed, but I didn't think it was important, and it tends to increase my connection with Rook, so I didn't bring it this time. He did say he'd be in a deeper trance."

"Keep trying," Tondra whispered. Then she cocked her head. "What's that?"

Lorcas listened for a second. "Rook," he replied. The grinding was distant and brief, not constant, but he was sure of what it was.

He turned back desperately to Zumar. They might have to abort the attempt. It would be worthless to confront Rook without having awakened Zumar. Besides wasting their time, they would never get a second chance once Rook realized what they were up to.

He felt Tondra against his left shoulder. She lowered the Sword into the crypt, holding it horizontally. The light of the candle played along it, creating patterns like he had seen in Raine's ceremony, tendrils curling and licking across it as though the blade itself burned. The reflection lit the interior of the crypt, filling it with illusory fire.

Suddenly Zumar's eyes snapped open.

"He's awake!" Lorcas hissed. Tondra withdrew the Sword and leaned over the rim, staring.

Lorcas quickly stuck the candle to the edge of the crypt's lid. "Zumar!" he whispered urgently.

Zumar did not move, but Lorcas could see by the light in his eyes that his focus was becoming stronger.

"He was groggy last time and he may be worse this time, but we don't have time to wait for him to come around," he told Tondra. "Help me get him out."

Lorcas grabbed Zumar's shirt at the shoulders and dragged him into a sitting position. Tondra leaned in as best she could and got one arm around his back. Together they scooted him further down the interior, and then Lorcas grabbed him in a bear-hug and dragged him out while Tondra managed his feet and legs. They tried to stand him up, but he was unresponsive, although he seemed to be supporting his own head. Tondra grabbed the chair Tomash had been using and Lorcas let Zumar down onto it.

"Zumar, I'm sorry to be dragging you around, but we have to go quickly now that you're awake," Lorcas explained hurriedly. "Rook is camping out down in the depths of the castle with no intention of leaving any time soon. We're taking you to Mira. She's agreed to take you across the lake. Things could get interesting in the next few minutes, but we've got to get you out and down to the cove. I need you to work on trying to wake up and control your body."

Tondra stood by the chapel door. "I thought I heard more grinding," she said nervously. She readjusted the Sword in her hand and looked out towards the King's Garden.

"All right, let's go," Lorcas said. "You lead the way with the Sword. I'll tell you what route to take."

He worked his arm behind Zumar's back and under his arms and heaved him to his feet. Fortunately, Zumar was not heavy, but his shorter stature made supporting him awkward and Lorcas had to stoop, which was hard on his back. Zumar seemed to have

82

regained some control of his body and Lorcas could tell he was trying to support himself, but he was still unable to truly walk. Lorcas moved forward, half lifting and half dragging, and they made it to the chapel door.

It was going to be harder than he thought proceeding like this, Lorcas realized. He considered trying to carry Zumar across his shoulders in a fireman's carry, but many of the doorways and hallways were narrow and low, and he was afraid it would be more awkward and thus slower. Even the path through the garden was narrow, only a single track, and he turned sideways, dragging Zumar partially behind him. Tondra stood holding the door to the Keep, the Sword glinting in the moonlight.

"How are you doing?" she asked as Lorcas squeezed past her. "Is he waking up at all?"

"A bit," Lorcas gasped. "He's trying. But I'm going to have to rest from time to time. I'm not going to be able to drag him the whole way."

"That won't do. We have to hurry," Tondra said. She stepped to Zumar's other side, wrapped her free arm around his back, and adjusted his hand loosely across her shoulder. She was about the same height as Zumar, and Lorcas felt the relief as she stood straight, taking some of Zumar's weight.

"I may have to drop him suddenly if I have to use the Sword," Tondra said. She held it in her right hand, blade to the back to avoid waving it around in front of them dangerously.

"I understand," Lorcas said. "Let's go."

They crossed the Keep much more quickly than they had the garden. Lorcas could feel Zumar's hand gripping his shirt now, and occasionally the Messenger attempted a staggering step. They reached the first stairway and made their way down laboriously.

"Go right," Lorcas gasped at the bottom. "It's longer, but there's a ramp, or at least there was last time I went that way."

Tondra didn't answer, but she turned according to his directions. As they descended the ramp, Zumar began to move his legs independently, although he still wasn't supporting himself completely.

"He's getting better," Tondra panted. "Do you feel Rook, Lorcas?"

"I don't know, and I don't want to alert him," Lorcas said, "but I don't feel him as far as I can tell. In fact, he's oddly quiet."

"Good," Tondra replied. "I'm sure I heard him before. Could he be waiting for us somewhere?"

"Of course, he could be," Lorcas said. "Let's hope not. Zumar, how are you doing?"

"For God's sake, don't let me think about him!" Zumar gasped.

"You mean Rook?" Lorcas readjusted his grip and hurried Zumar around a corner and down another ramp.

"Don't say that! Distract me!"

"Uh…" Lorcas glanced at Tondra.

Tondra pulled her arm out and left Zumar to Lorcas to manage. She took a few hurried steps in order to lead the way and flipped the Sword back around to a forward grip.

"All right, Zumar, I'll distract you," she said. "Have you been lying there aware that Tomash was sitting just feet away, suffering, and you didn't say anything?"

"It's not that simple," Zumar complained.

"Seems pretty simple," Tondra snapped. "You didn't have a problem summoning Lorcas."

"Only because he happened to be there when the light was right," Zumar asserted. "It couldn't have been easy to wake me tonight, and you see how I am now. Most of the time I've been semi-conscious."

"Well, okay," Tondra said, with a slightly teasing tone. "I suppose I can forgive you. Do you understand what we're doing?"

"No." Zumar shook his head. He was walking on his own now, but Lorcas gripped his upper arm to help him balance and move him along.

"You're going to Mira," Tondra said. "Lorcas told you that when we first awakened you, but I guess you don't remember."

"No. Does Mira know this? Did she tell you it's okay? Is she sure?" Zumar demanded. "Wait! Did you hear that?"

Lorcas slowed for a moment. He had heard it, or felt it, too. More grinding, although only for a moment, and a sudden intake of air, a rush of wind. In the depths of his ears there seemed to be a pounding like the sound of a heartbeat, but it wasn't his heartbeat. The throbbing was too slow and powerful.

"Don't stop!" Tondra urged. "Keep going as fast as you can!"

They reached the end of the ramp and arrived at the top of a narrow flight of stairs, barely illuminated by a series of windows to the south. Lorcas let go and followed just a step behind Zumar in case he stumbled or fell, but Zumar took the stairs without a problem. From there they were back in familiar territory, the route Lorcas usually used to access the top floors.

The next stairway was on the opposite side of the balcony. They ran together, feet echoing on flagstone floors. There was no point in slowing themselves down in order to be quiet if Rook was already awake and moving.

Suddenly Lorcas staggered. It was as if the entire building melted for a moment. For a few seconds he felt as though he was in some carnival fun-house where the walls were distorted and the floors rolled under his feet. He threw out an arm to steady himself, but his hand sank into the wall as though it was a damp sponge, or, he realized in a fleeting impression, cold flesh. He jerked it back, his mind flashing to a similar instance when he'd returned to his own form after flying.

Ahead of him Tondra and Zumar flailed around on the balcony as though they were running on soft sand. Then, in a flash, it was over. Everything seemed as solid and stable as ever.

Zumar scrambled to his feet from where he'd fallen against the rail. "I'm sorry!" he gasped hoarsely.

"It's not your fault!" Lorcas said. "Go!"

They gained the top of the next stairway a moment later and ran down. This one was wider, but the stone was polished like marble and slick. Lorcas slipped and nearly fell several times, only catching himself with the handrail. He knew they were still five stories at least above ground level. He had to make a decision now; did they continue down this way, or try to detour to a smaller, but possibly faster, side route where they didn't have to round half the floor to get to the next stairway each time?

"Go right!" he yelled. "Head for the stairwell in the northern turret!"

Ahead of him, Tondra skidded around the corner, followed by Zumar. There was a quick ripple through the stone like the pattern in a pond after someone threw a rock, but Lorcas kept his feet this time. They crowded together as they hurtled down the steep stairs, taking the turns from one floor to another at full speed. Finally, they reached the ground floor, and Tondra threw open a small door behind one of the columns in the Banquet Hall.

A few moments more and they were outside. They rounded the side of the building and stumbled along the path in the dark towards the bridge.

As they reached the bridge, Lorcas paused and looked back at the looming dark castle. It seemed to him it shimmered like an illusion, incorporeal, or at least losing its hard edges. He scanned it from side to side and top to bottom, but he saw no sign of Rook. But what else could explain the changes that had come over the building? Even now, he thought he saw it undulate and waver. For a moment it seemed to him that the entire castle was about to rush down the hill.

He turned again and hurried after Tondra and Zumar. If he was going to have to confront Rook about his removal of Zumar, at least now it would be out in the open where he felt he had a little more advantage. Perhaps the confrontation wouldn't occur until he returned, when Rook would certainly feel Zumar's absence from the world.

They made their way along the wall at a more controlled pace now that they were clear of the castle. Lorcas brought out his flashlight to help them navigate the dark forest and the steep path to the cove. The boat was there below, white against the dark sea. Tondra clambered up over the large boulder at the bottom and turned to give Zumar her hand. She heaved him up, and they stepped off onto the prow of the boat as Lorcas scrambled up behind them.

"You're late," Jason said as they crowded into the cabin. He backed the boat off immediately.

"Sorry," Lorcas said. "It took longer than I thought to wake Zumar up. Have you all met before?"

Tondra eyed Jason. "Tondra Sivitko. I spoke to you when you were up here before, interviewing people about Korrin Bright and Bob Dover."

"I remember. And you must be Zumar. You avoided my interrogations before," Jason said with a smile. "You don't look so good."

"Excuse me, I've been dead for a while," Zumar snapped.

Jason laughed shortly. "Where's your beastie, Lorcas?"

"He hasn't shown up yet, but that doesn't mean he won't," Lorcas replied. "Get us to the tower quick."

Jason turned his attention to the GPS unit and steered them off the coast. As they neared the tower, he brought the throttles back. "Now how are you going to get onto that thing?"

"You'll have to get me close enough to grab it," Lorcas said. He threw a couple of bumpers over the side as Jason maneuvered closer.

Lorcas leaned over the rail. It was not going to be easy with the boat moving up and down with the swells and the tower disappearing and reappearing in the shadows. But as he reached out for it, the water seemed to sink slightly into a bowl-shaped depression and the waves stopped sloshing over the top, leaving the steeple more exposed. The boat teetered on the edge as though it was about to drop into a whirlpool.

He made several attempts before he both got a good grip on the top and got up his guts to scramble over the rail and step off onto the lip he knew must be there. It was a more stable position than he had thought, and he was able to let go with one hand and crouch to feel around for the release mechanism. He opened the hatch and laid out the little deck.

"I've got it," he shouted. Jason, who had allowed the boat to drift off a short distance, brought it back to the tower, and Lorcas put out a hand to help Zumar off. Zumar ducked inside immediately.

"We have to go," Lorcas told Tondra and Jason. "Try to wait for me, but if things go bad, do what you have to do to protect yourselves. I'll be safer in the tower and the tunnels than you will be out here."

Tondra nodded. "I'll take care of things. We'll see you soon."

Lorcas climbed into the tower and secured the hatch, then began his descent down the ladders after Zumar. The green-tinged light was enough for them to see their way, and they took the now-familiar route in silence except for their hurried footsteps on the mossy stone.

Mira's boat arrived swiftly after Lorcas summoned her, which he did by agitating the water with his hand, since he didn't have the Staff. In the few minutes before she came, he tried to calm himself and lower his heart rate and breathing to closer to normal, telling himself that things were going well so far.

"I've been expecting you," Mira said as she stepped out. "How are you doing, Zumar?"

Zumar nodded in greeting. "Still recovering."

"Did you have trouble with Rook?"

"Not really," Lorcas replied, "or at least, not in the way I thought we might. Of course, there's the possibility I'll have to deal with him when I get back."

"I trust that you will be able to do so. You are capable. But for safety's sake, we will depart now," Mira said. "Once Zumar is completely outside of Rook's influence, I suspect Rook will realize there is nothing he can do." She smiled and offered a hand to Zumar.

Zumar took it willingly, but suddenly Mira stiffened and stood stock still. She dropped his hand quickly, her expression stony.

"He cannot come across the water," she stated.

"What? Why not?" Lorcas asked incredulously.

"He knows why," Mira replied. She was still standing face-to-face with Zumar.

"But what are we supposed to do?" Lorcas demanded frantically. "I can't take him back out there!"

"No," Mira said, turning away from Zumar at last. "He can stay here in the borderlands. But I cannot risk taking him across the water to my world at this time."

"Why not? Will he be safe here? Where could he stay?" Lorcas persisted.

"He will be relatively safe here, although not completely. We will eventually have to come to some other conclusion. But for the short term, it is the only solution. There is a cabin a bit further up the path we took the other day, past where we turned back. It is called the Woodcutter's Cabin, a place that exists on the edge of the tales of humankind. It will provide shelter and some few amenities. It will be easy for you to locate him, Lorcas, when you come. And you will have to return here, Lorcas, because I see that I have been mistaken about some few things. Unfortunately, I am not infallible. There is more to this than I realized."

Lorcas spread his hands. "I have to go! God knows what Tondra and Jason are dealing with out there! I have to rescue them and deal with whatever the fallout will be."

"Yes, go now," Mira said. "Remember that you have more power than you think. Although less, perhaps, than I have assumed."

Mira turned and strode to the boat, stepped in, and disappeared quickly into the mist. Lorcas and Zumar were left alone.

"Zumar, I don't know what's going on," Lorcas said. Mira's words were not encouraging, nor what he had expected to hear.

"I expect I do," Zumar said grimly. "It's not the Sazh that's the problem, it's me. We haven't time to discuss it at the moment."

"No. I have to go. Be as safe as you can. Go to this Woodcutter's Cabin, and I'll be back."

"All I can do is apologize," Zumar said. "That, and hope it's not too late." He turned sharply on his heel and hurried towards the edge of the forest and the path that Mira had indicated. Lorcas turned as well, the opposite direction, and made his way back to the tower as quickly as he could.

He scrambled up the ladders and threw open the window at the top, not sure what to expect. The boat was there, bobbing gently on the swells. Everything seemed peaceful. Rook was not there.

Rook's absence made Lorcas perhaps more nervous than he would have been dealing with the threat head-on. It had to happen; Rook had to be coming at some point. What would he choose to do to answer this insubordination? Rook had more than one technique available, and all the time in the world.

He heard Tondra's voice and the boat immediately began to putter closer to the tower. Jason brought it up alongside and Lorcas grabbed the rail and managed to step on. He turned back to the tower and leaned over the side to make sure it was secured. As he flipped the catch, the water surged back over the top.

"Let's go," he said as he made his way to the cabin. "Zumar is safe, or safe enough, for the time being. Let's make sure we stay that way as well."

"Where do you think Rook is?" Tondra asked as Jason swung the boat around.

"I don't know. Try not to think about it," Lorcas said. "I don't know what's going on with him lately. There are things Zumar needs to tell me, things that may help us all understand. I'll go talk to him when I can."

Jason kept them well off-shore to avoid bringing any attention with the motor noise. The eastern sky was just beginning to lighten as they made a slow arc back to the cove. Lorcas gazed up at the outline of the castle, strangely silent, and the black shapes of the wall and nearest houses.

At the very end of the wall he saw two people, silhouetted with the earliest morning light behind them. One was much shorter; that one, he thought, given the profile, was likely Kara, although what the young girl was doing up and around at this hour he did not know. He had seen her standing in that very place before. The other silhouette he did not recognize: tall and slender, with just a hint of the fiery red of the sun tinging tousled hair.

He kept an eye on them as Jason brought the boat in to the large rock in the cove. He and Tondra scrambled off, and Jason backed out quickly and turned to the south.

Lorcas led the way up the steep trail with Tondra just behind. At the top, his breath coming hard, his heart pounding, he wound his way through the woods to the furthest reach of the wall. It was barely dawn, but he could see well enough now to identify the figures.

One was indeed Kara, but the other was not a member of the Fell Ken. At least, not a current member. His face was familiar, in an oddly different way. He looked to be in his early 20s, with blond unkempt hair tinged with red, and his clothing seemed to be that of a medieval traveler. He did not move as Lorcas came up to him face-to-face.

Kara looked up at Lorcas with a triumphant expression. "He's back," she said.

CHAPTER SIX

In a moment Tondra jumped forward. The Sword flashed. The very tip of it paused just below Dirk's chin, pricking his skin. Dirk did not move. His pale eyes did not even flick in Tondra's direction; he continued to stare at Lorcas, eye-to-eye as they were nearly the same height.

"You're not welcome here," Tondra growled.

Dirk stirred for the first time, momentarily breaking eye contact with Lorcas. "If the Lorecaster commands it, I will go," he said softly, "but I will take my brother and sister with me when I leave."

Lorcas put out a hand towards the Sword, and Tondra lowered it slightly. "That's a change," he sneered, "you taking orders from me."

"It's been many years," Dirk replied. "I was a child, and mistaken about a few things. You did me no favors, but I admit my error. Since then, I have traveled many long roads and learned many things. Besides, you and the Fell Ken need me. If it was not time before, certainly it is now."

Lorcas glanced at Tondra. It was true that they had dealt harshly with Dirk, and since then they had been unable to determine exactly what had occurred to bring him to that point or what had happened to his parents.

"It hasn't been that long, only a year," Lorcas said, "but I see that you've grown a great deal."

"It's been seven years in the time that I experienced," Dirk replied.

It certainly seemed that Dirk had been away longer than a year, given his growth and the odd change in his manner of speaking and clothing. Who knew how time moved once one crossed Mira's lake? Where had he wandered, and what might he know?

"All right, then. The time's of no consequence to me. Why have you returned? How did you get here? What do you want?"

"As for why, it must be that you need me," Dirk said. A shadow crossed his face. "I ceased to search for a way home at last. I realized I could return only when called across, so I must indeed have been called. I walked through a mist, and this place was on the other side."

"I don't necessarily believe you," Lorcas said, "but I don't disbelieve you either. I think sometimes maybe we do find our way when we cease searching for it. Perhaps we have an opportunity to right a few wrongs from the past. There's information you may know that could be valuable. Your sister and brother have been seriously affected by both our actions." He nodded at Kara, who stood clasping her hands, glancing worriedly from one to the other. "You were once Fell Ken. If indeed you take orders from me now and not from whoever was handling you before, then you will do as I ask."

"As for that, I can promise only that I will not confront you," Dirk said. "There are other ways to accomplish what must be done, and I know you will find it in your best interest for us to cooperate."

Lorcas scowled. Dirk obviously wasn't trustworthy. He was skating around the questions, as bad as Rook. "Look, I'm very tired. We haven't slept tonight. I must have time to think about how to deal with you, and there are other issues I have to attend to. We'll lock you in the cabin where we kept Jack last year; it's been repaired and should be harder to escape from, although I suppose you might have learned a few tricks in your wanderings. You'll be cared for, and you can visit with Kara and Saber. After we've gotten some rest, we'll question you. Depending on the answers you give, we'll make a decision."

"I, too, need rest," Dirk said a little bitterly. "I have had none for seven years; and as far as being locked up, my life has never been my own, and it will be little change."

Lorcas glanced at Tondra. Despite his suspicion, he felt a jolt of guilt. He had been a part of Dirk's former life, at one point a role model and then later responsible for his banishment. Dirk's tone revealed how he felt, even if his words were neutral.

"Don't let him fool you," Tondra said harshly, as though reading his thoughts. "He's making you feel guilty. It's manipulative. Let's put him in the cabin and we'll deal with him later."

She walked a few steps away from Dirk and Lorcas followed, keeping an eye on the two Katzbalgers. Tondra pulled out her cell phone and lowered her voice. "Alan has the key to lock the cabin.

We'll need to let him and Tomash know what we did tonight anyway."

"Yes, but let's keep it within the Entourage for now," Lorcas said, "both what we did and what we're doing. The rest of the Fell Ken will be happy to know that Zumar's alive, no doubt, but they'll be puzzled as to why we're hiding him from Rook. They may like Zumar, but they're here because of Rook, and they've sacrificed a lot for him. They're going to be confused, and I'm not sure myself how this is all going to play out."

"I agree," Tondra said. "Just us for now."

The morning sun was becoming stronger and people would soon begin to start their day. Lorcas gestured for Dirk to walk in front of them. He and Tondra followed. The cabin was unlocked, and they escorted Dirk inside quickly, out of the public eye.

"I'll get Alan to bring food and anything else you might need, Dirk. What's in your bag?" Tondra asked.

Dirk swung a leather satchel off his shoulder. "Look if you wish. It's only clothes and a few small possessions. No weapon."

Tondra upended the bag on the bed. As Dirk had said, there were a few articles of clothing, a few stones of some type, some personal items, and one gold coin.

"The tracking coin that used to belong to Terry," Lorcas said. "I gave it to him for guarding my house. I suppose it will work again now that it's back in our world." He rolled the stones around a bit, but nothing seemed amiss. "I don't think there's anything dangerous here. Might as well let him keep it."

He glanced at the door as Alan walked in, looking as though he had been awakened by Tondra's call. Alan and Dirk locked eyes for a long moment.

"I brought the key," Alan said as he finally turned away. "I feel like there are things going on that I've been left out of."

"I'm sorry, Alan," Tondra said. "I'll explain in a little bit. I haven't had any sleep, but I know you have, so we'll need you to keep guard today while we get some rest. Then you, me, Lorcas, and Tomash will need to talk. And I suppose Raine, if we can find her and get her here."

"I can work on that," Alan said a grudgingly. "I have, indeed, had a mysteriously good night's sleep. As for talking, there will certainly need to be some."

Tondra avoided his gaze. "I'll need you to keep Kara with you. She can't be allowed to talk. Make up some reason for her to stay with you, some task that I need her to perform. Fortunately, I've been mentoring her, so her foster parents should find it easy enough to believe."

After Alan locked the door Tondra headed for her house, leaving Alan and Kara outside the cabin. Lorcas walked slowly to his own. He paused for a long moment, gazing up at the castle, concentrating on what he felt, but there was no hint of a call, nothing at all. The lack of response didn't make him feel any better. In fact, he felt even more on edge, as though he was waiting for it all to happen. There were other decisions to be made, but he would need to get some rest before he could make them. The charges of adrenalin overnight, the constant need to be on guard, the unexpected events, had all served to wear him out.

He slept until early afternoon, fitfully despite his exhaustion. When he got up, he had a text from Tondra from about a half-hour before.

"Went to check on Dirk. Found him sleeping or passed out. Couldn't wake him. He was breathing so I left him alone. Contact me when you're awake."

Lorcas put the phone down without replying to give himself some time to think. Showered and dressed, he made a cup of coffee and had some lunch; he'd skipped breakfast altogether. He sat in the living room and once again searched tentatively for Rook in his mind. Once again, he felt nothing except a heavy sense of foreboding.

When he was done with most of the coffee, he stuck his phone in his pocket and walked down to Tondra's house. Tondra was sitting outside on a lawn chair in the sun, as if waiting for him.

"Hey," he greeted her. "Have you had a chance to talk to Alan and Tomash?"

"Yes, I told Alan what we did before I went to sleep, and told Tomash when I got up."

"What do they think?"

"Alan's upset, of course. Somewhat less upset than I thought. Kind of like he was going through the motions. I almost wish he'd just lose it. Instead, he's just being stoic and withdrawn. He's making me feel worse."

"I'm sorry. I'm sure he can understand why we wanted as few people as possible involved in the rescue to avoid alerting Rook," Lorcas said. "He's a reasonable man, he'll forgive you. You can blame it on me."

"Oh, I did," Tondra said with a wry chuckle.

"As for Dirk, it's a surprise to all of us. How did Tomash take it? He must be excited."

Tondra shook her head. "When I talked to him an hour ago, he just seemed kind of flat, with no real emotion at all. Maybe he doesn't believe it, or he's been sitting up there in the chapel so long that he can't imagine what he's going to do now. Maybe he's upset that Zumar didn't contact him first when he spent all that time waiting for him. But he's kind of been like this ever since he went to Mira's realm. He went up to the castle and he hasn't come back yet."

"I can check on him if you want," Lorcas said.

"If he doesn't come back by himself, one of us should, eventually," Tondra said. "Let's give him a little time, though. Besides, we need to discuss what we're going to ask Dirk and how we're going to satisfy ourselves that he isn't a danger. Or that he is."

"I definitely want to know what happened to his parents and who convinced them to do what they did. And we need to know what he meant about us needing him now."

"But when I went to check on him I couldn't wake him. The questioning may have to wait a bit."

"Do you think he's safe enough locked in there?" Lorcas asked.

"It's hard to say. If he can summon Rook or some other power, of course a cabin won't be able to contain him."

"True," Lorcas said, "but if he's going to sleep for a while, maybe I can take some time and go visit Zumar. I might be able to get information from him or from Mira that will help us figure out how to question Dirk. And I definitely need to know why Mira refused to take Zumar over the lake."

"Sounds good, if you're up to it," Tondra said. "Ask Mira about waking up someone who's been wandering for seven years. I can sit here and keep guard and apologize to Alan and Tomash a few more times."

"Whether I'm up to it or not, I should probably go," Lorcas said. "I'll tell you what I find out. Don't worry about Alan; he'll come around. And I'm sure Tomash will too, once he's over the shock of it."

He took a deep breath and turned once again to the castle and the now-familiar route to Mira's realm.

When he arrived at the cavern, he passed the pool and continued up the broad path through the forest on the far side. As he walked the cavern seemed to grow, opening out and becoming lighter, indistinguishable from a heavy forest outside with a misty sky overhead. Somehow there was a different feel to it, as though he had exited Mira's borderland and entered another.

Eventually he came to a small log cabin, neat and solid, tucked beneath large trees. He assumed it was the Woodcutter's cabin: there was a large, heavy axe half-buried in a stump in front. But Zumar didn't answer when he knocked, and he was reluctant to bring attention to himself by shouting. After a few minutes of searching the general area and walking further along the path, he returned the way he'd come.

Mira was waiting for him on the shore. He raised a hand as he emerged from the woods. She didn't return the gesture, but she waited placidly, watching him until he arrived.

"Where is Zumar?" Lorcas asked.

She shrugged. "The borderlands are large and varied, and he can go many places. Time fluctuates here, not as much as across the lake, but it is still different from yours. I'm sure he will return eventually, although I cannot guarantee when."

"Okay," Lorcas said, "then I'll have to ask you, because there are some things I need to know now, and I can't wait. Why wouldn't you take him across the water like we agreed?"

Mira turned abruptly and strolled along the shore. Lorcas followed at her shoulder.

"Well?" he pressed when Mira did not answer right away.

She turned and scrutinized him, looking deep into his eyes.

"I should have realized," she said thoughtfully. "When I first saw the construction, the castle, I thought it strange. It is not a thing I would expect to be manifest by someone like you and your Fell Ken, someone of your time and place. But I had not had direct contact with Zumar and only met him briefly, and then only when my attention was on another. I assumed from your stories, from your bond with Rook, and from the fact that it was you who first crossed into the borderlands, that the manifestation was yours. But I was mistaken."

Lorcas shook his head in puzzlement. He did remember Mira's initial look at the castle the year before, when he thought she scoffed at it, but the significance of that escaped him.

"I told you I suspected that Zumar was able to pass into other worlds prior to his association with Rook," Mira continued. "I called him a sprite, a mischievous spirit of the borderlands, and have not paid attention to how he came to be. In fact, I did not much care, and only agreed to take him across my lake to help you and your people, with whom I've had long association. But I am not a mind-reader nor infallible, and it was only when I took his hand that I knew otherwise."

"What did you know?" Lorcas pressed urgently. "What is he?"

"As for that, it is difficult to give him a name. He is an Earth spirit, an immortal, much more powerful than the sprites and imps, but undisciplined and untutored, and therefore dangerous. His powers, largely unrealized, rival those of the ones you name 'Allies', including me. Of course, even such spirits must have a beginning, and it's likely he was born as he told you, into the time and place he related. But because he then met his demise so young, he had little time to develop before he became associated with Rook, and no guidance. He has the capacity to align himself with the good, but he was not presented with that opportunity, and thus identified with the chaotic and destructive. I will not take him to my personal realm, especially when he contains the Sazh. The two together have united, most unusually, to form a unique co-entity, half fire and half earth. I now believe he could indeed lead Rook, or others like him, into my realm, either accidentally or for other purposes. And I do not want Rook there. For that matter, I do not want Zumar there. There is room only for me, and not for another with such powers as he harbors, whether he is aware of them or not."

She gazed out across the lake before continuing. "This may have other implications. It may be that Rook could only have been initially drawn forth by an entity such as Zumar. If so, that indicates that Rook may have come from some much further and darker place than I have assumed, and his plans may be much more drastic than I realized. All worlds change from time to time, and so, even though I regret Rook's growing influence in your land, I have not seen it as a thing with which to interfere. But my suspicions are growing, as is my interest."

Lorcas hardly knew what to ask as Mira paused. He knew he didn't like what he was hearing, but the full implications were beyond him. Finally, he stammered out a question.

"But what does this mean for Rook and the Fell Ken? Whatever Zumar actually is, or was, how does it affect our relationship with Rook and what's going to happen in the future?"

Mira considered. "Contrary to my previous belief, you are not the primary manifestor of Rook, Lorcas, and thus you have less control than I thought. You are a conduit, yes, and by now a powerful second.

You have been imbued with various powers through bonding rituals with Rook as well as by the earth magic of the Fell Ken. But Rook was built on the back of Zumar and brought forth into your world by him. Undoubtedly Zumar has controlled much of what has occurred according to his own whims and desires and to fulfill some agreement with Rook."

She walked slowly once again along the shore of the lake near the trees. "Think about it. If Rook was a manifestation of yours, things would certainly be different. Why the form of the castle? Why has everything proceeded as though it was centuries ago in your time?"

"I assumed it was because Rook had slept all those years and he was trying to create something to make his people comfortable, but all he knew was what we had been back then," Lorcas said as he followed her.

"But the same can be said of Zumar. If he was the guiding force behind Rook's manifestation, then of course what Rook knew would be filtered through the mind of a man who died 600 years ago," Mira said.

"That's true," Lorcas agreed. He'd never felt he had anything to do with how the castle was created or formed. All he'd done was collect the stones and assemble them. "But then, is Rook unable to go on without Zumar? Is Zumar permanently bound to Rook?"

Mira considered for a moment. "Zumar is not permanently bound to Rook. The evidence for that is that he did not die even when he wished it and when Rook withdrew his support. Now he is aware that he has an existence apart and aside from Rook, whereas before he may have believed that it was Rook who sustained him. As for Rook, as he has grown in power, he has apparently separated himself from Zumar. Perhaps he realized that Zumar would one day become aware of his true nature, and he feared it, because loosed from any bonds and obligations, Zumar might become dangerous to him. This is why he was content to allow Zumar to die, and hoped it would happen if he withdrew. If it did not occur, he could at least keep Zumar imprisoned within himself to effectively prevent him from functioning."

"You mean he intended to keep him within the crypt, just lying there unable to do anything?" Lorcas asked with a shudder.

"The castle as a whole is Rook himself," Mira replied cryptically. "As for the rest, the control of the direction the Fell Ken will take and how they as a people will proceed still rests upon you, of course. That is wholly different from what will become of Rook. But you may not be able to accomplish what you want without Zumar if that direction includes the desire to be rid of Rook. As for how he manifested the spirit of Rook and why he made Rook into what he did, you will have to ask him yourself."

"And I shall tell you, since I currently have no choice."

Lorcas and Mira turned. Zumar stood just within the cover of the trees. He came towards them.

"Would it surprise you to hear that my mother told me when I was a child that one afternoon, she fell asleep upon a hill outside our town with her back against a rock, and that when she awoke she knew herself to be with child?"

Mira smiled slightly. "That is a common way for a child of two worlds to be born, especially an earth elemental. When did you know?"

Zumar shrugged. "I don't remember. I knew quite early that I could walk within my dreams while waking, and I often entered the worlds of mists to see the fantastic creatures I encountered. Some were funny, some were terrifying, but they accepted me as one of their own. And I could leave those worlds whenever I wanted and return to my own."

"You say "worlds"," Mira noted. "You could enter several?"

"Many," Zumar agreed. "It seemed that I could pass from one to another, traveling through borderlands and choosing which entry I wished to take, yet always find my way back to my own when I wanted."

"A most unusual quality," Mira said.

"Is it?" Zumar asked. "I wouldn't know. There was none other like me that I knew. As a child, some said I had a good imagination, that perhaps I would be an artist. My father said I was a day-dreamer, and apprenticed me to a wood-worker. The wood-worker beat me, and eventually I ran away back to my mother. My father was not a vindictive man despite his suspicions, for he believed I was not his son, in which he was correct. He did not force me to return, but instead sent me to relatives in the north hoping I would make a good marriage and create a solid business connection. I found that area to my liking; it was heavily connected to the borderlands, and I was able to come and go as I wished."

"This was the area of the Cornerstone?" Mira confirmed.

"Yes. I went about my life, entertaining the girls and working with my kinfolk. I was by then quite good at certain sleight-of-hand tricks, and I could add a bit extra to them by sending things into the mist and retrieving them later, either for my own use or to play jokes by returning them. And I also found that I was unusually good at escaping from incidents in which others were injured or even killed, by simply being elsewhere. Eventually it was to prove my downfall, as I was branded a witch. They sought to rid the community of one they considered dangerous, as well as one who was a bit too successful with his flirtations."

"That's very similar to what you already told me," Lorcas said.

"Not too different. After I was thrown in the pit under the Cornerstone, I regained consciousness slowly. At first, I attempted to move myself out of the grave and into one of the borderlands, which I thought was much more likely to be possible than escaping into my own world. But I had too little experience or power. It was as if I could open only a slit into those worlds, not large enough for me to pass through. But eventually I became aware of another entity in the rock above me."

"And that was Rook?" Lorcas asked.

"I only knew it was another being. I had no idea of his form or shape. I knew him to be out of place, trapped outside his own lands, just barely existing in ours. It was as if a small part of him had entered our world and become stuck, unable to return and unable to continue to move out. It seemed that he was just the spark of a being, or a leftover of one who had previously existed, like me. Over time we learned to communicate. He used me as a kind of anchor and began to pull himself further out, and the connection between our worlds slowly opened. At first, I was afraid his energy would harm me, but in fact I felt stronger as he became more complete. As the castle was built, he became able to move from one stone to another and he was able to draw me along with him, increasing my freedom. But he needed a map upon which to build himself, a framework upon which to develop. So he grew along the plans I set out, the things I knew or could imagine he might be."

"He took your knowledge of the world and of stories and legends and molded himself to fit," Lorcas said.

"Yes," Zumar admitted. "Of course, I also tutored him on how to interact with humans and set myself up as his interface with them. There is more to my story, but it can wait. Right now, you must know Rook's true plans."

"That is vital," Lorcas agreed. "I am going to have to face Rook when he confronts me about removing you from the castle. He will undoubtedly feel betrayed again. And I can't honestly say this time that I wasn't aware I was betraying him. In fact, I trusted you over him, and I'm not the only one. Tondra had no qualms about it, and I know Tomash is dissatisfied with how things have gone."

"One thing you must know," Zumar replied. "What Rook has said was filtered, always, through me. I bent the truth when it suited my purposes in order to lead you along a certain path, towards Rook's development and eventual independence from me."

"But I've spoken to him directly as well," Lorcas pointed out. "He promised me the opportunity to create peace and a world with no terrible wars. I've always understood that there would need to be changes to the world in order for that to come about."

Zumar nodded. "Even when Rook spoke to you directly that was in a way shaped by me, as he learned from me how to communicate with you and what kinds of things to say and avoid saying. I know you do not understand the kind of changes that Rook will make. When he is done there will be no more strife, that is true. But neither will there be any world, not in the way you think of it. Rook is ripping a hole between his world and yours. As this hole grows larger and larger, his world comes further and further into yours."

"You mean that rather than Rook existing in our world as a kind of leader or controlling force, eventually his world will entirely overrun ours?" Lorcas asked.

"It will be as though the world has been turned inside-out: his now the one on the outside, and yours on the inside, within the mists, receding. It's already begun. You know when we explored the depths of the castle, we often heard other creatures scuttling around in the dark. Those were the small residents of his world, the ones that could fit through the openings he has made. And you told me about a stone you found, and a new chapel."

"You called it an egg," Lorcas recalled.

"Yes. Another being similar to Rook is waiting to emerge, to help speed the ripping open. And so it will go, becoming easier each time, more of them, faster and faster, pouring forth, until all of your world has been swallowed up by theirs."

Lorcas felt his stomach lurch. "What would become of humans in such a place?"

Zumar shrugged. "Your world will be only a haunted shadow of itself. You will be like furtive little animals, out of place, hiding in dark corners. Most humans will not survive. Only a few, the Fell Ken, will live, each set protected by their own Rook, to watch the rest of society dissolve. Eventually the world of humankind will recede into the mists, pushed away like many of the worlds I've walked in, always in danger of disappearing altogether."

"But why did you go along with this once you understood it? Why did you continue to help Rook and deceive us? Ours is your world, too. And other than the Sazh, why have you changed your mind now?"

Zumar turned and looked over the lake. "I only ever wanted freedom, freedom from Rook and freedom to be allowed to live my life, the one that was taken from me so early. I have been a prisoner, trapped by him and within him, for centuries. I wanted to develop Rook's strength until he could survive on his own without me, and I without him, and then disengage myself from him. I thought perhaps I could then go on about my normal life. But eventually I realized there was no place for me here, in this time, in this world, and that I would never be free of him and what I had created while I lived here. My alliance with Rook was thus both selfish and ultimately useless. When I failed to die when he withdrew his support and I was infected with the Sazh, I knew I had a power I had not realized before, as well as responsibilities to the Fell Ken who I led along this path. I do not know where, if anywhere, I do belong, only that it is not in the world into which I was born. Yet you are right, it is my birth world, and it would be wrong to continue to allow Rook to destroy it. And if we are to stop Rook from continuing this process, we're at a critical point: your discovery of the egg means the next stage is imminent."

"That reminds me," Lorcas said, "Dirk is back."

Zumar looked alarmed. "How did he find his way?"

"He said he was called. He said the Fell Ken need him now and that he couldn't have found his way back otherwise."

"He's right," Mira said. "It's very difficult to find one's way out of the lands in which I left him without a call."

"I'm beginning to suspect what he is here for," Lorcas said grimly.

"Yes," Zumar said. "Each new Rook will have its own group of Fell Ken to help it along. Each one will train his own Entourage to suit his purposes, starting with a young king or Lorecaster chosen by the previous Rook and tutored to communicate with and obey the new one. You need to stop that next egg from emerging, or you may never have the opportunity to even consider which way you want to go."

"Can't you stop it?" Lorcas demanded. "If you brought him out, can't you put him back?"

Zumar shook his head and took a step back from Lorcas's vehemence. "That time is long past. I would need help, if that's what you want to try to do. Serious help, not only from you and the Entourage. And we would need a plan. There isn't time for that right now."

"What if the Entourage refuses to help this emergence? Could that keep Rook contained at the stage he's at now?"

"Maybe temporarily. But whatever the eventual decision, stopping this next emergence is critical to buy us time."

"How can I do that?" Lorcas asked desperately.

"First of all, do not under any circumstances allow Dirk to go there. Also be suspicious of his siblings, and of course his parents if you can find them. Dirk needs help; he won't be able to trigger the emergence alone. But I have my suspicions about his sister and brother. They are undeveloped and unprepared, but I believe Kara to have the beginnings of a new Lorecaster within her, and Saber a new Messenger. The little one sees through the mists, that I know. The three of them might be able to pull it off."

He paced for a moment. "Are there any guardians of the chapel?"

"There is a monk," Lorcas said. "He showed up there the second time I went."

"They are here, then," Zumar said cryptically. "They may help you under certain circumstances. There is too much for me to tell you right now; go and assure nothing is happening to the new stone."

"I won't know how to stop it if there is," Lorcas said, "but I can at least make sure Dirk is secure and that the Entourage understands what the future will be like."

"I will come with you," Mira said.

Lorcas paused, surprised, as he turned towards the path.

"Zumar's words confirm my suspicions," Mira said. "I now believe that your world may become untethered in time if Rook is allowed to continue. And that is a thing neither I nor inhabitants of many other worlds would want."

Lorcas frowned. It was another of Mira's cryptic expressions, and he no longer had patience for them. "What does that mean, 'untethered in time'?"

"Your world serves as a kind of anchor, a stable place around which many other worlds move and intersect. If your world were to become untethered, what Zumar terms being 'turned inside out', it would fade into a shadow world. It would no longer be able to serve as an anchor; traffic back and forth between lands would become impossible and we would all become isolated in our own territories. My power would recede and I would diminish. There has been evidence of fluctuation of time around Rook already, in the event you call the Rising when the construction moved suddenly forward. Therefore, although I have little agency in your world now, I will endeavor to advise you well at the very least."

"Then let's go," Lorcas said. "I think we'd better hurry. Good-bye, Zumar, for now, but I suspect there is much more to discuss."

"Indeed," Zumar said.

CHAPTER SEVEN

Lorcas's phone beeped as soon as he exited the castle. He pulled it out as he walked and glanced at the screen. It was a message from Jason Japert. Actually, he saw, there were several messages. But he didn't need to listen to them; down by his house, he could see Jason's sedan. Whatever he wanted Lorcas to know, it was important enough that he'd come up in person.

Tondra met him halfway down the slope. "I've been watching for you," she said as she arrived.

They both looked up as a large silver raven glided up over the edge of the cliff. As it approached, it morphed seamlessly into Mira.

"Hello, Mira. I don't suppose you've come to fetch Dirk back?" Tondra greeted her.

"Unfortunately, no," Mira said with a smile. "Now that he's passed through the mist once, the likelihood is that he could do so again with much less problem. Also, I doubt he would trust me."

She turned and looked up at the castle. "I had intended to arrive in the casement where I met you before," she said, "but I found it inadvisable."

"I don't blame you," Tondra said. "Things have gotten weird in there lately." She turned back to Lorcas. "What did you find out from Zumar?"

"Many things, but I left before I got the whole story. Is Dirk still in the cabin?"

"As far as I know. Why, what did you find out about him?"

"That he was telling the truth," Lorcas said.

"What?" Tondra fell in beside them as Lorcas and Mira headed down the hill. "About being the replacement King? That can't be true!"

"Not exactly. But the only real mistake he made was thinking he was supposed to be the King here. He's not."

"Where else would he be?" Tondra asked.

"At the new chapel, where the new stone is," Lorcas said grimly. "A whole new Rook is scheduled to emerge there, and he'll need a new group of Fell Ken and an Entourage to take care of him. He needs a nice young King who can withstand his inexperience in dealing with humans, who he can train easily to his personal ways."

"Since when is there more than one Rook?" Tondra demanded. "I don't know anything about that."

"I didn't either," Lorcas said, "but Zumar did. Good thing he was imbued by the Sazh, otherwise I don't know if we would have found out before it actually happened."

"Now that we do know, can't we solve a lot of problems by just sending Dirk over there and letting him start up his own new Entourage?"

Lorcas glanced at her. "Maybe. But I'm pretty sure we don't want a second Rook, given what Zumar told me about the first one. There are a few, ah, details that have been left out of the story."

"I see. You're proposing we stall any further development. Rook isn't going to like that."

"I know. But you and I know we've got some doubts. We might as well admit it. Tomash has expressed some doubts to me, too. I don't know if he's said anything to you, but with you, him, me, and Zumar all feeling the need to consider new information before going forward, that's most of the Entourage."

Tondra took a moment before answering. "Tomash has hinted at a few misgivings, it's true. I guess I'm willing to stall until we can get all of us together and discuss things. We need to bring Alan and Raine into this, and eventually we may need a Council of Fell Ken convened." She squinted. "Is that Jason Japert's car?"

"Yes. There are a few things besides what I learned from Zumar that you should probably know."

Jason got out of his car as they approached, but stood uncertainly outside the wall as the trio approached. Lorcas opened the gate and waved him in.

"Jason Japert, this is Mira," he said. "I've mentioned her."

Jason nodded. "Nice to meet you."

"And I already know something of you," Mira said. "How did my potion work for you?"

"Your potion?" Jason glanced at Lorcas.

"The one I gave you the other day," Lorcas told him.

"Ah, that. I didn't realize it came from, well, wherever you come from, ma'am. Anyway, it worked well."

Lorcas gestured to Tondra. "You know Tondra already."

She reached out to shake Jason's hand. "Glad you could join us on dry land."

Japert flashed a grin. "Sorry to show up unexpectedly." He sobered. "I left you a couple of messages, but when I didn't hear back, I got a little concerned."

"Sorry, I was out of range. I haven't listened to them. What's going on?"

Jason hesitated and glanced at Tondra.

"It's okay," Lorcas said. "Given what I just found out myself, she needs to know everything that's going on."

"I just wanted to run some info about the church property and the monastery by you and see if it means anything."

"Good. Hopefully that will help fill in some of the pieces. But I think we need to take care of whatever Mira wants to do first. Anything else can wait."

"I should see this new stone and monastery," Mira said.

"Me too," Tondra put in.

"I do want to talk to Dirk, too," Lorcas said. "I need to know what, if anything, he knew about his parents' plans for him and how they managed to keep that information from us."

"He may be sleeping like before," Tondra replied. "Very deeply, like almost in a coma."

Mira nodded. "Not unusual for someone who has just crossed through the mists after long travel. I may be able to help awaken him, but as Lorcas said, I cannot stay here too long. Therefore, I wish to see the stone first. It is more important to me. And besides, it may be best to leave Dirk in sleep for right now. When he sleeps, he does not awaken another Rook."

"The new chapel is nearly a two-hour's drive away," Lorcas said. "Can you go that far?"

Mira raised her eyebrows. "There is no restriction on where I can go in your world. There are entrances to mine, and to others, in many more places than here, for one thing. My only limitation is how long I can stay. Therefore, we should go now."

"If you're going to the church again, I should go along," Jason put in. "It was a little creepy last time. And we can talk about the property on the way."

"I guess we'll all go, then." Lorcas shrugged. "Whose car?"

"Let's take mine," Tondra said. "It'll be more comfortable than cramming all of us in yours, Lorcas."

"True, and I'm not sure Jason's will make it up the hill without bottoming out, so I guess that's the best choice."

Tondra hurried off to bring her SUV around. Jason pulled a few things out of his car, including his windbreaker and shoulder holster. He grinned. "Back in bodyguard mode."

When Tondra pulled up, Lorcas got in the front to act as navigator and Jason and Mira got in the back. Jason helped Mira buckle her seatbelt, which seemed to amuse her.

"Alan isn't home," Tondra said. "I didn't want to leave him out of this again, but I don't know where he is. I texted him and just asked him to call me. I haven't told him anything about the chapel yet, only about Zumar. If we want him to join us, you'll have to give him directions when he calls back."

"I can do that, or we can wait for him somewhere if he calls before we get there. Meanwhile, in the interest of not keeping any more secrets, Tondra, I think you've figured out that I took your advice and asked Jason to help us out with some investigation as well as the escape," Lorcas began. "Now let me tell you what I learned from Zumar."

As they continued on down towards Seaside Heights, Lorcas described for Tondra and Jason what he'd heard from Zumar, including Mira's assertion that he was an Earth entity separate and apart from Rook.

"How powerful is he?" Tondra asked Mira over her shoulder.

"It's hard to describe power, since it exists in many forms," Mira said, "but I would place him at the level of some of those you call Allies. I have known a few like him. I am quite sure that only one such as he could have accomplished what he has. I can also verify that he is inhabited, albeit temporarily, by the spirit of truth you call the Fire Ally. It may be this that has turned him away from Rook, but it seems to me that he has developed at least a small conscience. He himself told us that it was his desire to live as a human in your realm that led him to form an alliance with Rook after the death of his human body. Seeing his life more clearly recently, he despaired and attempted to end it, unsuccessfully."

"I'm not sure how to feel about this," Tondra said. "If he has some sort of peer-level alliance with Rook apart from being just the Messenger, then it seems that his goal should be to encourage us to continue, not to stall."

"I don't blame you for your suspicions; this is information that must be considered carefully, and I would not influence your decisions," Mira said.

"And yet, you've come here," Tondra pointed out. "You must have some preference."

Mira laughed shortly. "Of course. Besides my concern that your world will become untethered and fade into the mists of time, there are things I can obtain in your world, physical items mostly, which are useful to me in my life. Objects have power, and they often change as they pass from world to world. I pay for what I take in knowledge."

Tondra glanced in the rear-view mirror. "Certainly we still owe you for your help with Tomash and Dirk. I'm not sure how much more I want to owe you. We're racking up quite a debt."

"I never ask for that which one cannot provide," Mira replied.

"It's not a matter of 'can we', but rather 'do we want to', I expect," Tondra said. "This is a lot to take in. I suppose we'll have to decide whether to support or oppose this new Rook and what it might mean for the world pretty quickly."

"Which reminds me," Jason said, "I found out who holds the property the chapel is built on."

"That's right," Lorcas said. "Who is it?"

Jason pulled a small notepad out of the pocket of his windbreaker. "Names are Dalibor and Elena Katzbalger. That mean anything to you?"

"Katzbalger?" Tondra said. "Those are Dirk's parents."

"Yes," Lorcas said. "Somehow that doesn't surprise me, now that I know what the chapel is for. How about the monastery? Same?"

"No," Jason said. "I couldn't find any official record for the monastery, even though I can extrapolate the plat number. There are no buildings of any kind registered in that area. The land itself appears to have belonged to a foreign corporation at one time, but that was way in the past. I couldn't find any recent records for it. What should be the plat number somehow just doesn't exist in the database."

"That's weird," Lorcas said. "Is it possible that the monastery and the chapel aren't actually connected?"

"Doubtful, with that monk showing up," Jason replied. "I'll keep working at it."

"So why did Dirk think he was supposed to replace Tomash, then, and that he didn't need you, Lorcas?" Tondra wondered. "Why didn't he know he would be the King at the new chapel? Obviously, his parents knew about this place if they own it. That suggests they knew what it's for."

"The only thing I can imagine is that they hadn't told Dirk the entire plan before they disappeared. Zumar hinted that Kara is destined to become the new Lorecaster, and Saber the new Messenger. If Dirk at least knew that, he might have assumed he didn't need any of us, only his siblings. But this is all speculation. We'll have to ask Dirk." Lorcas turned back to the road. "Slow down. The turn should be coming up soon."

When they arrived at the new chapel Tondra parked in the same spot Lorcas had, an obvious flat area just north of the stone on the edge of the forest. The four of them got out cautiously, but it was as quiet as it had been before.

"Wow," Tondra said. "I see what you mean. The resemblance is uncanny."

"Not strange if it's simply modeled on yours," Mira said. "It would have been constructed to mimic the original."

"What do you think, Mira?" Lorcas asked. "Is it telling you anything?"

Mira frowned slightly and approached the stone. She laid a hand upon it. "This is a conduit to the realm from which these stone-spirits come, awaiting their manifestation in your world. It is the same as yours; it contains a being in potential, an idea, empty until it is formed in the thoughts of an entity with the power to manifest it, like Zumar, and brought forth to inhabit this more material world."

"I thought Lorcas was the 'manifestor'," Tondra said.

"As did I," Mira admitted. "But now I would say that Rook was a set of ideas, Zumar manifested them into a physical form, and Lorcas provided the direction."

"That's very esoteric," Tondra said. "The question is, I think, now that we have a better understanding of how Rook got here and what his intentions are - at least, according to Zumar - do we want to allow someone to manifest a new Rook?"

"Indeed, that is a question," Mira said, "although a logical continuation of that question would be, do you want to allow the Rook you already have to complete his plans?" She left the stone and walked towards the chapel. The door, as before, was locked.

"I have the key." Lorcas pulled the chain over his head and fit the Key in the lock.

The door swung open to the cool, dark interior. Mira stepped in first, walking quietly on the flagstone floor. Tondra examined the entry table and scanned the windows. Lorcas and Jason, having been there before, stood by.

After Mira made a circuit, she returned to Lorcas. "Interesting. There is less connection to the old ways here. It is human-built, and unfinished. But I am interested in meeting this monk you spoke of. Where can he be found? Must we go to the monastery?"

"He just kind of appeared last time," Lorcas said. "If he came from the monastery he made extraordinarily good time, since he seemed to be on foot."

"He might not need to come over land," Mira said. "Perhaps he can pass through the mists and reappear here. In fact, I rather suspect he can. It would explain why the monastery cannot be found on your maps: because it does not exist in this time or place, or is veiled in some way."

"You say that so casually," Jason remarked.

Mira smiled. "You are not familiar with me. But you must suspect the truth, that I am myself of another world, beyond the mists. It is no strange thing to me that creatures can come and go from one to another. At one time, many hundreds of years ago in your reckoning, but little time to me, it was much more common. My kind and those like me walked at will within your realm. We had regular contact with certain people, generally kings and mystics, those set apart from the others, and those who understood the power of the elements. But over time they have become scarce, and our access to your world has become limited. Our land draws further away, and only those with both power and desire, like me, can still pass through the borderlands and visit yours for a short time."

"How about Rook, then?" Jason persisted. "Is he like you?"

"Yes, and no," Mira said. "His spirit was able to access your world through some rift, but he was nothing then, as Zumar noted. Zumar gave him form, and with that his strength began to grow. Paracel, and later Lorcas, gave him direction and purpose, in accordance with their own prejudices. But he also has his own will. He desires, most likely, to stay in this physical form, with the freedom to roam your earth and to transform it to his liking, along with his relatives. He does not want to return to his spirit form or to his own world. This world is preferable, and truthfully, he is not the only one to consider it so."

She broke off abruptly and tilted her head. "He comes," she whispered.

A chill ran up Lorcas's spine. He turned to the open door. As before, a shadow passed over it, throwing a shade larger than the being that cast it. The monk, or a monk at least, appeared in the doorway, swirls and tendrils of mist dissipating around him.

Jason stepped in front of them protectively, but Mira motioned him aside with a wave of her hand. She made her way forward to meet the monk as he approached soundlessly from the other direction. They stood toe to toe, the monk's dark hood concealing his face.

Mira lifted a hand. "I know the lands in which you walk," she said quietly. "Long has been your toil."

"And long has it been since you have been seen in this world, Lady," replied the monk in his harsh whisper. "Your presence gives me some comfort."

He turned slightly to face Lorcas. "You, heir of Paracel. I know not whether to celebrate your return or dread it."

"Why?" Lorcas asked cautiously.

The monk exhaled with a sound that grated like chalk on a rough board. "We know not whether you come to raise another, or to gather the power needed to end the first. Thus, I know not if you are friend or foe."

"Why don't you show yourself?" Jason demanded, stepping closer. "Why are you hiding underneath that big cloak?"

"You would not like what you would see, should I reveal myself," the monk replied.

"That's probably true," Mira cut in. "Let him hide himself for the time being, until you understand what he is and are ready to accept it."

"That sounds ominous," Jason said.

"Perhaps," Mira said. "Many things seem ominous to those who do not understand them. I will let this creature himself tell you who he is, but I can tell you this: he has not lived on your earth for many years. Centuries, in fact."

"But he lives here now," Lorcas said.

Mira shook her head. "You misunderstand. He does not live on this earth now, either."

Slowly her meaning dawned on him. "You mean...he's dead?" He peered at the robed figure.

"Yes, in a way. He is dead, but not dead. He is one whose mission drives him on until its fulfillment. He cannot rest until his task is done."

"The undead. He's a zombie," Tondra whispered, stepping up next to Lorcas.

"Okay," Lorcas said, "that's not so bad. I mean, it's not that different from Zumar or Raine. I suppose at one time I would have found the idea scary, but now I'm really more interested in who you are, or were, rather than what you are."

"I used to have a name, when I lived," the monk replied, "but that name died with my mortal being. If I remembered it, I would not speak it, for it is not good to call the dead, even if that is oneself."

"Then we'll call you 'the monk'," Tondra said. "What connection do you have to this chapel, and are you here to aid us or oppose us?"

"It is within my power to help you," the monk said. "I cannot steer you along a specific path; you must make that decision for yourself. I will tell you this: I am not the guardian of this chapel. I can be summoned by your presence in it, but I do not come to protect it. Or you."

"Yet you're one of us, either Fell Ken or Koen, obviously. Otherwise, you would have no interest in this little piece of property," Lorcas pointed out.

"I am, indeed, very interested," the monk replied.

"I'm guessing from what you've said that you're very interested that it doesn't develop," Tondra said. "You're here because you're watching it. You're keeping track of what's going on with it. That would make you more closely aligned with the Knights rather than us, the Fell Ken, wouldn't it?"

The monk turned and moved slowly, as if contemplating. "Many centuries ago, in my time, there were events similar to ones that have occurred in the last few years in this area. There was the rise of an entity, a demon, who burst forth from the Inferno, the Netherworld, into our own. He lurked within the stones, such as no natural creature can endure. Over time he corrupted the alchemist known as Paracel. Long he lived, aided by his unholy spirit. But in time he came to regret his actions and to suspect the motives of the demon."

"I've guessed at this," Lorcas said.

"In that time," continued the monk, "the demon was known to devour those with whom he was displeased. I belonged to an order formed by a part of the family to attempt to purify the castle in which he lived, to extract the family he had entrapped and send them to their God with honor in death."

"You're referring to the raid on the castle in which the Fell Ken were mostly all murdered," Lorcas said, with a glance at Tondra. "Then you were involved in the killing of most of my ancestors."

"I do not apologize. Paracel at that time had been working for a number of years to make preparations. He laid many traps and created many Objects of Power and coded books intended to inform those in the future who might encounter the same being, or one like it. With his help, we entered the castle and, with the aid of those who had come to our side, put all within to the sword, with our prayers and exhortations, that they might avoid eternal damnation."

"How nice of you," Tondra sneered.

"Of course, the demon rose up and tried to stop us," the monk continued, unperturbed. "Without the support of the family and Paracel, he knew he would be forced to return to his own world, or at least become a shadow, doomed to remain within the stones. In his rage he killed many of the Knights who supported our order, and thirty-three monks, including myself. But in the end, he was defeated and returned, with his familiar, to his own land forever, or thus we hoped."

"If Rook killed you, how is it that you have survived in this form?" Tondra asked. "Usually those who endure in some form or another do so at Rook's will. Those he kills as an enemy don't retain any form."

"Paracel had gathered together many Objects of Power, as I said. In his final act, Paracel became a conduit for the power he could call through his objects and allies, and in so doing sacrificed himself, but gave a kind of life to the monks, an animation. Thus we have survived through the centuries, tasked with assuring that the demon does not rise again."

"He did not call upon me," Mira said.

"No," the monk replied. "If he had, perhaps the effort would have been more successful."

"You knew him?" Lorcas asked, turning to Mira.

"Of course. But I met him only once, outside the castle, where he journeyed in the woods. It was at that time I offered him the Sword, as I saw that he was invested in the old ways, and in that time passage back and forth was becoming more difficult. I also instructed him in the making of the Mirror and Needle. At the time, he had the Staff, which I believe he made himself, and a ring, likely the one you have now. I did not see him again, and I knew nothing of Rook, or I might have made myself more available."

"Paracel used the Staff," the monk said. "He believed it channeled his most powerful forces. But in this he was mistaken, I think. At the end he used the Ring."

Mira nodded grimly. "Forgive my interruption," she said. "It is in the past, and of little consequence now."

"Maybe not, but maybe so. It's information I might need to know. But all this makes it seem that you are in fact allies of the Knights, whether or not Paracel joined you in the end," Lorcas asserted once again.

"No." The monk shook his head, or the hood of his robe. "We are intended to stay hidden from either side of your family until the need should arise. While we are here to stop the demon from rising again, we have found that family bonds run strong, and your two 'sides' have been fluid over time. So it has been to our advantage to remain hidden from either."

"All right," Tondra said, "now we know a few things. But I have a feeling you can answer a few other questions for us, like perhaps what happened to the Katzbalgers."

"I would answer these remaining questions. But I would like some assurance that my conversations with you will not be used against me or the rest of the monks by the Fell Ken, who might wish to oppose me. I require some symbol of your good faith."

"Like what?" Tondra asked.

The monk nodded at Lorcas. "Give me the Key."

"You asked for it before. My answer is the same," Lorcas said. A cold chill ran down his spine. Automatically, he reached for where the Key hung around his neck.

"It will do you no harm to allow me to keep this Object of Power. You are in possession of others. But it will assure that you do not call forth the demon. Every time you turn the Key in the door of the chapel, it brings him forth a bit more. He feels your power and knows his time is soon. You have turned it three times already, and also used a pattern of power to increase its strength. It has summoned one from the mists who is to begin the transformation."

"Summoned one from the mists? Do you mean Dirk?" Lorcas asked.

"I do not know the human name, only that he has re-entered the world and that his presence is an ill omen suggesting the time is near. Give me the Key to forestall it, and to earn my trust."

"You summoned Dirk back," Tondra said, glancing at Lorcas.

"Not intentionally," Lorcas replied. He addressed the monk. "I won't give it to you, but for the time being I promise not to turn it in the door. I also promise not to try to increase its power or summon any more of the new Entourage if I can avoid it."

The monk bowed slightly. "For now, I must accept that compromise. I am not a man of violence, except when I find it necessary."

"Same," Jason said casually.

"Your weapon would do nothing to me, except, perhaps, leave an inconvenient hole," the monk said to him. "But although I and my cohorts could likely stop any action you might take, I can do nothing to the Lady, nor would I try. Also, it would be harder for us to capture the Lorecaster, who is imbued with much power of the demon, than you, a mortal man. But not impossible. There have been others from the Fell Ken who have visited here, and not left."

"Like who?" Lorcas asked. Jason still stood in front of him, but he believed the monk: Jason would probably not be able to protect him in this circumstance.

"Two, those you name the Katzbalgers, whose actions would certainly have eventually opened the rift to allow a new demon to emerge here. We hold them at the monastery, both to stop the emergence and as an incentive to you to cooperate with us."

"Are they alive, that is, in the real, original sense? Rook told me he'd eaten them to gain power, and Dirk insinuated the same," Lorcas said.

"They are alive," the monk said. "We keep them safe, but imprisoned. In the future a bargain might be had, but we will exact a steep price."

"What if we don't want them released?" Lorcas asked. "Maybe we could bring Dirk here, and you could have him, too."

"Are you set upon not allowing the emergence of this demon, then?" the monk asked. "If so, there is more I will tell you, and I will provide you aid. But if at some point our task is complete, we, ourselves, will cease to exist, and experience death and welcome release in the traditional way. Then we would be unable to hold anyone, although at that point it would likely be unnecessary."

"I'm not set on anything," Lorcas said. "I don't have all the facts, and besides, it's not completely my decision. It will have to involve the Entourage and the rest of the Fell Ken. But for right now, I'd say we don't want this new Rook to emerge until we know a lot more and have made an informed decision about the future of the earth."

"I agree with that," Tondra said. "We've operated on half-facts and poor information ever since Perry and Delva died, and apparently at the whim of Zumar. Going forward, I want good, solid knowledge. No more flailing around. We get everything from

Zumar, everything from Dirk and the Katzbalgers if we can, as much as we can extract from Rook, and then we make a deliberate plan. We present it to the Fell Ken at a formal Convention and we go forward from there."

There was a moment of silence as the small group stood contemplating the monk.

"Is that a vehicle?" Jason asked, cocking his head.

Tondra took a step towards the door. "A diesel truck, from the sounds of it. Is there any other way out of here?"

"Unfortunately, no," Lorcas said.

"Whoever it is, it's too late to hide the car now," Tondra said. "Shall we go and meet them?"

"I guess," Lorcas said.

The vehicle stopped abruptly, and seconds later a door slammed. Before they could reach the entryway, a figure loomed in the door.

"Well, well, well," said Jack Bright. "What an interesting little collection we have here."

CHAPTER EIGHT

Jack stood for a moment surveying the group, his eyes moving from the monk to Lorcas, to Tondra, to Mira, and finally to Jason.

"Well, Jason, are you going to tell them you've been acting as a double agent, or am I?"

Jason flushed. He turned to Lorcas. "That isn't true. He's making it up. He's trying to stir the pot, that's all."

Jack smiled smugly. "Maybe. But if Jason hasn't been passing information on to me, how do you think I know about this little meeting?" He turned slightly, his eyes following the monk, who had moved slowly towards the back and side of the group.

Lorcas stared at Jason, unsure. He had been deceived and betrayed enough during his life. The suspicion came easily and quickly.

Jason spread his hands. "Seriously, Lorcas, it's not true! If it was, would he tell you? He'd be playing his hand. Remember what I told you about my integrity being important to me? At the very least I owe you for getting me the poison cure. Besides, I'm a crappy liar."

Lorcas took a deep breath. It was true, Jason seemed to be about the most straightforward person he'd ever known. And Jason was right that Jack certainly wouldn't reveal an agreement like that - it would be too valuable. There must be another explanation.

"You have a connection to Rook yourself now," he pointed out to Jack, "and also to Mira. Maybe you could just feel that something was happening and you discovered it the same way I did."

"Or maybe there's a more mundane explanation, like a tracking device on my car," Tondra put in. "The Knights haven't been watching us too obviously lately, but I doubt they'd just forget about us."

"Damn," Jason muttered. "I should've checked for that."

Mira took a step closer to Jason and looked him up and down before turning to Lorcas. "I sense no duplicity," she said. "He drank water I prepared for him, and I therefore have some connection to him now. I am confident that Jason Japert is truthful."

Jack shrugged. "Ah, the Lady. There's little that gets by you. But I'm surprised you've gotten yourself involved in this matter. It seems of little consequence to you. Perhaps it's just amusing, watching us earth-bound creatures struggling with our limited future."

"Attempting to throw doubt on me, as well," Mira said with a smile. "I'm sure Lorcas and Tondra are familiar enough with you to put little store in your comments."

"That's right, I'd trust Jason any day over you. So," Tondra pushed, "how did you know about this place? Do tell us."

"As usual, I know more than you about your own history," Jack said. "Remember, I have a lot of Fell Ken books. I had many of the books you needed to undo a poisoning. I had Paracel's book that described the Rising. There are many more."

The monk spoke for the first time, from behind Mira's shoulder. "Yet you have not been here before."

"How would you know?" Jack squinted at the monk as he stood in the dark recesses of the chapel. "Maybe I snuck up here at night."

"We know whenever anyone approaches the chapel," the monk said. "Night or day makes no difference to us."

"So you've never been here before, and we don't accept that Jason told you about it," Tondra said. "Yet you happened to show up today when all of us are here. Interesting. Were you just out driving around with your antenna out for the Fell Ken?"

"I vote we go take a look at Tondra's truck and remove anything suspicious," Jason said. "Won't help with today, but it will help in the future. And I'll look at all the vehicles that belong to anyone Fell Ken later and take any tracking devices off them as well."

Jason moved deliberately towards Jack, who took a step to the side, out of his way. "You're wasting your time," Jack said as they filed past him. "I don't need a tracking device to know what's going on with the Fell Ken. But if I did track any of your vehicles, I certainly wouldn't show up when all of you are here. I'd just pinpoint the location on a map and come later when I could take a look in private."

At Tondra's vehicle, Jason lay down on his back and scooched under the front bumper, then under the middle of the chassis, and lastly under the back. "Here it is," he announced. "I think. Magnetic."

He stood up and displayed the small device, fixing Jack with a smirk. "Whattaya got to say about that, huh?"

"I'm as surprised as you are, actually," Jack replied, peering at the object in Jason's hand. "I didn't put it there."

"I bet," Lorcas said.

Jason sobered and took a closer look at the object. "Kind of weird," he said. "I'm not positive it is a tracking device. Something that shouldn't be there, though." He handed it to Lorcas.

Lorcas took it and immediately felt a jolt of adrenalin. "It's a tracking coin," he said.

"A tracking coin?" Jason asked.

"It's a Fell Ken coin that allows anyone with access to the castle to track where anyone with one of these coins goes on a map."

"Who has access to the castle and access to these coins?"

"Not many of us," Lorcas admitted. "Jack has his own coin, but I know for a fact that it's just been sitting in one spot for more than a year. I've seen it on the map. This isn't it." He didn't mention the other coin they had attached to Jack's truck; he didn't want Jack to know about that one, since he hadn't found it and they were still able to track the truck with it. "But if he didn't put it there, who did? Who else would want to track where Tondra goes?" Lorcas demanded.

His question was met by silence. Jason gingerly took the device from Lorcas's palm. "I think I'd better hold onto this for now," he said. "You may need my services yet."

"Now that we agree that I'm not a liar..." Jack began.

"You lied about me," Jason said.

"...I don't believe I've been properly introduced," Jack continued. "I know all of you but this fellow here." He waved at the monk.

"And yet you are not surprised to see me," the monk replied.

"No, no," Jack said. He squinted as though bringing up a memory. "Of course, there are stories. As I mentioned, I have a lot of books. And with nothing better to do, I have made a habit of exploring satellite images of the area and visiting places that pique my interest. I'm still the Director of the Knights of the Inner Circle, and it's my duty to pinpoint places that are associated with the Fell Ken in one way or another. But it seems to me that you and I are on the same side, unless I miss my guess, so I do wonder why you're consorting with the enemy."

"I'm here to determine what they are engaged in and to dissuade them from proceeding, if possible," the monk answered, with a slight bow.

"That's very nice of you," Jack said. "Considering what I suspect they're up to, I'm not inclined to be as tolerant."

"If it becomes necessary, as it did last year, we will take other action," the monk replied calmly.

Lorcas stepped back and looked the monk up and down. He had allowed himself to let his guard down, but it was obvious the monk, and any others he might be able to summon, was still a threat.

The monk bowed slightly again, this time to Lorcas. "Do not be alarmed. Although your presence here and the use of the Key awakens and calls the demon, I will honor your vow not to do so at this time. I am no threat to you unless you take direct action. Of course, I also know that the person chosen to lead this emergence and his stewards are not here to take on the role, so I am less concerned."

"You mean Dirk and his family," Tondra said, then glanced uncomfortably at Jack.

"Oh, you're not telling me anything I don't know," Jack smirked. "I'm sure Rook took Dirk on as a protege, or tried to, to prime him for the next step. Remember, I was there at Cliffview when some of the stuff with Dirk was happening, and I picked up quite a lot. The little dude stabbed me, or have you forgotten?"

He turned to Lorcas. "As far as an emergence, the monk only confirms what I suspected: you've managed to move things far enough along that you're expecting a second branch, or even a second being. And Dirk was tasked with providing a human face for this new thing, someone to make it more palatable to the world in general. Who better than a young kid to make a monster seem harmless?"

Lorcas shrugged. As usual, Jack was either a step ahead of them or he was doing a good job of faking it. "I don't think you have to worry about it right now, Jack. Dirk may have been elected as the new King for this emergence, but his skeleton Entourage are too young to be able to fulfill their roles, and his parents are, shall we say, not around."

"Maybe," Jack said. "What does it take to call forth a demon, to put it in the monk's terms? You did it, Lorcas, just you and Zumar. The rest of the Entourage were ready to go, but they didn't have anything to do with the actual emergence of Rook into the world. And before, Zumar did it with just Paracel. It seems to me it only requires a Messenger and a Lorecaster, or perhaps a Messenger and a King or a Lorecaster and a King. So whether or not Dirk's Entourage are ready, you can stand in for them."

Lorcas exchanged a glance with Tondra. He wasn't going to start admitting their doubts to Jack, let alone reveal what they now knew about Zumar.

"Good thing you sent Dirk packing beyond the mists," Jack added. "Like you said, I guess I don't have to worry right now, unless you're planning on trying to raise this new one yourselves without him."

There was silence for a long moment. Jack raised his eyebrows, crossed his arms, and rocked back on his heels. "Oh, don't tell me. He's back."

"Whether he is or isn't, it's none of your business," Tondra snapped.

"It's very much my business, and I expect you'd flatly deny it if he wasn't. But I wonder then, why didn't you bring him with you? Surely you want to get on with it."

Suddenly Jack spun around and took a couple of strides out the door. Lorcas, Tondra, and Mira followed him quickly. They could see Jason near Jack's truck.

"What are you doing there?" Jack demanded.

"Me? Oh, just looking at what could be the basis for a couple of nice pipe bombs," Jason said innocently.

"Yeah, well, I have to do what I have to do," Jack growled.

"You won't be blowing anything up today," Jason replied. He pulled open the truck door and grabbed a couple of items off the floorboard in front of the passenger's seat. Jack strode over to him, his face flushed, but Jason took a couple of steps back with the items and brushed his open jacket aside.

"You really going to shoot me, Jason?" Jack demanded, but he stopped short.

"Doubt it," Jason said with his customary grin. "You've got Lorcas and Tondra right behind you. I expect the three of us could mob you and hold you down without resorting to any other means, if necessary."

Jack glanced back at Lorcas and Tondra. After a moment he settled his shoulders and gestured to the truck. "Certainly not worth arguing over," he said.

"No, I agree," Jason said. He walked over to Tondra's truck and carefully put the items inside. "Not rigged yet," he explained to Lorcas and Tondra. "He was probably either just casing the place and he carries supplies with him, or he planned to rig things out here."

"Either way, now we need a guard for the chapel," Tondra said.

"Destroying the chapel will not stop the emergence," the monk said from where he stood, a few steps outside the door. "You cannot destroy the Cornerstone that way, and the chapel is merely a human marker, a place for ritual and gathering. Would that it was so easy."

"Good to know," Jack said. "I won't waste my time on it. But, reading between the lines, maybe you know how the Cornerstone itself, and the entity, can be destroyed? Since you know what won't work, what will?"

"We hold some such knowledge," the monk said, "but we will not reveal it for fear it might be circumvented."

"That seems a bit counter-productive," Jack said. "Perhaps you and I can discuss a few things in private."

"Is that another vehicle?" Tondra broke in. She tilted her head and stared down the hill.

"Sounds like," Jason said. "Popular place all of a sudden."

"Oddly popular, for folks who aren't planning some event," Jack said. He, too, turned to look down the road.

A moment later the vehicle appeared. It stopped short, but within full view of the little group. After a moment the truck moved slowly forward a few more feet, then the ignition was switched off. The door opened, and Alan stepped out cautiously.

He didn't say anything, but stood looking over the group from near his truck. Lorcas's mind went through a cascade of thoughts. He, and as far as he knew, Tondra, had not told Alan about the new chapel or the new cornerstone. And Tondra had not told Alan where they were going, only asked him to call her, which he had not done. So how did Alan know they were there and how to get to the property?

Jason nodded. "I guess this belongs to you," he said. He stepped forward and offered Alan the tracking coin. Alan took it in his open palm, his face expressionless.

Tondra stared at Jason and then back to Alan. "I have a few questions," she said stonily.

"You have questions? I have questions!" Alan snapped, a flush running up his neck to his face. "Why have I been left out of this little assembly? Why was I drugged and left out of Zumar's removal from the castle? Am I or am I not a part of the Entourage? What is it you're trying to do, or trying not to do, here?"

Jason held his hands out. "Everybody calm down," he said. "You can blame some of it on me, Alan." He glanced quickly at Lorcas, as if signaling him to stay quiet. "You see, I'm a little bit of a bulldog, and once I get hold of something I don't let go. So while some folks might think I wrapped up the cases of Korrin Bright and Robert Dover, in truth I've still been investigating. I've been going into the backgrounds of all of you folks, and if you think you've got questions, well, I've got a few of my own."

Jason continued, ticking off the points on his fingers. "Alan Bistry. Born: nowhere that I can find. Grew up: nowhere. Lived: nowhere before Lafayette.

Educated: who knows? According to any records I can find, you appear suddenly in Lafayette, meet Tondra Sivitko, been together ever since. Not a Fell Ken, not a Knight, but a member of the Entourage and in one of the highest positions in the Fell Ken. Who the heck are you, really?"

"I'm sorry about your failure of an investigation," Alan replied caustically. He turned to Tondra again. "You've been listening to this guy? If you wanted to know any of this, why didn't you ask? I've told you parts of my background. You never seemed to be too curious about the rest. And you left me out of Zumar's rescue, now you've left me out of whatever is going on here, which appears to be a meeting with our arch-enemy, because of something some suspended two-bit detective thinks?"

Jason smiled slightly, but he didn't reply or appear to grow angry.

"There's more to it than that," Tondra said cautiously. "In fact, Jason hadn't told me any of this before now. You told me you'd changed your name, and I trusted you with that and never pushed you for details, it's true. Maybe I should've asked you a few more questions over the last few years, but we've been overwhelmed dealing with the Fell Ken's business almost to the exclusion of everything else. But I'm curious about why you thought tracking my truck was the right way to find out why you were being left out. You could have asked me."

"And what would you have told me?" Alan demanded.

Tondra paused. "Maybe nothing," she admitted, "but I guess it's time now. I happen to know you were the last person to see Zumar before he attempted to kill himself. And afterward, you were the one who urged us to leave him be. Add to that the fact that you were the one who brought Dalibor and Elena Katzbalger in when we needed guards for Jack, and that Dali was your personal friend. It seems to me there are things you should have known and passed on to us, but you didn't."

Lorcas raised his eyebrows. His mind began to catalog a host of new suspicions: Alan, the one who had arranged the Coronation, including where everyone stood and when the new Entourage moved up to the dais; Alan, who had given Terry Bell the tracking coin, and who had access to all the coins, as well as all the Fell Ken internal records, information, and plans. Alan had been the one who had convinced the rest of the Entourage to allow Terry to continue seeing Lorcas; Zumar had been opposed to her from the beginning. And of course, Alan had been with him when the two of them discovered Zumar in the crypt, and he had been the one who eventually suggested that Zumar be left in peace and not be resurrected. Alan had a habit of leaving Lorcas out of the loop, like when they discovered that Jack had the coins, and when he had picked up two additional coins and given Zumar a cell phone.

On the other hand, though, Alan had been seriously injured protecting him and Zumar from Don Bright, and he had dedicated the past few years to the affairs of the Fell Ken with very little reward. He had been injured during the collapse of the original Keep, too, and it seemed unlikely he would have orchestrated his own injury. And in the end, it had been Alan who had exposed Terry's duplicity, despite his original acceptance.

Lorcas glanced up to find Alan watching him, his arms crossed.

"You know that Zumar made the decision for himself!" Alan retorted. "As far as leaving him in peace, why not? Give him the authority to make a few of his own decisions!"

"It's true, Zumar told me he made the decision for himself, and why," Lorcas confirmed to the rest of the group. "He never implicated Alan in pressuring him."

Alan replied in a somewhat calmer tone of voice. "I did know what Zumar was going to do before he did it. I didn't do anything to help him, but neither did I try to stop him. My reasons were as I told you then: he had lived a long life and no longer felt useful in this one. I knew Rook wouldn't resurrect him because Zumar told me that Rook had guaranteed to grant him this last wish when the time came. I didn't know, of course, that Raine would invoke the Sazh."

"Or that Zumar is probably immortal, or close to it," Lorcas told him. After all, Alan had not been privy to their discussion in the truck on the way. "But why did Zumar confide in you? I wasn't aware you had that close a relationship."

Alan laughed shortly. "Perhaps not, but you really knew very little about what Zumar said or did, much less about what I do in my spare time. Zumar and I were closer than you knew."

"Not only Zumar," Tondra said. She was still glaring at Alan. "Dali was a good friend of yours. You're the one who suggested him when we were guarding Jack. And I saw something pass between you and Dirk when you came in to the cabin."

"Are you really accusing me of somehow betraying the Fell Ken? Or Rook?" Alan snapped. "That would hardly be true if I helped Dirk and the Katzbalgers, would it? In fact, I would be helping Rook, whereas it seems to me you're considering hindering him! Why do you think I showed up here today? I didn't expect all of you to be here," he said,

142

gesturing around, "but I knew that Tondra and Jack were here together, and I wanted to know why."

"That's interesting," Jack said. "How, I wonder, did you know I was here?"

"How did you know Tondra was here, for that matter?" Lorcas interrupted, hoping to distract Jack. "I mean, the only way to use a tracking coin, as far as I know, is to view it on the map in the Keep. You weren't home when we left; Tondra tried to include you today. And you haven't had time to go home, go to the Keep, see where we are, and drive here."

"That wasn't hard to get around," Alan scoffed. "I installed a peephole camera directly across from the map and hard-wired it to an antenna. Cell phones and electronics don't work inside, of course, but the Keep is on top now, so I just ran a wire through a little gap in the stones and put the antenna outside. It can't be seen from the King's Garden, but you could probably see it from the forest side of the castle if you were looking for it. I transmit the camera via wifi to my laptop at my house and monitor it on my phone."

"Uh, how many of these things do you have deployed?" Lorcas asked suspiciously. Alan crossed his arms, but didn't answer.

There was a moment of uncomfortable silence. It was Mira who broke it.

"Your group, it seems, is in need of honesty. Perhaps all of you should, in turn, receive the Sazh!"

Lorcas took a deep breath. "I'm not sure we're in need of quite that much honesty, but I agree that it seems we've all been keeping things from one another. We need to be on the same page. There are serious decisions we need to make quickly, and we need to lay everyone's position out on the table."

Mira moved closer to Alan and peered at his face. Alan looked away after a moment and rolled his eyes.

"And now you're going to tell them what you know, I assume," he said.

"No," Mira said, "I will let you do the telling, if you wish. I will only assure them that you are wholly human now. What an unusual group of people you all are!"

"'Now'?" Tondra said, gaping at Alan. "What were you before?"

"Well, Mira? Go ahead," Alan said. Another flush ran up to his face, but this time, Lorcas thought, it was less anger than embarrassment or discomfort.

"No," Mira said mildly. "I will only say that it makes sense that he would seek out those who have some contact with the borderlands, such as the Fell Ken, and it's likely that Zumar knew this. Certainly, your Raine knew something of it; you have told me, Lorcas, that she positioned Alan at the West, the direction of water, in the Turning Ceremony."

She turned abruptly and raised a hand before Lorcas could ask another question. "My time in your world is up for now. I must return to my own."

"We'll drive you back to Cliffview right away," Tondra said stiffly. Lorcas saw that she avoided Alan's eyes completely.

"No, no," Mira replied. "There is another entrance I can use not far from here. I will go with the monk; it is along his route, and he knows the place. I have the information I need, and I trust I will be of some use once your decision is made. I am sorry I won't be able to help question Dirk, but you now know what you need to ask, and probably know the answers already. Come." She gestured to the monk, who turned to walk beside her, and without a backward look they receded rapidly over a rise behind the chapel and then disappeared completely, leaving the little group in awkward silence.

Jack, Lorcas noticed, was leaning on the bed of his truck, one arm along the rail, grinning broadly. He was obviously enjoying the falling-out of the Entourage. Lorcas felt a surge of anger, directed at Jack, but, he realized, engendered as much by his own failings as by anything the Knights had done. At least it was all out on the table now, but they had little time to sweep up the pieces and try to put themselves back together. They all needed to be in agreement about the next step, and he felt that there was very little time in which to make that decision.

In the silence, a cell phone buzzed. Tondra reached for her pocket.

"It's Tomash," she said. She flicked the phone with her thumb, then, with a glance at the group, put the phone on speaker and held it out flat. "What's going on?"

"Where are you?" Tomash demanded. His voice, Lorcas thought, sounded sharper and more alert than it had in a long time.

"Hard to explain," Tondra replied. "I'll fill you in later."

"Do you have Dirk with you?"

"No, why?"

"He's gone. I walked by the cabin and the door is wide open. He's nowhere to be found."

"Shit!" Tondra swore. "How did he get out?" She met Lorcas's eyes.

"Easy enough if Rook wanted it, I suppose," Tomash replied. "Speaking of which, he's awake, and he's not happy. He knows Zumar is gone, and he knows you didn't tell him about it."

"What is he doing?" Tondra asked.

"Steaming," Tomash said, "literally. The castle looks really weird."

"What do we do?" Tondra demanded, looking around at the group.

"Let's think," Lorcas said. "Dirk will be on the way here, most likely. If Rook released him, it'll be because Rook wants to move things along. But Dirk can't drive and he doesn't have a car, so he's on foot, and it's a long way unless he knows some underworld routes and he can still access them."

He spoke towards Tondra's phone. "Tomash, do you know where Kara is?"

"Kara? No, but I can check around."

"If she's not there, it's likely Dirk took her with him. That'll slow him down."

"I think I need to go," Tomash said from the phone. "I'll look for Kara if I can, but I might be busy."

"Hold off on dealing with Rook if you can," Lorcas said. "We'll get there as soon as we can."

Tomash disconnected the call, leaving Lorcas to wonder what he would be busy with. He had known they would have to deal with Rook's discovery of Zumar's escape sooner or later. He just hoped Rook would hold off and not take his anger out on Tomash, who was perhaps the least culpable of all of them in the deception.

"We'll need someone to guard this place and stop Dirk when he gets here," he said to the group. "Hopefully the monk and his buddies will be able to tuck him away for the short term with some help."

Tondra stared at him. "Do we want to stop him? From what we've found out, this is the next step. Alan is right: if we support Rook, then this is the way things are going to go. Dirk starts a new Entourage and a new Rook emerges. We move on towards our goal. If we don't support Rook, then I don't know what we do."

"I don't know either," Lorcas admitted. "I just want to stall Dirk for the time being, until we have time to think about what Zumar told us and what we've found out today. If we decide to go forward, then we can always release Dirk and let him do his thing."

"Unless the monks refuse," Jack pointed out. "I'll help you stop him. I'll even be the one who stays here and deals with him when he arrives. But I won't help you release him later and I won't go against the monks."

Lorcas hesitated, considering. "It's a chance we'll have to take," he said finally. "I'm not ready for this next step. None of us are, except maybe Rook."

He turned to Alan. "Alan? You haven't heard what I found out from Zumar, although I suppose you may already know it. We obviously need to know something about you. I don't know if or why you worked with the Katzbalgers behind my back or why you thought you needed to conceal what they were doing from me. But you and I have worked together for several years now. I've trusted you with many things. You've worked for what you believed to be the good of the Fell Ken, I have no doubt about that. Will you trust me now?"

Alan studied the ground for a moment, but then he met Lorcas's eyes. "For right now I'm willing to stall. I may know more than you realize about Zumar and Rook. I've got my reasons. If I get to Dirk first, he will most likely accept my assistance over the rest of you, and I may be able to bring him back."

"Shake on it?"

Alan stuck out a hand and Lorcas gripped it for a moment. Then he turned to the rest of the group. "We need to go to Cliffview and deal with Rook. We'll leave Jack here to intercept Dirk if Alan can't find him first, Jack and Jason, because if things go wrong, I don't want Jason at Cliffview. This isn't his problem. If we decide to go forward with Rook, then we'll try to make it back here before Dirk and do what we have to do to support him before the monks get to him."

"Allies again, until we're not," Jack said wryly. "You better go, then. I'll get Jason back to his car when things settle out. Providing things go my way. If they don't, he's your problem."

CHAPTER NINE

As he began to climb into the passenger side of Tondra's truck, Lorcas hesitated. He knew the devastation of finding out that someone you cared for was not who you thought they were.

"Do you want to go with Alan?" he asked. "I can drive your truck."

"No, I really don't," Tondra said, "but thanks for asking."

"All right," Lorcas said as he closed the door and tucked Jack's PVC pipes under the seat. "Then we're heading for Cliffview. It's going to be you and me and Tomash facing down Rook and trying to explain what we're doing."

"I'm ready," Tondra said, "although that last part might be difficult since I can't say I really know at this point."

"The first thing to do is figure out whether he's just mad about Zumar, or whether he suspects something else. Let's not deal with anything we don't have to. If he does know that we have doubts about continuing with the new emergence, I'll try telling him that if he expected us to help the new Entourage, he should have told us what was going to happen. I'll try laying the blame back on him. I'll tell him the monks thwarted us, as well. All you'll have to do is support what I say."

"Yes, but you'll have a harder time explaining why Zumar didn't want Rook to know he was awake and why you and I helped him escape into the borderlands without involving all of the Entourage."

"True," Lorcas said. "Tondra, I need to know: what about Alan? Whoever, or whatever, he is, he apparently supported Dali, Elena, and Dirk behind my back, and you obviously suspected something."

"It's true," Tondra said after a moment. "I have suspected something. I knew he was close with Dali and Elena, and I found it hard to believe he didn't realize what was happening with them. I knew he was close with Zumar and I knew he supported Zumar's decision to die. I felt like he should have warned me about Dali and Elena and about Zumar's feelings. That's why I didn't want to include him in Zumar's rescue or tell him we knew about the chapel. Of course, now I think that he probably already knew about the chapel himself."

"But your suspicions obviously weren't strong enough to tell me," Lorcas said. "You can't have thought he was dangerous. And what do you know about where he came from?"

"I wouldn't have let you be in mortal danger," Tondra said. "I would have taken action if I had any idea at all that Alan was dangerous in that way. But like he said, he might have been keeping secrets, but what he's been doing has been in line with supporting Rook and the development of Rook's world, so he can't be accused of betraying us in any meaningful way. I can also believe he didn't realize Dirk would challenge you after his parents were captured by the monks, that he didn't realize Dirk and Rook's story about eating Dali and Elena wasn't true, and that they were, perhaps, just trying to conceal the existence of the monks and the monastery from the rest of us."

"Yes. But his origins?" Lorcas pressed again.

"I can't say I haven't wondered," Tondra finally admitted. "What he told me about his past seemed sketchy, kind of incomplete or shallow, like it was a story that hadn't been completely developed. No pictures, no relatives. He told me he had changed his name, but I didn't really care about that. I asked him if he'd murdered someone or something and he just laughed and said, "No, pretty much the opposite." I thought maybe he'd been involved with a cult and didn't want to talk about it, that maybe he would even be in danger if they knew where he was. I made the decision to trust him. I was in love with him, you know? We've been together for seven years, and we've grown a lot together. I know people can grow apart, like you and Carol, but for us it's been the opposite, more of a settling in, something solid and dependable. At least I thought so until now."

"As for that, we've obviously all been keeping things from each other," Lorcas said. "Do you have any idea what Mira meant about him being human now?"

"Not really, but if he is, or has been, something else, Mira would know. Remember what she said about Raine? Raine used Alan as the representative of the West, the water direction, in the Turning ceremony. Mira would know another water spirit when she saw one. There have been other things, little things, that point that way, too. But we can talk about that later.

Right now, we need to think about how we're going to deal with a pissed-off Rook."

Tondra drove on in silence, but in truth, Lorcas couldn't focus his mind on dealing with Rook. He watched the side-view mirror displaying Alan's truck close behind them, until Alan turned off on a small side road before they arrived at the intersection near Copsberg.

"Where's he going?" Lorcas wondered.

"That's an old gravel road that leads up the coast," Tondra said. "It'll be slower than the route we're taking, but it's possible that Dirk will follow a direct path straight down from Cliffview to Seaside Heights, then continue south."

"He can't have gotten very far," Lorcas said. "If he's got Kara with him, and maybe even Saber, they won't be traveling very fast."

"Maybe," Tondra said, but she didn't sound convinced.

They passed the deserted gas station and turned north, with Tondra keeping her foot on the gas and the big pickup roaring along the wider, more open road well over the speed limit. It still seemed to be taking a long time, but Lorcas wasn't looking forward to dealing with Rook anyway. He stared out the window, watching the rolling farm fields and copses of dark trees roll by. If Rook was allowed to continue, according to Zumar, all this would eventually be gone. If it wasn't destroyed outright, it would recede into some sort of twilight land, a land of mists like Mira's realm, like, he realized, Cliffview Estates, with its constant crown of fog, was becoming. He thought of the bright, sunny day when he and Terry had taken his UTV up the coast, of the sparkling sea below, the rocky cliffs, the cool shade of the forest. He knew Zumar was telling the truth; after all, he had the Sazh. All that would be gone eventually if Rook and his kin were allowed to continue.

Lorcas was startled out of his reverie by his cell phone. He grabbed for it and flicked the screen. It was Jason.

"Jason. What's up?" he said as he answered, then put the phone on speaker so Tondra could hear.

"I think you'd better come back here," Jason said.

"Why? Are you having an issue with Jack?" Lorcas demanded, internally cursing himself for having left the two of them there alone.

"No, that's not it," Jason said. "Alan's back."

"He is?" Lorcas glanced at Tondra, who slammed the heel of her hand on the steering wheel in frustration.

"Yep, and he's got Dirk and his little sister and brother with him. Picked them up and brought them straight back here."

Lorcas groaned. "Why did he bring them there? How did he get to them so fast?"

He grabbed for the support handle as Tondra slammed on the brakes and rattled off onto the gravel shoulder. "We forgot about the tracking coin," she said. "Dirk had one, and Alan would be able to see it with his monitor. Of course, Alan knew where Dirk was all along."

"All's I know is they're back here, and I thought you didn't want Dirk here," Jason said.

"I don't," Lorcas said. "Did Alan say anything else to you?"

"No. Do you want to talk to him?"

"Yeah, put him on," Lorcas said.

"Hello, Lorcas," Alan's voice said a moment later. "You're probably wondering what I'm doing."

"I thought we agreed to trust each other," Lorcas said reproachfully. "You should bring Dirk back to the castle, we'll stick him back in the cabin, we'll deal with Rook, and then you and I will go to the Borderlands to talk to Zumar so you can hear what he has to say yourself."

"No, I told you I would bring Dirk back. I meant back here. Our duty to the Fell Ken and Rook is to support the next stage. We can make any further decisions later."

"You don't understand. You haven't heard what Zumar says will happen, and we know he's telling the truth because he has the Sazh. You said you would trust me on this. Besides, you'll have to get through Jack and the monks if you want to go through with it," Lorcas warned.

"As for the monks, I don't think they'll be able to stop us with the tools they have at the moment," Alan said, "and Dirk and I can probably deal with Jack. Dunno where Jason will come down, though."

"At least wait until I get back there," Lorcas begged. "Saber is five, so you don't really have a Messenger, and you know I'm now the one with the strongest connection to Rook and his world. Trying to go it alone could be dangerous to all of you, or impossible."

"That's true," Alan said. "I will wait. I did promise to trust you for the time being, and I'm still on board with that. I'm just preparing."

"Let me talk to Jason again," Lorcas said, and waited while Alan gave the phone back.

"There you go," Jason said. "I'll stall as much as I can, but I don't know what all I can do."

Lorcas turned to Tondra. "Tondra, we have to go back."

"We can't!" Tondra exclaimed. "We can't leave Tomash to deal with Rook by himself!"

"Call him," Lorcas said. "Tell him to get in his truck and head this way. We'll talk him through the directions to the new chapel. Then he'll be away from Rook. Tell him to bring the Sword and my Staff."

Tondra nodded and grabbed her phone.

"Jason, just hang in there, we're coming back," Lorcas said. "Keep yourself safe."

"Will do," Jason said.

Lorcas put his own phone on the dash as Tondra greeted Tomash and put him on speaker. He listened as Tondra rapidly explained some of what was going on.

"Tomash, you've got to get out of there. We can't come back right now. Get in your truck and head this way."

"No," Tomash said.

"No what?" Tondra demanded.

"No, I'm not leaving," Tomash said. "I'm not going to flee and leave the Fell Ken here with Rook with none of the Entourage to deal with him. I'm the King, this is what I'm here for, whether I want to be or not. We're supposed to be the interface with Rook on behalf of the Fell Ken. No one else from the Entourage is here, so that leaves it to me."

"Tomash…" Tondra began desperately.

"That's it," Tomash interrupted. "Do what you have to do. I'll be here with the rest of the Fell Ken. I'm not leaving."

"You're not strong enough to stand up to Rook alone," Tondra protested. "He's going to be angry."

"I won't be completely alone," Tomash said with a short laugh. "Raine's here. And now I have to go. I'm going up to the castle. Things are happening there, and it's my duty to deal with it. Love ya, sis."

Tondra stared at the disconnected phone in her hand. "What do we do?"

"We go back to the new chapel," Lorcas said grimly. "We have to stop what's happening there first, or we'll be dealing with two Rooks."

Tondra put her head in her hands. "Oh God! I just want this all to be over with!"

"Completely over?" Lorcas asked cautiously.

Tondra sat back, shook her hair out of her face, and took a deep breath. She looked straight out the window. "Yes. I can't take much more of this. In the last few years, I've lost my mentors, nearly lost Tomash, thought I'd lost Zumar at least once, nearly lost Alan twice and who knows what's going to happen with that, and worked full-time just to keep the Fell Ken in one piece and away from the Knights, never knowing who was betraying who. And I have to say, some of them are not that grateful."

"I know some of that is my fault. Maybe all of it," Lorcas said.

Tondra shook her head. "No. If you didn't bond strongly with Rook, it's because you weren't the right one, which means the rest of the Entourage probably aren't the right ones, either. That's not your fault. It's Zumar's, probably, or Rook's, or the timing, or I don't know. I do know that not being strongly bonded with Rook has meant that you've made decisions from a more human standpoint. And more and more, I think that's a good thing."

"So what do you want to do?" Lorcas asked carefully. "I mean, if you, if we, can't take any more of this, and we're not sure it's right or that we're the right ones to do it, it sounds like the best decision is to just stop right here."

Tondra nodded slowly. "I've been coming to that conclusion."

"Then at least you and I are on the same page," Lorcas said. "After what I heard from Zumar, I don't think I can continue to support Rook. I'm tired, too. At one point I thought we could save the world from itself. That's what Rook promised. Now I think we're helping destroy it. And even if our society ends up collapsing like the Romans at some point in the future, you know what? It's our right to do that to ourselves. Our destiny has to be our own, not under the control of some entity from another world."

Tondra glanced at him. "That's what he promised you," she said. "That's what you want. You feel responsibility for the rest of the world, so he told you he'd fix everything. That's what Mira meant about you manifesting what you wanted in Rook. But it's not what he told me."

Lorcas stared at her. "Rook told you something different?"

Tondra nodded. "You know the rest of the Entourage, and some of the rest of the Fell Ken, have had private conversations with Rook," she said, "or maybe you don't know. You certainly know he spoke to Zumar. Now we know what he promised Zumar: freedom from his imprisonment within Rook and to be able to live a normal human life in our world. What I wanted was to revitalize the Fell Ken, to create a self-sufficient community where we could talk openly about what we know of the world that most people don't, teach our children our own ways, and live good lives supported by others like us. He promised me that. And Tomash? You know what Tomash wants?"

"Not to be King," Lorcas said.

"At least not to have the responsibilities of Kingship. He has never been interested in the weight of leadership. Rook promised him that he will find a soulmate, someone he can settle down with, have a couple of kids, and spend his life exploring and traveling and not being stuck in some boring, repetitive job. The perks without the duties."

"He's promised each of us something different," Lorcas mused. "We've all manifested what we wanted to hear, or at least pretended to ourselves that he was leading us in our preferred direction. But what did he promise Alan?"

"That I don't know," Tondra said. "When we've talked about it at all, he's only agreed with me. I imagine he promised Dali and Elena power, the ability to run a fiefdom of their own with their kids being raised as royalty, free from the constrictions of the current Fell Ken system, as long as they'd give him Dirk to develop into the new spokesman for the new emergence. But I can't imagine Alan wanting power. He's just not that type."

"In a way, it doesn't matter," Lorcas said. "Whatever it was, it can't override our responsibility to our own world and we still can't allow Rook to turn it inside-out and disconnect us from the borderlands."

"No," Tondra said. "That has become very clear."

"Then let's go back," Lorcas said. "This is what we have to do."

Tondra put the truck in gear and made a U-turn. "What are we doing?" she whispered. "Can we stop what we've started at this point?"

"I don't know," Lorcas said truthfully.

He watched Tondra as she geared up the pickup and floored it along the road back toward Copsberg. Her momentary lapse was the closest he'd ever seen her come to despair. Now her face looked relaxed and calm, as though she had made the decision and that was that. At one-point Lorcas had found her unforgiving and distant and had done his best to avoid her. Now he realized he took comfort from her strength and decisiveness. And he realized something else: Tondra and the rest of the Entourage meant more to him than Rook did. The decisions he had to make had to be made with them foremost in his mind. He felt a measure of peace and clarity as he held that thought. It was a direction, a route that he could follow, not some straying path upon which he was lost. For the first time in four years, he felt like he knew, and would know, how to proceed, no matter the consequences. An odd calm washed over him.

Tondra took the dirt road up to the chapel at a good speed, and Lorcas clung to the support bar over the window. She stopped just a bit behind and off to the side of Jack's truck, and the two of them surveyed the scene.

The monk had returned without Mira. He stood menacingly in the door of the chapel, arms crossed, hood lowered. To his left, Jack and Jason leaned against the outside wall in a slice of shade. Alan stood a bit further off by himself, mirroring the monk's posture. Dirk sat squarely on the cornerstone, facing east. Behind him, Kara and Saber perched on the rock. None of them changed position as Tondra and Lorcas exited the truck.

Lorcas walked around to the front of the cornerstone, which put him in the approximate middle of the group. Dirk stirred, as though pulling himself out of a deep meditation.

"I assume you've brought the Key," he said. "It will be useful in what is to come. It will help bind Kara to the new master here."

Everyone wanted his Key, Lorcas thought, first the monk and now Dirk.

"Do not give it to him," the monk said. "It holds your power, the power of the Lorecaster, and your soul.

He who holds the Key is the Lorecaster. If you give it to him and he presents it to Kara, she becomes that person for this castle, and her soul will replace yours in the Key. Without redemption, yours will be lost. He will then have all things necessary for this emergence, King, Lorecaster, and Messenger, even if they are inexperienced."

"I'm not going to hand it over," Lorcas said. "That all sounds like a bad idea."

Dirk shrugged. "No matter. You can remain the Lorecaster and take on that role for this emergence as well as the original. I agreed to that long before now, when I believed Rook's castle was to be mine. Kara and Saber are still too young to act in their eventual roles in my Entourage. I will need help. Together you and I can begin this new stage, even without a Messenger. You only need devote yourself to the task and allow the new one to follow the thread of your connection. I'm sure we can do it."

"I'm afraid you're mistaken," Lorcas told Dirk. "I'm not here to try to start a new stage. I'm here to stop it."

Dirk scowled at him. "Alan told me that, but I'm surprised to find him correct. You were chosen for this. You agreed to dedicate your life to this. You are the one who found the stones and built the castle."

"That may be, but I didn't understand the true scope of what was going to happen. Now I do, and the fact is, I don't want it. Zumar, who's been with Rook for 600 years, doesn't want it. It isn't right. This next step cannot be allowed to happen, and I won't help it begin."

Dirk stood slowly. "I have gained a great deal of experience and knowledge of the other worlds in the last seven years. I am prepared to bring this emergence forth myself if I must. You cannot stop it now."

Tondra stepped up shoulder-to-shoulder with Lorcas. She looked around. "Maybe not, but we're going to try. I doubt the monks will let this happen if they can stop it. Jack doesn't want it to happen, and I doubt Jason does. And Lorcas and I stand together on this."

"Tondra," Alan said quietly. "What are you doing?"

"Alan!" Tondra replied. She spread her hands. "This has to stop now. Look at us. We've all been sneaking around behind each other's backs. Lorcas contacted Jason and woke Zumar without telling the rest of us. I helped Zumar get to Mira and knew about this new chapel, but I didn't tell you or Tomash about it. Raine did the Turning ceremony and invoked the Sazh without consulting anybody, as well as cooperated with Jack. You've kept secrets. You tracked Terry without telling Lorcas or anybody else but Zumar. You've tracked my truck. You went behind Lorcas's back to support Dali and Elena. Zumar, of course, has been manipulating all of us all along to get what he wants. With the possible exception of Tomash, we've all been deceiving each other. Are we all just a bunch of dishonest people who betray our friends? Or is there something else going on?"

"What are you suggesting?" Alan asked.

"Maybe it's Rook," Tondra said. "Maybe it's his influence directly, or maybe it's at least partly because our families have been primed to lie and conceal his existence from the Knights and from the rest of the world for generations. I'm not sure. All I know is that I don't like it, I can't deal with it anymore, and this isn't who I want to be."

She took a few steps closer to Alan. "Look. What we know from Zumar has changed everything. I don't care who you are or where you're from, Alan.

161

You've always stood by me. That's what matters to me. You've believed what I believed, done everything you can to support me and the Entourage and the whole of the Fell Ken. I know this seems like a drastic decision, but I promise you it's not. Please, Alan, stand by me now. The only way forward is toward a more normal life, for you, for me, and for everyone, with humans the number one priority. This is what's right for all of us."

There was a long silence. Alan dropped his defensive stance. "I don't know," he finally said quietly. "You're right, we've all deceived each other. I am who I am because I refused to deceive, because I stood up for what I believed was right, and I was banished for it. And yet here I am, betraying my own morals, my own past, to support this thing because of my own motives. Am I wrong? I don't know anymore."

"We've all been wrong," Tondra said. "I don't know exactly what you did that brought you here, but it sounds like it was a good thing, and that's the Alan I know. Please, all I'm asking is that we stop right here, get everyone together and tell everyone's truths. And that whatever we do in the future, we do it for us, the people, and anything we do for Rook comes second."

Alan studied the ground as though struggling to make a decision. Kara and Saber huddled together on the cornerstone behind Dirk. Dirk stared piercingly at Alan as though willing him to support his side. Lorcas allowed his vision to travel over the group, taking in their expressions one by one. And then, as his eyes traveled over the monk in the doorway, his focus shifted to the land beyond the chapel.

Quietly, very quietly, they came. The monk was no longer alone. His compatriots, the thirty-three who had died at the siege of the castle, flowed silently, like a wave of darkness, around the sides of the chapel.

Dirk leapt to the front of the cornerstone, pushing Kara and Saber behind him.

"You won't be able to take me as easily as you took my parents!" he growled.

"No, indeed," said the first monk. "You have traveled in the other lands, and your connection to the demon is stronger than that of your parents. Also, our tools are limited. Nevertheless, we will try if we must."

Lorcas crossed his arms. "Funny, I thought you told me you gave your parents to Rook and he ate them."

Dirk gave him a sideways glance, but Kara looked back and forth between the two of them in confusion.

Saber walked purposefully around Dirk and straight up to the first monk.

"Do you know where my parents are?" he asked.

"Yes," the monk said, his hood bowing further as he bent his head. "I can take you to them."

"Me, too!" Kara exclaimed as she rushed to join Saber.

The monk looked up, his dark hood oriented to Dirk. "Come," he said softly. "You are in fact only a twelve-year-old boy. Your time in the other world has not changed that. Your family awaits reunification. Your parents yearn for you; your brother and sister will go to them. You stand alone; no one here will help you in your quest. Yet if you renounce this demon, you will surely be forgiven. That, in the end, is the most important thing."

Dirk pivoted to Alan, but Alan stood stock still and made no move to go to Dirk's aid. Dirk backed up a few steps, until his legs came up against the cornerstone. He turned slowly once again to Lorcas.

"You are the Lorecaster, the one chosen to guide Rook into this world and prepare the way for those to come," he repeated deliberately. "You know this is the way, the only way, for us. You know that any other way will lead to the destruction of the Fell Ken and to your own abandonment by the greatest entity any of us have known. You know you won't be able to live without him, or you won't want to. You consented to binding your soul to his. You must take this next step, and the time is now. Right now."

Lorcas took a few steps closer to Dirk and the cornerstone. He felt the buzzing in the back of his mind that signaled Rook's presence, or the presence, he now realized, of Rook's world. He knew Dirk was right. He had experienced Rook's withdrawal in the past and he knew Rook protected him from experiencing the pain he would otherwise have suffered. He knew he was still bound closely to Rook and in many ways the experience had been amazing. Rook had brought him to the Fell Ken, given him his community, trusted him to rebuild the castle.

He shook his head to clear his thoughts. Were these even his thoughts? He could no longer tell. And Mira had loosened those bonds with Rook; they were not as tight as Dirk imagined. His conversation with Tondra in the truck came back to him, and with it his new resolve to make his decisions for the people, and not for Rook.

He looked up and found himself within a few feet of Dirk. Dirk's eyes burned with the heat he had seen there before, a fever, or, he thought, an infection: an infection with Rook. He felt no anger or hatred for Dirk anymore. The monk was right: he was nothing but an overgrown deceived twelve-year-old. He felt only pity.

With a sudden lunge, Dirk dived for him, his fingers clutching at Lorcas's chest where the Key hung. Lorcas leapt backwards instinctively and Dirk stumbled over the corner of the rock, fell short, but then scrambled back to his feet.

In one motion, Lorcas slid his fingers under the chain around his neck, pulled it over his head, and slung the Key in the direction of the first monk. It was almost instinctive; he had no idea if the monk could, or would, catch it. But a bony hand snapped out of the sleeve, the chain caught on the fingers, and the Key swung down, suddenly many times larger than it had been as it lay around Lorcas's neck. The monk held his hand, or what remained of his hand, palm up, the Key describing an arc like a pendulum at the end of its chain.

Dirk's momentum propelled him forward and Lorcas fell backwards heavily, Dirk's weight on top of him. Lorcas brought his hands to Dirk's chest and gave him a powerful shove, using the ground as leverage. Dirk flew off of him sideways, then rolled to a sitting position and up onto one knee.

Dirk stared at the monk and the dangling Key, then spun around to Lorcas again as they both gained their feet. "You fool! You've given away the power of the Lorecaster! You have none now, none! You fail as a Lorecaster! You intend to face Rook? How do you think you're going to do that now? He will know you are nothing, a puny, normal human who dared to defy him! You think you win here today? You have no idea how badly you have lost!"

"I realize that," Lorcas said, although until that moment he hadn't really. "I renounce my role as the Lorecaster. I'm doing what's best for us, for the people, from now on. That includes you, too, Dirk, whether you realize it or not. That's what I've learned these last few years. That's what I learned from Zumar. It's us, the people, who count."

Tondra stepped up beside him. "Yes!" she said. "And whatever happens, we're still the Fell Ken. Nothing can take away what we've all been through together or what we know. We'll all stand together."

She turned. "I know Zumar will support Lorcas and I. And I know I can count on Tomash and probably Raine as well. Alan? You apparently chose to be human in the past. You chose to live life as one of us. What do you choose now?"

Dirk turned. "Alan, help me!" he pleaded. "You know this Lorecaster won't be able to complete his tasks!"

Alan raised his eyebrows. "Yes, I do know that," he said thoughtfully. "We've known since he wasn't able to sacrifice Terry. Rook played it off as a trick to get him to sacrifice himself, but we knew that wasn't the original plan. That's when some of us, your parents included, began to look at other ways to move things along."

Alan turned to Lorcas and Tondra. "As for me, I guess I've seen Rook as a kind of redemption. I failed to do what was expected of me to support the world into which I was born, and I was banished for it. Here, I wanted to prove I could do what was needed, and my reward was to be a life in a world other than this one, this mundane human world without special powers. But over the years something has happened. I've discovered that this world isn't so mundane. It's the anchor for many other lands, and interestingly enough, a lot of inhabitants of those lands want to come here. Obviously, Rook does. I think that says something. There's more here than meets the eye. I've found part of it."

He moved closer to Tondra. "Now the time is up. I have to decide who I am, and who I'm going to be. I supported Rook for selfish reasons. That's not redemption. It's a mistake. In fact, Dirk, Lorcas is stronger than I am. He gave himself up to Rook to save Terry, not knowing what would happen. He gave up the Key to the Monks, not knowing what would happen. He did those things because he felt they were right, not for any personal gain. And that's the kind of power I want to be associated with. Maybe someday I'll have a little bit of it myself."

He raised his chin. "I lost the other world long ago; I just didn't want to admit it. Now I choose this world, and these people. I choose to be human, forever."

Dirk slammed his hands on top of the cornerstone, as though willing it to break apart, to open to allow the new emergence. But nothing happened, although Lorcas felt a jolt in the buzzing in his head. Dirk could not do it by himself, Lorcas realized. He needed tools and he needed people. He didn't have them. And Dirk himself must have realized it, as he collapsed to his knees, his forehead upon the cold stone between his outstretched arms.

CHAPTER TEN

"Nothing will happen here today," the monk said with a note of finality. "Today, the demon sleeps."

Lorcas looked at Jack, fully expecting a sarcastic onslaught. But Jack remained silent for a long moment. The grin he had exhibited while watching the argument amongst the Entourage was gone, replaced by a much more serious expression.

"You know, Lorcas," he said quietly, "I think you and I have an opportunity to do something really great here. Imagine if your legacy, our legacy, was not bringing Rook and his kin out into our world, but instead bringing our two families back together, ending a feud that started 450 years ago. Dirk says you're a failure as a Lorecaster; I agree. That's not a bad thing. It's because you just can't become an evil sorcerer and betray your own species, which is what Rook wants and needs. Same with the rest of the Entourage." Jack nodded at Tondra and Alan. "Even Zumar's not evil; he's just strange and, I admit, unfortunate."

He paused and looked around. "As for power, I suspect you have more than Dirk would like to admit. There's a great deal of power in dedication to doing what's right, in the support of friends, in the desire to protect your family, as Alan has noted. Rook hasn't managed to destroy the Knights yet, despite our lack of Objects of Power and our reliance on the mundane. And I doubt Paracel left you with nothing.

"Imagine what we could do as a united front. If we stopped using a lot of our energy to oppose and stalk and spy on and, you know, bomb each other, we could do some real good in the world. There's a lot of energy and intelligence in both the Fell Ken and the Knights. Determination, the ability to stick to a cause for generations. That kind of experience and knowledge could be put to other uses. You and I could go down in family history as the ones who stopped the violence, as uniters rather than dividers."

"Maybe," Lorcas said, "but I'd have to convince the whole of the Fell Ken to suddenly give up their beliefs and unite with their arch-enemies."

"Same here," Jack replied. "I didn't say it would be easy. But I am saying that it's worth a hero's try, and it starts with talking to each other and laying out all the possibilities. We call a truce, we share documents and knowledge, we use our combined strength to tamp Rook down to a dull roar, and we go from there."

"It might not be as hard as you think," Tondra put in. "But please, please, if we've stopped this thing at least for the time being, let's go. Tomash and Raine are back there with Rook, I can't get him on the phone, and we have no idea what's happening. We are a two-hours' drive away. We have to leave now!"

"Yes," Lorcas agreed, turning away from Jack. Tondra flipped her keys impatiently in her hand. "At least some of us need to go back to Cliffview. Let me think for a moment."

He scanned the group assembled there. Jack held his hands up as Lorcas's gaze fell on him.

"Forgive me, but truce or no truce, I'm not inclined to go face down Rook with you at the moment," he said. "I need to discuss things with the Council of Knights and I don't see how I'd be of any help. I'd just be a liability."

Lorcas nodded. "I agree. Jason shouldn't come, either. This isn't his fight. You said before you'd get Jason back to his car. Will you still do that?"

Jack nodded, but Jason stepped in. "Hey, wait a minute! You left me here before to guard the chapel, but it doesn't seem like that's necessary any more. I'm a part of this thing now, and I want to see what happens!"

"Okay, Jason, it's up to you. We've still got to take care of Dirk and the kids, though," Lorcas said hesitantly. "I don't want to have to have one eye on them while I'm trying to deal with Rook."

The first monk, who had been standing with the Key still swinging, suddenly withdrew his hand into his sleeve. The Key disappeared with it. The monk took a few steps closer to Dirk and the cornerstone, but he addressed Lorcas.

"There we may be able to help. With the voluntary return of the Key, you have greatly increased our desire and our ability to assist you, both by providing information and in other ways," the monk said. "We now own this chapel, and all that this Key opens. You may have ceded the personal power of the Lorecaster, but with your decision you have gained allies."

171

Lorcas turned to the monk, emboldened. "Don't think that just because I've returned the Key to you, I've suddenly started to believe the way you believe," he said. "I've never been particularly religious, and I haven't started now. I won't condone the wholesale slaughter of my ancestors to achieve your goal, and I won't support any kind of movement in that direction. Any help you give me, you do so of your own free will, but you stay away from the Fell Ken."

The monk inclined his head. "I understand. I will not withdraw my offer of support, because our end goal has become the same. But we will limit our support to what we can do here and to any advice we may be able to offer. We have no plans to do away with the Fell Ken. Times have changed, and we have learned much in the ensuing centuries. Note that we did not murder the Katzbalgers, only imprisoned them. But if you want us to stay away from the Fell Ken, as you put it, we can release them now."

Lorcas hesitated, torn. "I don't really want to deal with them right now. We still need to keep this whole family away from the new cornerstone, or we'll be right back where we started."

"Then we will continue to hold them until you request their release, or until the stone demon has been defeated, at which time our presence will no longer be necessary."

"What can you do with the kids?" Lorcas asked.

"We will do as I promised. We will take them to see their parents, as they desire."

"And what does that mean?"

"Our monastery is behind a veil, as you may have discovered. They must pass through it to get there, and they will not be able to find their way back without help. Nevertheless, it will not harm them. Their parents are in deep sleep at the moment, but can be wakened.

When the time comes, we can return them to you to deal with as you wish. Until then, fear not, they will be safe."

The monk nodded at Dirk, who still sat collapsed upon the ground, a shoulder against the cornerstone. "Pity him. Everything he has been raised to do, everything that has occupied his mind for what in his experience has been seven years, has come to naught. He has not had the opportunity to grow and learn in the manner of your people during this critical period of his life. We can remedy this, at least in part."

"How?" Lorcas asked suspiciously.

"We can return him through the time he spent wandering in the other worlds. At the end, he will be much as he was when he left. He will have the opportunity to live that part of his life again. He will forget much, although not all, of what he experienced. Reunited with his family and with a different course laid out for his life, he may, perhaps, become a useful member of your society."

Lorcas looked at Dirk. "How do we do this?"

"It is done," the monk said. "Already the spirits of these children wait within the veil. We have only to collect their bodies."

As he spoke, Kara and Saber walked silently to Dirk. Each took one of his hands, and he rose obediently and followed them to the chapel. As the three arrived at the door the crowd of monks began to withdraw, and the children and Dirk went with them like foam sucked back by a wave retreating along the beach. In moments they had disappeared.

"I hope that's the right thing to do," Tondra said worriedly as she stared after them.

"At least they will all be reunited," Lorcas said. "If the monks keep their word, they'll be returned to us at some point. Now, we've got four of us to get back to Cliffview, and two trucks. Who goes with whom?"

Tondra hesitated. "I'll take Jason," she said. "I'd sure like to hear Alan's story, but I think it will take more than the drive to Cliffview to discuss. Maybe he can give you the basics, Lorcas, if you ride with him. If you trust him enough."

Lorcas studied Alan, who met his gaze. "Yes, I do. I think he proved something here."

Tondra turned and hurried to her truck, and Jason jumped in beside her. She had the vehicle turned around and headed back down the road in seconds. Alan started the engine in his truck, but Lorcas raised a hand to tell him to wait. He approached the lone monk, still standing by the chapel.

"There are things I need to know," Lorcas said. "How can I contact you when I want to?"

"Come to this place," the monk said. "We will know, as we always have. I will come. There are things I can tell you that will help in your struggle."

"I hope so," Lorcas said. He strode back to Alan's truck and jumped in. Alan took off as he was buckling his seatbelt.

"Tondra's got a head start, and she drives like a maniac," Alan said with a nervous chuckle. "We won't be able to catch up."

"No problem," Lorcas said. "I doubt she'll do anything before I arrive. She just wants to make sure Tomash is safe. Now I need some answers from you. You're going to have to tell me everything if you want me to trust you."

"Yes, boss." Alan flashed a quick smile but kept his attention on the road. Lorcas didn't return it; Alan had called him 'boss' a few times in the past, usually when he was questioning a decision or subtly reminding Lorcas that he wasn't actually the boss. But Alan also didn't smile much, and Lorcas decided it was probably intended to be light-hearted, or at least it was the result of nervousness and not meant to be snide.

They drove on in silence for a few minutes, Lorcas waiting Alan out. Finally, Alan settled himself a bit and began, with a quick, this time serious, glance at Lorcas.

"There's not an accurate name for it in any human language," Alan said, "similar to how there's not a good name for what Zumar is, or Rook is. All the terms I've heard for beings like me are frankly wrong or very limited in scope. Maybe the closest is 'Vodanoy'; they're supposed to be water spirits in Slavic mythology, but they're also supposed to live underwater, which we don't, and they're supposed to be old men with green beards, covered in scales. And they're supposed to be able to transform into fish, which we can't. We're more water-adjacent than water spirits. My people are very human-like, but we live in a very limited world, almost just a borderland. We have a close association with water, which we use as a medium for our limited skills, which you would call 'magic', perhaps. We're very protective of our little realm, and that's where the problems lie."

"I'm glad you don't actually have scales hidden somewhere," Lorcas said. "I assume you're more like Mira, then."

"Yes, but no. Mira is a powerful entity who controls a huge realm, and she interfaces easily with many other worlds besides her own, including yours. Her borderlands - the area where the lake is and more - are similarly huge and connect to many other places. My people are humans who at one time, long, long ago, slipped through the mists into another small world and occupied it. We have little power, and most of us don't care to interface with this world at all, although there are a limited few others we travel to."

"What did you do that got you kicked out?" Lorcas asked.

"I mentioned that we're very protective of what we have. When someone strays into our land - usually someone from this world, because other worlds know of us and leave us alone - it's our responsibility to make sure that person can never reveal us or somehow open up a more accessible doorway between our two realms. Therefore, that person can never go back."

"Do they stay there, then, as prisoners?"

Alan glanced at him. "No. We have no interest in maintaining prisoners, and if one escaped it could be a disaster."

"I see," Lorcas said, feeling a slight chill run up his back. "You kill them."

"Yes." Alan nodded hesitantly. He paused as he slowed to turn north at the intersection. "It's a rite of passage. Each one of us must know how to lure the trespasser into our waters, and how to make him drown himself. I was educated in the methods of transfixing a person so he didn't realize what was happening. But when it came to actually going through with it, I refused."

"I'd think that would be a common thing," Lorcas said.

"No. We're raised to do it. It's part of our culture, and it's emphasized that it's for the protection of our homeland. Most of us view it as normal. It's rare for someone to refuse. But they say it runs in my family; some people believe there are humans from this world mixed into my family fairly recently. When someone does refuse to drown an interloper, there's a choice to be made: accept drowning, or accept banishment to this world, with no way to locate or pass back through the veil into the homeland. I chose banishment."

"And the person you refused to drown?"

"Unfortunately, I was unable to save him," Alan said. "I was thrown into this world with nothing, nothing at all. Often those of us who are banished remain marginalized, homeless, in mental wards, or in prison. But I had known for a while that banishment was a possibility, and I was determined to make a life here. It was rough for a few years, but I learned about this world, I got on my feet, and I even, eventually, went to college, got a degree, and started making a good salary for myself. But something drew me to this area, some hint of connection with the other worlds I was now locked out of. When I met Tondra I knew immediately that she had a connection to at least one other world. I wanted that. I harbored some tiny hope that maybe I wouldn't be stuck here forever, that maybe I could work out a way to gain access to at least one other world outside this one, one I thought might be more suitable for someone like me."

"But back there you said you now realize there's more to this world than you thought," Lorcas reminded him.

"Yes. For one thing, there's Tondra. My original interest in her was because of the connection I could sense, but that's long since become secondary. She's my family, and Tomash is like a brother. Then there's the rest of the Fell Ken and the Entourage. It's my community, and it's actually a much stronger community than the one I came from. In truth, why should I want to go back there, or to any other world? Here I'm mortal, it's true; while my people aren't immortal, our lifespans are much longer than yours. But there's something to be said for quality over quantity. This world is in many ways richer, perhaps because its people live such a short while. They have to make up for that with invention and entertainment and culture. Rook promised to give me access to other worlds, a thing I longed for, but I no longer need that. I'm happy here."

"Okay," Lorcas said. "Now I understand at least the basics of who you are and where you're from. How about Raine and Zumar? Did they know who you are?"

"Yes and no," Alan said. "Mira certainly knew something the moment she met me, but she didn't care, and I took pains to stay out of her way so I wouldn't come to her direct attention. She can't tell specifics without direct contact with a person, or at least some intense study. She had to study me a little more closely to begin to figure out who I was, and then she probably guessed, or came close enough. She never told you, because she couldn't have known if you knew or cared or if you'd chosen me specifically for your Entourage because of my association with other worlds. As for Raine, she's always been water-adjacent, and now that she's just a spirit she can sense others who are like her. She knew I was a water-adjacent the same way she knew Tomash and Tondra are fire people and you're an air-adjacent. She didn't know specifics."

"And Zumar?" Lorcas persisted.

"He could certainly tell I wasn't altogether human. He knew that I'd walked in borderlands, but I never told him where I'd been or where I was from. He might have guessed; he may have visited our land himself, but him being who he is, he was allowed to look around and take his leave. We were drawn together, even if we didn't directly discuss our past experiences. It's something you can sense in others, the way I could sense something special in Tondra, and then in the Fell Ken in general. And Zumar felt more comfortable with me than with you, because you were

178

the one he really had to manipulate into bringing Rook out. I was just a side-kick to Tondra."

"I never saw you as just a side-kick," Lorcas said. "You've been an important part of the Entourage. You've risked your life for me and been injured in the process. That's why I'm so surprised that you went behind my back and collaborated with Dali and Elena in this whole attempted coup thing."

"Sorry about that," Alan said, glancing at Lorcas again. "Things weren't supposed to go that way. The monks got in the way and Dirk went rogue, with Rook's support, I'm sure."

"How did you know about the chapel and the new emergence when the rest of us didn't?"

"As I said before, when you couldn't sacrifice Terry, some people began to have doubts that you could carry through with the Lorecaster's tasks. There was some discussion among a few of the Fell Ken about your bond with Rook and your overall knowledge of your position. I had become friends with Dali and Elena when I met them after they moved to Cliffview to be part of the Fell Ken. They felt called to move here because they believed Rook was reaching out to Dirk, despite how far away they were."

"I know Dirk believed he was in touch with Rook," Lorcas said, remembering. "He told me that himself."

Alan shrugged. "Maybe it's true. It definitely became true once they arrived here. Dali and Elena immigrated here from Europe before their kids were born and lived with a small group of Fell Ken who have some different ideas and traditions than the ones around here. Over time, groups tend to pass on knowledge that varies from other groups and develop their own interpretations of how things will happen. Of course, Dali and Elena knew some of these stories; they'd been hearing them all their lives. The one they liked to speculate about the most was the idea that eventually there would be Councils or Districts, which is logical when you look at it. It would make sense for some of the authority of the Fell Ken to be delegated as things start to spread out over a larger area. It's something we've considered in future planning for the Fell Ken, as well."

"That's true," Lorcas agreed. "I heard Tondra mention it kind of in passing a few times. I guess I could have been more involved with the day-to-day running of the Fell Ken. Maybe then I would have realized what was going to happen. But I left it all to you."

"As you should have," Alan said. "That's why there's an Entourage. The Lorecaster isn't supposed to have to do it all. There are definitely some things about the future of the Fell Ken and Rook that you don't know, but that we should probably have included you in. But you seemed very stressed a lot of the time, and like I said, there were some doubts about your ability to guide things in the future. I want to emphasize that Tondra never had those doubts. I kept this from her as well as from you. It was me and Dali and Elena that kind of extrapolated from what we knew."

"And Zumar?" Lorcas asked. He felt gratified to know that Tondra had remained firmly in his camp, but it stung that Alan and others had not felt they could include him in their speculation.

"Zumar wasn't involved in it. I plied him for information a few times, but he didn't really know much about how Rook's future development would go, or if he did, he didn't tell me. It appears he concealed what he knew about the end result from me, anyway, so maybe we weren't as tight as I thought. And he's more loyal to you than you might think. Remember, it was he who supported you on the bridge when you first came back from Mira's and Dirk confronted you. The rest of us were asleep."

"What did you extrapolate, as you put it?" Lorcas asked. He felt a bit of relief that surprised him, knowing that Zumar, despite their occasional head-butting, had been in his corner.

"Dali and Elena came to the conclusion that Rook was prepping Dirk, and probably Kara and Saber, for some future role. We didn't know exactly what at first, but it was logical to assume that they would be important to some future expansion. They figured it must be a kind of fiefdom, a little kingdom they could call their own, with their kids ruling it, answering maybe to some kind of overall leadership council but otherwise independent. This fit with some of the stories and legends they knew. They started feeding this stuff to Dirk. I agreed with them about the probable future management strategy for Rook's expanding domain and I agreed that Dirk seemed unusually connected, but I didn't think it was anything that was going to happen any time soon. I thought we had time, and I wasn't particularly worried about you being a good Lorecaster or a crummy one. No offense. I thought we were past the part where you needed to be intimately involved anyway. I figured the Entourage could take it from here."

"But how did things get messed up?"

"Dali and Elena found the new cornerstone. I don't know exactly how. Maybe they were drawn to it or Rook made some sort of suggestion. They did spend a lot of time looking around, trying to figure out where the new faction would be located. It seems that it's findable by those who are looking for it. Once they found it, things started coming together. They figured that it would be the site of the new fiefdom they believed Dirk was being primed to lead. But they didn't tell Dirk that; they came to me and we discussed it. Once again, I didn't believe it was anything that was going to happen any time soon. But I think they warned Dirk that his time was coming. Then there was the thing where Rook set up the sword-in-the-stone event for him right before he stabbed Jack, probably drawing on what he knew of our legends. That sealed things for Dali and Elena; they knew he was meant to be King. They obtained the land and began to build the chapel, modeled on what they knew of ours. At some point the monks noticed, set a trap, and grabbed them. Rook must have been able to tell, and when he was furious with you for going to Mira and allowing her to loosen his bond with you, he called Dirk. He lied about 'eating' Dali and Elena to conceal the existence of the monks. I'm not sure what he told Dirk, but he must have made it sound like it was a good thing. Dirk would have known that Rook had used that term about bonding with you. Of course, his parents would eventually have explained that he was meant to be King of the new area and that he would have his own Rook-type beast to support. But they were gone, and they hadn't told him that in advance, so he assumed he was going to replace this Entourage. Rook either didn't understand Dirk's confusion or he played along to get to you."

"Either one is possible," Lorcas mused. "Sometimes I think he's manipulating everything and playing three-dimensional chess with us, and other times I think he really doesn't understand us enough to be able to communicate what he wants or plans."

"Anyway, I was asleep when Dirk made his move," Alan said. "I would never have supported that, and I did support you tricking him into going to Mira. At that point I thought he was dangerous and with his parents gone, I didn't see how he could rule some minor fiefdom that I didn't believe was going to be established any time soon anyway. I had other things on my mind, too. I knew Zumar wanted to die. I wasn't sure he could, knowing what I knew about him and people like us. But I supported his decision and his desire to get it done quietly. I didn't encourage him to do it, I just didn't discourage him."

Zumar had as much as confirmed that, so Lorcas believed Alan on that point. "Yet when Dirk came back, you immediately jumped back into supporting him," Lorcas pointed out.

"No, I jumped back into supporting the emergence of the new Rook," Alan corrected. "I believed Dirk was the one Rook wanted to use to do that, and I believed it was in the best interest of the Fell Ken to do it. Also, of course, supporting Rook was within my own best interest, as I've admitted. And I knew you wouldn't support it. I've watched you over the last year, and I've seen your suspicion growing and I've felt you pulling away from Rook. To be fair, I've heard Tondra and Tomash express some doubts too. If I was leaving you out of things, I also knew I was being left out of some things myself. That's why I tracked Tondra's truck; I was trying to figure out exactly what was going on and what I was being excluded from. And I wanted to hold onto my dream of someday regaining some of what I lost when I left my homeland."

"And now? You seem to have changed your mind pretty quickly."

Alan hesitated. "No, not really. I've gone back and forth. I needed a little bit of time to digest what Tondra said, and remember that I don't know all the details about what Zumar told you. But I had to make a decision. Nobody was going to wait for me to weigh everything. I knew at that moment that what I want is to do what Tondra wants to do. I also saw you stand up and act on your convictions. That's how I could wish I'd behave, and how I have behaved in the past. I was proud of the actions I took leading to my banishment. I wasn't ashamed that I'd acted on my own moral convictions. I saw you do the same. So I threw in my lot with you. There's no going back now."

"No, I don't think there is," Lorcas agreed. "I still feel like you did things behind my back that you shouldn't have and that I was left out of some important conversations, even though I admit I could've inserted myself into the Fell Ken management a bit more."

"Then let me say this now," Alan said. "I apologize. It was wrong, and it came from selfishness. No excuses. If you want, you can expel me from the Entourage. I'm not sure what's going to happen between me and Tondra anyway. It's my own fault."

"Apology accepted," Lorcas said. "Don't go anywhere. I have a feeling I'm going to need your help."

It wasn't a mere platitude, Lorcas realized. Somewhere deep inside he had a feeling that Alan's part in the Fell Ken wasn't quite finished. He wasn't sure if he just couldn't consider the dissolution of the Entourage, but he knew he didn't want Alan to go.

The truck began the last of the climb towards Cliffview, winding through the trees along the newly-graveled roadway Rook had torn up the year before. They took the final turn and the houses and the hill upon which the castle sat at the edge of the ocean cliff came into view for the first time.

"Uh-oh," Alan said as he stopped the truck abruptly outside the gate.

"That's one way to put it," Lorcas said, staring up at the castle. Or rather, he stared up at what had, at one point, been a castle. It really couldn't be described as that anymore, because a castle was a building, and this was not. This was an entity, wholly and completely inhabited by Rook. There was no separation anymore; one was the other. As he looked, the entire thing shook itself slightly and settled on top of the hill, and he could feel the earth move with the tremors it created.

"What do we do?" Alan asked.

"We've got to find Tomash and Raine," Lorcas said. He could see Tondra's truck stopped inside the gate, near her house. "We need the whole Entourage together. Things are going to get interesting."

CHAPTER ELEVEN

Alan pushed gently on the accelerator and the truck moved slowly forward once again. Lorcas didn't bother getting out at the walk-through gate to his own house. They traversed the wall to the electronic main gate and Alan opened it with his phone app to let them in. From there they drove the short residential road to the main route through Cliffview Estates and turned off at Tondra and Alan's house. Alan pulled his truck into the driveway; Tondra's SUV was parked alongside the house on the gravel. They both got out cautiously and walked to the front door.

The door was standing open and Tondra and Jason were lurking just within, out of view of the thing on the hill, but able to see at least part of it. Lorcas and Alan crowded in with them.

"Have you seen Tomash?" Lorcas asked immediately.

"No," Tondra said. "He isn't at his house, we checked. He's not here either, and neither is Raine. I'm about to go walk the neighborhood and ask if anyone's seen them. A lot of people are hanging out and talking. Someone must have noticed where they went."

"I hope they're not up in the castle," Lorcas muttered, peering out.

"I'm not sure you can be in the castle anymore," Tondra said. "At least, I don't want to think about what that might mean."

"Is the Sword here?"

"No. I left it here, but it's gone. I checked for it at Tomash's house and couldn't find it."

"Hopefully Tomash has it, then. I'm going to get my Staff."

"What then?" Tondra asked.

Lorcas hesitated. "Then I guess I'm going to go talk to Rook," he said, grimacing. "It has to be done."

Tondra slipped out the door and around the corner, moving swiftly towards the lower neighborhood. Lorcas followed a minute later, leaving Alan and Jason at the house. He was in full view of Rook as he walked quickly to his own residence, but he couldn't tell if Rook had noticed him or not. He had no idea how well Rook could see through the increasing fog, but he suspected it was better than humans could.

He felt some measure of relief as he entered the front door and closed it behind him, but he knew he couldn't escape the inevitable. He grabbed the Staff and allowed himself a minute to think. Unable to put it off any longer, Lorcas took a deep breath, blew it out, and opened the door. He walked deliberately towards the bridge over the chasm, although he was no longer sure exactly how to approach Rook.

Once across the bridge he paused and stared up. It seemed unwise to go a lot closer; he'd be subject to

188

any loose stones, dislodged by movement, that might plummet from the upper stories.

At first, he couldn't see where what he had come to know as Rook's head was located, but in a minute, he saw movement from where the chapel had been, on the highest level closest to the sea. Rook snaked his head, chapel and all, down along the western side of the castle, then created a bend and brought it back to the south and to within a few feet of where Lorcas stood.

It was hard to maintain his position when what had been an entire building approached him of its own volition, but Lorcas was determined to stand firm. He let his eyes roam over Rook's body, taking in the softening of the edges, the outline of limbs, the sealing of seams and filling of crevices, that concealed the form of the castle and made Rook look more like an animated, purposefully-shaped giant boulder.

Ruefully, he thought of all the books and other items within what had been the building. They would never be accessible now. But as he thought that, his eye was caught by a pile of items partway down the hill. He squinted and studied it carefully. He could see stacks of volumes, pieces of the old suit of armor, Zumar's crypt, and, surprisingly, leaned up against the mound were the four sets of directional windows from the chapel, minus the Control Panel, and Terry's memorial stained-glass.

Rook's head swayed slightly towards the sea.

"I don't do windows," he said. His voice, as usual, sounded like water rushing over rocks in a deep chasm, with a background tone of tumbling boulders grinding against one another. Now, though, the voice was powered by a body the size of a skyscraper. The grinding was like fingernails on a very large chalkboard, and Lorcas shuddered. He could also see tendrils of dark mist, which he had encountered before, and steam rising here and there, shrouding Rook's new body in fog.

"I see that," Lorcas replied as casually as he could. "You seem to have had a metamorphosis."

"Hmm. Good term. Like a butterfly developing from a caterpillar, is it not? I would agree. And like a butterfly, my main purpose now is to reproduce."

Lorcas didn't reply. If Rook didn't know already, he wasn't going to point out that the 'egg' was not going to be hatching any time soon. All this talk about eggs and reproduction also caused him to fleetingly wonder if he should still be calling Rook 'he', but he quickly decided it didn't matter.

"I was wondering when you were going to come and tell me what you've done with the Messenger," Rook said.

"I'm pretty sure you know what happened to Zumar," Lorcas said pointedly.

"Well, yes," Rook admitted. A few extra puffs of mist emanated from various locations. "Raine, the water-seer, infected him with one of your Allies, which are no friends of mine. At some point he woke up, although he was able to conceal it from me, since I remained sleepy due to my metamorphosis process. It takes me a while to wake up when I'm in such a phase. And then you removed him, probably taking advantage of my state, which you discovered during your uncalled-for visit. I suspect you took him to Mira, as she calls herself to you. But I cannot tell if she allowed him to enter her realm. He is a rather unusual creature, especially in alliance with the Sazh."

"You're exactly right," Lorcas said. "So it wasn't necessary for me to tell you what happened. You already knew."

"Perhaps, but it's considered polite to keep one apprised of major changes in personnel," Rook replied with an amused air.

"You've told me before that you don't care about the inner workings of the Entourage," Lorcas pointed out.

"So I have," Rook agreed. "I could be irritated with you for this interference, but truthfully, as you can probably see, it's of little consequence at this point. Other things in which you've recently interfered are of considerably more consequence."

Here it comes, Lorcas thought. He didn't care for Rook's verbal games, so he elected to be straightforward.

"You mean Dirk's return," he said.

"Of course. I cannot directly remove one from Mira's realm, but I can provide a beacon for one who is seeking. I set it immediately after you took him to Mira, as I wanted him to be prepared for the next stage. It took until now for him to follow it here, but eventually you added a bit of wakening power to the new site, and that provided the extra light he needed to be successful. So helpful of you, it seemed. But then you rudely locked him in the small house, which of course I found easy to open. I provided him with a nice rapid passageway to his new domain. Now, however, you appear to have thwarted him again."

"Maybe we wouldn't have if you'd explained what was going to happen instead of just expecting us to follow along blindly," Lorcas responded. "All I know is that Dirk tried to unseat me and the rest of the Entourage after we brought Tomash to Mira for healing and you accused us of betrayal. When he returned, I made sure he couldn't try that again."

"As for that, it was the Messenger's task to keep you informed about the process, and if he stopped communicating with me in the manner to which we were accustomed, it was not my fault. You, also, could have built your bond with me and thus known yourself about future developments. I gave you that opportunity many times. I opened myself to you and took your essence into mine. If you had chosen to, you could have used that bond to do many things: to learn my mind, to rise in your own power, to develop skills that most mortals do not have. It was your choice to abandon that, and therefore, once again, not my fault that you didn't know what was to come."

That was all probably true, Lorcas thought. He hadn't understood what sacrificing himself to Rook truly meant, and he was glad of that. Perhaps, had he known the benefits, he might have found them hard to resist.

"You have thwarted the emergence of my next relation, who is ready to begin his life here on this earth," Rook continued. "I can feel it. Dirk has been removed from this world, like his parents before him, and indeed the younger ones, who I intended to tutor, are also gone. You yourself refused to provide the necessary support. Why have you done this?"

"Because I didn't want your 'next relation' to emerge, at least not at this point," Lorcas answered truthfully. "Whatever the reason for my lack of information and understanding, I do not know what I need to know. I won't support something without specific details and a plan. And I believe you concealed this from me on purpose; you've known since I went to Mira that my support for you and your plans has been waning. And you likely know that Zumar has described for me what the world will be like when you're done with it and how your development will change this world, and many others, forever."

Rook remained quiet for a minute. "You know," he finally said, "despite the interference of the Water Ally, I can still feel your mind to some extent. You are still bound to me. Much I can infer, and much I have observed. I know, for example, that you no longer hold the Key. It was the first gift the Messenger insisted we provide for you, a thing he had obtained in the past and which he believed to be valuable. I trusted him on that point, but I now believe the power of the Key helped hold your essence away from me. A curious betrayal by the Messenger, so early in this development. I assume you have returned it to the monks, from whence it came."

Lorcas remembered what Dirk had said just a few hours ago. He had given away the symbol of the Lorecaster, and Rook would know he had no power. Yet it seemed Zumar had been at least partly responsible for his remaining apart from Rook over the years. As Rook had noted, it was a curious betrayal, but one that was a bit eye-opening, now that he knew it. Zumar had been ambivalent as far back as the very first layers of the chapel about re-empowering Rook and duping Lorcas into supporting him.

"You know I don't have the Key, yet you're talking to me like normal," he noted.

"I care nothing for the Key," Rook scoffed.

"You don't?" Lorcas asked. This seemed in contrast to what Rook had just said.

"It is meaningless to me, especially as it is now gone. It is one of your Objects of Power, a human game you play. It was a thing stolen long ago, and it was brought here along with the Cornerstone. As for its uses, it has perhaps interfered with some things, but at this point it is of no consequence. You will have to ask Zumar more about it when you see him next, which I assume you will."

Lorcas didn't answer that. Of course, he did intend to see Zumar again, and the monks as well. He would ask one or both of them about the history of the Key, but for now it was interesting to know that it meant much less to Rook, if he was telling the truth, than Dirk had thought it did.

"I know other things, as well," Rook continued, lowering his voice. "You cannot hide from me. I know you will not support my further development. You want to get rid of me."

Lorcas swallowed. He stared at Rook's huge face, only feet away, unsure of what would come next.

"You cannot un-make me," Rook said casually. "Once a thing is created, it can't be un-created."

"Seems like Paracel and the Knights and monks did a pretty good job of un-making you," Lorcas pointed out boldly.

"Hmm, yes, but also no," Rook said thoughtfully. "What they did, after murdering most of the family who remained true to me, was disassemble the castle, stone by stone, in effect ripping me limb from limb. This forced me to retreat back to the one stone, the one you call the Cornerstone. My spark remained, compressed, but waiting for its time. But you'll never be able to do that again, as you can surely tell. I've come much further this time."

Rook shook himself, and Lorcas let his eyes run over the form of Rook's body. The castle's stones were no longer distinguishable, one from the other, except through occasional fine lines. Rook inhabited them all so thoroughly that he was them, and they were him. Taking a stone away, if it could be done at all, would be ripping a body part off. That option was, indeed, gone forever.

Rook stretched his neck, and Lorcas could see what remained of the time-control window panel in his throat, like a bright gem in a necklace. The weak sun through the clouds reflected off the glass and the gears, spinning wildly, sent shards of brilliant light dancing over Rook's chin and shooting off into the mists. After a moment Rook brought his head back down.

"Why do you hate me so?" he asked petulantly. "I am only another being, trying to make my life with my own kind. I have not abused you, at least not very much. I have offered you the opportunity to survive in the world I will remake, asking only that you support me as I need you and represent me to the rest of your people. I have offered you the things I know you desire: peace and prosperity, a better life, in your view."

A bit of guilt tickled at Lorcas's brain. He couldn't tell if it was his own feeling or one suggested by Rook.

"I have to say, in the past, offering the original inhabitants of a place the opportunity to survive in a remade world has not worked out so well," Lorcas said. "As for why we hate you, we, or at least I, don't hate you, exactly. We find the idea of you taking our world and turning it into something completely foreign to be offensive, and we feel like we didn't understand what the final outcome would be like when we agreed to go along with it. We feel deceived, and that's not conducive to love."

"I have not intentionally deceived you," Rook replied. "AS you know, I left most of the communication up to my Messenger, who knew better than I how to explain things to you. If he did not do it to your satisfaction, that is not my fault. I followed his recommendations. You should take any complaints up with him."

"Oh, I have," Lorcas said. "I know what Zumar did and didn't do, and you know I know, because you're aware he has the Sazh. That's why you were so angry with Raine when she invoked it: you realized that Zumar might tell us the whole truth, and that would be detrimental to your development. Having Zumar out of the way once he'd outlived his usefulness to you was the most convenient. But you wouldn't have cared about Zumar at all if you hadn't realized how we'd react to knowing the whole truth."

"Maybe," Rook said. "What do you expect me to do about it now? I'm here, I'm growing independent, and I need you less and less. In fact, I really don't need you at all anymore, and if you're going to refuse to cooperate any longer, that will be to your detriment. I don't have to save you, and remember what it was like when I removed myself from you completely."

Lorcas did, indeed, remember that experience. Despite Mira's work to decrease his bond with Rook, enough of it remained that he was sure he was shielded from his own emotions and the consequences of his experiences to some degree. He didn't want to deal with that again, but on the other hand, he realized that dealing with those kinds of feelings was part of the human experience. It wasn't fair or normal to be shielded from them. In addition, he knew, Rook's influence had changed their behavior towards each other, shielding them from guilt about deceit, and like Tondra, that wasn't the kind of life he wanted to live.

"What are you going to do now?" he asked. "If you don't need us, what's your next move without us?"

Rook paused. "I will let you consider your options," he finally said. "I will give you time to come around and agree to support me. After all, it is most convenient for me to have an experienced human interface, even if I can proceed without one. It is easier if there is little opposition, and that is best facilitated by the inhabitants of a world. Now go away and think, and I trust you will return having settled on supporting me.

If not, I will not wait forever. I have things to do, and I do not want annoyances in my way."

Lorcas nodded numbly. He, the Entourage, and probably the rest of the Fell Ken, had become 'annoyances' now. What would Rook do to rid himself of them? He couldn't see that Rook would simply allow them to go about their business; he would need them permanently out of the way and not able to actively work against him. Lorcas felt a chill. He didn't need it spelled out. Either they decide to support Rook entirely, or he would get rid of them.

"Okay," Lorcas said. "I'll take that message to the Entourage. We'll take a bit of time to think about it, and I'll come back and tell you what we've decided."

"Very well," Rook said, "but I hardly think you'll have to tell me. Although it is no longer automatic, if I concentrate, I'm sure I'll be able to tell what you know. Despite your best efforts, you remain bonded to me. Remember that: neither Mira, nor anyone else, has been able to sever that bond. No one is strong enough to stand up against me."

Lorcas had nothing to say to that, so he turned to cross the bridge once more. But then he turned back. Rook, who was withdrawing, paused.

"Yes?"

"Have you seen Tomash or Raine?" Lorcas asked. He didn't know if Tondra had found them in Cliffview, but it couldn't hurt to ask.

"Of course," Rook said, with a sly tone.

"I don't mean have you seen them ever, I mean have you seen them lately? Today?"

"I have," Rook said. "The King approached me as my metamorphosis became complete. Raine as well, although she did not dare address me; she is aware that I am not fond of her, given her transgressions in the past. We had a brief conversation, which may or may not have included information about what you were up to, Zumar, Dirk, and the new emergence. I may or may not have extracted what I needed. Then they left."

That sounded ominous, but Lorcas also new that Rook was happy to equivocate when he thought it might buy him something. In this case, Lorcas suspected, he was hinting again at his power and at the folly of opposing him. In reality, Tomash and Raine may or may not have had an encounter with him, and that encounter may or may not have had serious consequences.

"Fine," Lorcas said. "I can't assemble the Entourage to discuss our support of you unless I can find all of us, though, and as the King, Tomash is a pretty important part, whether or not you care for Raine."

"True. I will not disadvantage you," Rook said. "Goodbye."

Lorcas raised his eyebrows, but he turned without another word and made his way back down to Tondra's house, where Tondra, Alan, and Jason were waiting near the door.

"How did it go?" Tondra asked as soon as he arrived.

"He knows," Lorcas replied.

"Knows what?" Tondra asked.

"Everything. He knew when Dirk slipped into the mists when the monks took him. He knew what we did with Zumar too, he just didn't really care. He told me he would like the support of the Fell Ken, but he doesn't need it. If we refuse to support him, we become 'annoyances', in his words, and he'll want to be rid of us."

"That doesn't sound good," Tondra said.

"No. He's allowing the Entourage to discuss things and make a decision. Did you find Tomash and Raine? We'll need to assemble all of us."

Tondra shook her head. "I talked to Marek and Wyne. They last saw the two of them heading up the hill towards Rook as it became clear that something was going on. No one saw them come back down."

"Rook said he wouldn't interfere with our discussions," Lorcas said. "I told him Tomash and Raine are important parts of that. He agreed, so if he's got them locked up somewhere, maybe he'll let them go."

"How much time do we have?" Alan asked.

"I don't know. He didn't say. But I need to talk to Zumar and Mira again, maybe Jack, and hopefully the monks too, besides the Entourage. And whatever decision the Entourage makes, we then have to run it through the Fell Ken at large. I'm not sure what the response to that is going to be."

"Maybe better than you think," Tondra said. "Many Fell Ken weren't happy with Raine when she included them in the Turning ceremony without their permission. They liked Zumar and appreciated his memorial service, but they didn't care for Rook showing up in person. Many of them had never actually seen him. It was a bit of a shock. There's a lot of ambivalence among them. Only a few of them grew up really invested in Rook's re-emergence. For the majority it was kind of an abstraction, a part of their history but not much more. Those who joined us at Cliffview are perhaps the most devoted, but some of them did it because it offered them a close-knit community and a means of support. That's the most important thing to them, not Rook himself and his plans."

"That's good to know," Lorcas said. "Let's find Tomash and Raine."

"Definitely," Tondra said. "Tomash's phone still says he's out of range, though."

"That might mean he's in the castle," Lorcas said.

"Is that even possible anymore?" Tondra asked doubtfully, glancing up at Rook.

"Maybe. I'm not sure that Rook's body includes the underground parts. That's mostly open space. He kind of seems to be sitting on top. It's possible they're down in the passageways, although how they got there I wouldn't want to guess."

"But how will we find them and get them out? We won't be able to get to them the normal way anymore, obviously," Tondra said.

"No, but there are other ways into the passageways. We could go out by boat to Mira's tower and come back in, for example. But do you remember when Zumar and I were blob-hunting and we got trapped in a tunnel that came out up the road a way?"

"Yes, of course. Tomash cut you out with the Sword. Is that still there?"

"I'm not sure, but it can't hurt to check. And Tomash knows about it, so he might head that way if he couldn't find any other way out."

"But then why wouldn't Raine have just come to get one of us?" Tondra wondered. "She wouldn't be trapped. Is it possible that Rook has done something to them?"

"Of course, it's possible," Lorcas admitted. "If he wanted to use them as some kind of warning, though, I think he would have told me what he did with them. Otherwise, it's not much of a warning."

"Come on then, let's go," Tondra said. "You know where it is. Should we drive or walk?"

"We can walk," Lorcas said. "It's not that far."

The four of them started off together with Lorcas in the lead. He purposefully headed directly for the road outside the Cliffview wall rather than cutting up through the neighborhood. For one thing, the trees there would conceal them a little bit from Rook. For another thing, it would be less obvious where they were going.

The gravel of the new roadway ended on the east side of Rook's hill where the construction road had originally been built. That road had overgrown now, since it was used only as a path to the graveyard and the clearing beyond where Fell Ken would take their bows for target practice. Lorcas glanced up that way as they hiked past. As far as he could tell, the graveyard had not been incorporated into Rook's new body.

The road turned to a dirt two-track that eventually led out of the private property held by Cliffview Estates and into the state forest. It swung further east through the trees, leaving more room between the road and the cliff's edge. Lorcas squinted into the forest to the west, trying to remember exactly where to turn off to head back to the window. He recalled seeing it from the truck when he had taken Terry back up that way and trying to distract her from it.

Eventually he saw the familiar rise and the dark shape of the window. The little group hurried through the brush.

"Hey!" As soon as Lorcas squatted down in front of the low window, with its bent, half-sawn-off bars, Tomash popped up on the other side. Tondra, Alan, and Jason crowded around.

"It's about time you found us," Tomash said. "This thing's useless." He stuck his cell phone out through the gap in the bars.

"Why didn't you crawl out?" Lorcas asked.

"I may have lost some muscle since I've been sick, but I'm still a bigger guy than you," Tomash said. "You barely squeezed through last time and you scraped your back all up. I did try, believe me, but it just didn't work."

"Where's Raine?" Tondra asked, peering into the gloom behind Tomash.

"Right here," Raine answered from behind Tomash. "Let me by."

Tomash backed up and Raine threaded herself through head-first.

"Why didn't you just, you know, come through somewhere?" Lorcas asked her.

"I tried a few times, but I got lost," Raine said. "I didn't want to get too far from Tomash and lose him. Even if I'd found my way out, I don't think I could have led anyone back to him. It's crazy down there. I'm sure Rook was doing something to confuse us. He's been mad at me since I turned the Wheel. And besides, my ability to pass through things has decreased. I'm sure that's also his doing."

"Get me out," Tomash pleaded. "From what I saw earlier, I really don't like the idea of being in here."

"Do you have the Sword?" Lorcas asked. Last time, Tomash had cut him out with it.

"Yes, but I can't get a good angle on the bars from in here, now that they're bent," Tomash said.

"How much more room do you need?" Jason asked, his hands on his knees.

"Maybe a couple inches," Tomash replied.

"Stand back," Jason told Lorcas. "Let me and Alan yank on the bars for a minute. Then we'll switch out and you and Tondra can yank. Maybe if we take turns, we can start to shift them a bit."

Lorcas stepped aside, and Jason grabbed one of the bent bars with both hands and began yanking it upwards. Alan stepped in beside him and grabbed another.

"It's bending," Tomash said. "You can do it! Last time Lorcas was able to kick them out, but I couldn't get a good footing on them."

"Try that," Jason said, releasing the bar. Tomash stuck his hands through, then his head, but got stuck at his shoulders.

"Almost!" he said. "Can you hold the bars up just a bit?"

Jason and Alan each grabbed a bar again and heaved up on it. Tomash turned his shoulders a half-turn, and Tondra and Lorcas each grabbed a hand and pulled. Slowly, Tomash slid out through the bars.

"Ouch," he said, sitting up on the ground. "Tight. I'm okay. Let's get out of here."

Lorcas offered him a hand up. "I'm guessing your discussion with Rook didn't go too well," he said.

"It didn't go at all," Tomash said. He peered up through the trees at what could be seen of Rook's new form. "He hadn't transformed as much as he has now. We went up to your office, hoping he'd be there, and that's when things started going south. He showed up and told us we had agreed last year that he'd only communicate with the Entourage through the Lorecaster, which is true. But then things started to change all around us. The floor got squishy and started undulating, the walls started bending, it was crazy."

"Like when we took Zumar out," Tondra said.

"We ran out of the chapel and started down as fast as we could," Tomash continued, "but we couldn't find a way out. Eventually we were sure we were below ground and things got more solid, but then we couldn't figure out where we were. We've been wandering around ever since. I even tried to find the passageway to Mira's, but it's either gone or things have been rearranged so much that I couldn't get there. Then suddenly we were at this one passage, and I could see the window."

"Now what?" Tondra said. "At least we're all back together and can function as the Entourage."

Lorcas looked around at the little group. "I want to take Alan and go visit Mira and Zumar tomorrow. I need to finish the conversation Mira and I were having before she had to leave, and I need to find out if there's any other help she can give us. Alan needs to hear what Zumar has to say from him directly, because he doesn't know it all and he'll accept that it's the truth if Zumar and the Sazh say it is. And I need to know if there's anything else Zumar has been withholding. Jason, I don't suppose you could get your boat?"

"Probably not with this short notice," Jason said, "but let me check the schedule." He fooled around with his phone for a minute, then shook his head. "Some guys are going fishing tomorrow. Unless you want to go tonight."

"No," Lorcas said. "We all need to rest. I'll call Jack and see if he can bring the Natural Seize around. Tondra and Tomash, I'll need you to call an emergency meeting of the Fell Ken. It's too late tonight, so make it for tomorrow as well. I'll join you when I'm back from Mira's. Tomash and Raine, you'll need to know what happened, and what didn't happen, at the new chapel. The Entourage should get together this evening and make sure we all know what each of us individually knows. And we should make sure we all agree on the plan going forward. That way when Alan and I are gone tomorrow, you can assure the rest of the Fell Ken that we're all on board."

"What should we tell the congregation?" Tondra asked.

Lorcas thought for a moment. "They'll all have seen what's happened to Rook. Some of them might not be real thrilled about what they see. Rook was just an idea, something connected to their ancestors that might be a thing at some point in the future to most of them. They may have grown up knowing about him, but very few grew up thinking it was going to happen in their lifetimes. They've grown up in a modern world, not a medieval one, and they're not going to want to lose their amenities."

"We can make it clear that Rook is developing quickly, and that's going to mean major changes to the area, the Fell Ken, and the earth," Tondra said. They started walking back down towards Cliffview as she spoke. "We can tell them what the world will eventually be like and ask them: if you had a choice, would you continue to support Rook, knowing what we know about what's going to happen, or would you prefer to stop things at this point, or even go back a step? We'll take a vote. I'm pretty sure I know where the majority will come down, framed that way."

"It's the truth," Lorcas said. "Everything has to be the truth from here on out. No misleading anybody. No secrets. That goes for us in the Entourage, but also for what we tell the Fell Ken. No need to frame anything in any particular way. Just say it."

"As if from here on out we've all got the Sazh," Raine said.

"Exactly," Lorcas agreed.

CHAPTER TWELVE

"Seems you're alive," Jack said as he answered his phone. "Things must have gone well."

"Not that well," Lorcas said. "I need to go visit Mira. There's no way I can get there through the castle at the moment, or at least I don't want to try. Can we use your boat?"

"If by 'use my boat' you mean can I transport you in it, then yes," Jack replied. "Are we looking at going out in the dark?"

"No, tomorrow is fine. I have a few days," Lorcas said, hoping that was true.

"Okay, name the time. And can you guarantee me safe passage to the marina in Seaside Heights? If so, I'll meet you there. That will be shorter for you than coming down to Lafayette and I won't have to maneuver into that cursed cove to pick you up."

"Yes, I'll make sure you're safe from the Fell Ken. We'll be there at nine if that works for you."

"Fair enough. Just you?"

"Probably also Alan," Lorcas said. "Thank you."

"Ah, a new era of civility," Jack said. "See you there."

Lorcas pocketed his phone and finished packing a few things into a cardboard box. They were going to whip up some dinner at Tondra and Alan's house while they discussed everything that had occurred. Every person in the Entourage was going to get a turn to speak. Each of them had agreed to reveal their true feelings about what should happen next with Rook. They would go into the Fell Ken meeting the next day as a united front and with all the facts at their disposal to answer any arguments or questions the community might have.

Tomash and Jason were busy preparing some of the meal, with Raine looking on, when Lorcas arrived and deposited his box of items. Lorcas asked Tondra to send a general message out to leave Jack and his truck alone if he was spotted in Seaside Heights. She and Alan had already been working - together, Lorcas noted, although with little conversation - to set up the meeting and activate a message tree they had established in the past to notify the Fell Ken of critical issues.

With plates prepared, they sat in a circle in the living room with a few small tables and ottomans pulled up to support their dishes. Lorcas went first, talking slowly through things as they ate. He had decided to start way back with his thirteenth birthday, the 'gift' of the Cornerstone, and the disagreement between his mother and father that had led to him not knowing about the Fell Ken or Rook until he was an adult. This part of his story had been related to the rest of the Entourage second-hand by Perry and Delva, but they had never heard it from him, and he felt it helped explain why he had often been so confused and why not only Zumar, but also Perry, had fed him information slowly and in incomplete chunks. As he put the story together, a few things became clearer to him, including the probability that he was less likely to simply go along with Rook's plans than he would have been had he been primed for it since childhood.

Tondra and Tomash told their story next: how they'd been raised knowing the Fell Ken legends, the location of the Cornerstone, and how the stone was guarded. They had grown up around Perry and Delva, known Raine's parents, and been educated to play important roles in the Fell Ken organization. But neither of them had received any real instruction as far as dealing with an actual emergence; Lorcas's father's try at it had never proceeded very far, and it had been dealt with by the older generation. Tondra admitted that being thrown into the leadership of the Fell Ken had been overwhelming; besides a family, it was a business, and without Alan she wouldn't have known how to manage the day-to-day affairs of supporting the movement of people, the organization, or the finances. Tomash's story was briefer; he had never particularly wanted to be a part of the leadership of the Fell Ken at all. Now he had been attacked, poisoned, and expected to be an example for the rest of the Fell Ken when he had very little actual interest in Rook's development.

Raine's story was one all of them were familiar with except Lorcas. She had known Tondra and Tomash all her life. She had been raised by her grandmother Delva after the accidental death of her parents when she was very young, and Delva had initiated her not only into Fell Ken lore, but also earth magic. When she had found out that the spirit of the Messenger was trapped in the Cornerstone along with

Rook, she had felt sorry for him, and taken to going to the hill and reading out loud hoping to keep him entertained. Thus, she had developed a relationship with Zumar in her mind over the years, and when he was free to move around, she had wanted to make that relationship a reality. Her support for Rook had thus actually been more support for Zumar.

"I might have encouraged Zumar to try again to develop a Lorecaster and move out of the stone," she said, glancing at Lorcas. "If so, and he went through with it when in fact it was not the right time, that's at least partly my fault. It was a selfish desire to be able to be with Zumar. I realize that now, but at the time I felt that I was doing the right thing, helping him to become more whole and freer. I have only ever wanted to be an asset to you, not a liability. I can only apologize now."

"It isn't any worse than what the rest of us have done," Tondra said. "We haven't been good at calling on you to use your skills and knowledge, either. And Zumar ultimately made the decision to contact Lorcas himself. That was his choice, and not something you had control over."

Finally, it was Alan's turn. He told his story again as he'd told it to Lorcas in the truck. In the silence that followed, he turned to Jason, who sat listening without interjecting.

"What do you think about all this, Jason?"

"I have no idea," Jason said. "Frankly, it all sounds like bull, but I know some of it is true, because I've seen it. I know I'm not part of your organization, but if I can add my own opinion in here, I vote that this thing gets stopped. It all sounds like a bad idea from the get-go."

Lorcas looked around at the Entourage. There were a lot of nods and glances, one to the other.

"Are we in agreement, then?" he asked. "At this point, the new emergence should not go forward and Rook needs to be stalled and kept from developing any further at the very least, perhaps permanently. Do we need a vote?"

"I don't think so," Alan said. "I think it's pretty clear that's what we all want."

"Any objections?" Lorcas asked. He looked around, but no one spoke up. "Then that's settled. In that case I need more information from Zumar, whatever he knows about the Allies and the Objects of Power and how to use them to gain control of Rook. I propose to go to Mira's tomorrow during the community meeting, and take Alan so he can hear from Zumar himself."

"I don't really need to go," Alan said. "I believe what you're claiming Zumar said. But I wouldn't mind seeing him alive, and I'm not sure what I could add to the meeting anyway. I don't want questions that might lead to me having to reveal where I'm from. It could affect general trust in the Entourage, but I won't lie about it if I'm asked."

"Why don't you go, then?" Tondra said. "The Congregation will probably feel better believing Lorcas has some protection instead of being out on a boat with Jack by himself, even if we've done similar things before."

"Fine with me," Lorcas said. "That way I don't have to try to make polite conversation with Jack."

After a long evening, Lorcas made his way back to his own house. Jason was going to bed down at Tomash's house for the night, so he was alone. But somehow, he felt less alone than he had before; he felt he had the true support of the Entourage and all the cards were on the table. He knew they would stand with him, whatever was to come. What that was, he still did not know, nor did he know how to accomplish whatever they might decide was necessary. But at least he knew the members of the Entourage would tell him the truth now, the whole truth.

He tried to get a decent night's sleep. Of course, he was restless, and every noise from outside woke him up with his heart racing, wondering if Rook was on the move. He finally got up early and had some coffee, and dared look outside in the morning light. Rook seemed to be curled up on the hill in a heavy mist, possibly sleeping.

Alan knocked on the door a little before eight-thirty. "Your car or mine?" he asked. He edged inside the door as if he wasn't comfortable standing outside with Rook looming so near. Lorcas couldn't say he blamed him, although he got a little twinge of schadenfreude, since it was Alan who had until recently been Rook's supporter.

"Let's go in mine," Lorcas said. He grabbed his keys and hesitated for a moment, staring at his Staff leaning in the corner near the door. In the end he decided not to take it; what would he do with it on the boat, anyway? He was sure he didn't need it to summon Mira.

They drove in relative silence, Alan occasionally sipping coffee from a large travel mug he'd brought. He looked tired. Lorcas suspected he and Tondra had spent the night in conversation, and who knows how long they'd talked, trying to figure things out. He wasn't going to pry into how that had gone, but from Alan's appearance it had been rough and he'd gotten little sleep.

Jack was backing the boat trailer into the water when they pulled up. Lorcas parked in a gravel lot a few hundred yards from the marina's reserved parking spots and he and Alan walked down to the pier. Jack had already unloaded by that time, and he waved and jumped back in his truck, leaving the Natural Seize idling and tied off. A few minutes later he returned.

"After you," he said, gesturing at the walkway. Lorcas and Alan made their way to the boat, trailed by Jack. "Go ahead and board," Jack said. "I'll cast off."

He quickly untied the two lines he'd looped over cleats on the dock, threw them on board, and jumped on. He ducked into the wheelhouse and dropped the engines.

"Lorcas, can you tidy the lines?" he asked as he backed out. "Alan, come on in here. There's plenty of room, and it's a little rough today."

Lorcas coiled the lines up on the deck and then joined Jack and Alan inside. It was, indeed, a bit rough as they moved away from the marina and out onto the open sea. Once well offshore, Jack paused and let the engines idle for a moment.

"Good practice to wear a PFD in weather like this," he said. He opened one of the bench-boxes and pulled out three life jackets, checking the sizing.

Lorcas threaded his arms through the vest and zipped it up, then pulled the straps tight. "Of course, Alan can probably swim like a fish," he joked, although he realized Jack didn't know exactly what he was talking about.

"About that," Alan said as he fumbled with the PFD. "I actually don't swim at all."

"What?" Lorcas was shocked.

"Yeah, you see, if I'm swimming and another water spirit happens to notice that a banished water spirit has returned to the water in any way, he or she has the right to just come up and grab me and pull me under. It's considered a violation of the banishment. The only other option to banishment is drowning. Bathtubs even make me nervous."

"All the more reason to wear a PFD," Jack said, looking Alan over curiously. "It would make it harder to pull you under. Although, of course, hopefully we won't end up in the drink anyway. Something would have to go pretty wrong for that to happen."

Once Jack had secured his own PFD, he brought the Natural Seize up on plane and they started north along the coast. The trees of Seaside Heights gave way to broken cliffs. The choppy seas continued and a stiff breeze came up, blowing spray across the windshield. Jack turned on the wipers and leaned forward a bit over the wheel, one hand on the throttle levers.

He concentrated on managing the boat in the rough seas, which seemed to be increasing. Lorcas peered out the window. A heavy mist seemed to be settling over the water as well. He glanced back at Alan, who was sitting on the bench-box, hanging onto a grab bar as they rocked up and down.

"How are you going to get off onto this thing in these seas?" Jack finally asked as they neared the spot.

"It's going to be tough," Lorcas admitted. "Alan's never gone in this way before. I'll have to get off first and open it, then you can let Alan off and back away until we call for you. Do you think you can do it?"

"I'm a pretty good boat operator," Jack said. "I'm game to at least give it a try."

Lorcas pointed off the port bow. "There it is. You see it appearing in between the swells? Once we get there the sea will hollow out a little and expose it better. It's like it has some kind of sensor."

Jack swung the boat to the left and slowed, still trying to keep the prow into the rolling waves. As they neared the tower a hollow opened around it. Jack chose his line of approach and moved in closer.

But as they approached Jack shoved the throttle levers forward abruptly. He brought the boat off a ways, then turned back. "Sorry. It's weird. There's something happening with the waves. It's as if they're coming offshore instead of going in."

Lorcas stared at the water. He could see what Jack meant. The motion of the waves appeared to be emanating from the cliffs, rather than from the open sea. He had never seen anything like it before.

"Trying again," Jack shouted. A true wind had replaced the breeze, and with the waves slapping the hull there was a good bit of noise. He kept one hand on the throttle levers and gripped the wheel with the other, maneuvering in from the west now, trying to go against the waves.

As he approached this time the hollow seemed to expand. As Lorcas watched, he could see the water beginning to move in a circular pattern, around and around the tower.

"Jack! It's a whirlpool!" he shouted.

"It's okay!" Jack said. "It's just an eddy. It's not that bad."

The Natural Seize reached the edge of the eddy and Jack brought the boat over the rim and down the inside, sliding alongside the tower. Lorcas stepped partly out the door of the wheelhouse, holding the vertical handle on the outside. Just as he did, the speed of the water increased and the sides of the whirlpool seemed to rise higher.

"I'm going to have to take her out!" Jack yelled. He slammed the throttle levers forward again and the boat leapt up the wall of the eddy, going nearly vertical. Lorcas clung to the grab bar, trying to get himself back inside. All he could see was the deck of the boat and the water rushing to his left. He could hear the Natural Seize's engines straining as the boat seemed to continue higher and higher. He kept waiting to reach the rim, to feel the boat pitch forward and over, but it never came.

The next minute was confusion. Lorcas felt the stab of the cold ocean as he fell in. He tried to hold his breath, with no idea which way was up. The PFD shot him back to the surface in seconds and he gasped, taking in part water and part air. He had a fleeting impression of the Natural Seize on her side, coming over as though in slow motion, and over the roar of the eddy he heard the crack as the tower impaled her. Moments later the eddy disappeared, leaving him floating in a rough but normal sea.

The tower, too, seemed to have vanished. The Natural Seize lolled for a moment on her side, then rapidly began to sink. Lorcas paddled away as best he could, afraid that it might pull him down with it. He coughed violently from inhaling sea-water, still trying to catch his breath. He tried to ride the waves, looking around at the top of each one for Jack and Alan.

In a minute he heard someone yelling frantically. He was sure it was Alan.

He yelled back, "Alan! Keep shouting!"

He followed the sound of the voice, paddling as best he could in the PFD with the waves slapping him in the face at the top of each swell. Soon he saw Alan, with Jack approaching him as well. Lorcas allowed the waves to bring him closer, trying to conserve his strength. He was very cold.

Once they were all together Lorcas grabbed Alan's PFD with one hand and Jack's with the other. "Everyone okay?" he asked.

Alan and Jack both nodded. "I want out of here!" Alan said, his voice edging on panic.

"You're not going to drown," Jack said firmly. "No one's going to pull you under in that vest. You're much more likely to get hypothermia." He looked around. "If the waves are back to normal, we'll be drifting slightly northward and inland. We'll eventually end up somewhere around that state forest beach. But it's too cold to mess around."

Lorcas squinted up at the top of the cliffs, hoping someone up there might have seen what had happened. But of course, they were all in the Community Center at the meeting, even the kids. Only Rook could be seen, just slightly, looming on the hill.

"Have you got me?" Jack asked.

"What? Yes," Lorcas answered, tightening his grip on Jack's PFD.

"Okay." Jack let go of both of them and yanked at the pocket on the front of his life jacket. It opened with the sound of Velcro, and he stuck a few fingers in and extracted a thick zip-top pouch attached to a coiled cord. He held it up, squinting, and Lorcas could see a cell phone. His own, he realized, was still in his pocket, but probably ruined.

"Good thinking," he acknowledged.

Jack grunted and scrolled on the phone right through the pouch. Then he punched at the screen.

"Yes, this is an emergency," he said calmly into the phone. "My boat has gone down and three of us are overboard. We're all in PFDs and together. We're about three-quarters of a mile off shore just northwest of Cliffview Estates. I have a whistle and lights."

Jack listened and then looked at them over the top of the plastic pouch. "Coast Guard has a boat a few miles from here, heading our way. They'll snag us in just a few minutes."

Lorcas tried to keep himself calm and concentrated on gripping his companions' PFDs with his increasingly cold fingers. Alan kept looking down at the water as though he could see through it into the depths and anticipate an attack. Jack stayed on the phone, and also activated a bright blinking light clipped to his vest.

It wasn't long before they saw the red-and-white pattern of a Coast Guard cutter on the horizon. Jack raised a hand and waved and the boat slowed visibly and turned towards them. Lorcas saw several people moving on the deck as it approached them.

"Take this guy first," Jack shouted, pushing Alan forward toward the ladder that was mounted on the side of the cutter. Two of the crew reached over and grabbed Alan's PFD as he struggled to pull himself up. Lorcas went next, far from arguing with Jack about it. It was more difficult than he had thought, climbing the ladder with numb, cold limbs and sodden clothing, his heavy wet jeans interfering with his leg movement. He was grateful for the assistance of the crew.

Inside the cabin Jack answered questions while Lorcas and Alan were swathed in heat-reflective blankets. Lorcas was cold, but he could see Alan shaking violently.

The reality of the last hour began to set in. He responded numbly to the crew member who questioned him and examined him for injuries. He could feel, as he warmed up, bruising on one arm and thigh, but nothing he thought was more serious. He shook his head when she asked if he would like to be transported to a hospital via ambulance.

Jack and Alan turned down the offer as well. The Coast Guard cutter eventually brought them back to the marina in Seaside Heights. Jack discussed boat recovery with the crew before they left.

"I can get you a GPS location where the boat went down once I get home," Lorcas said. "That will at least give you a starting point."

"That would be great," the Coast Guard officer said. "That area is not that deep, at least compared to some spots off the coast. We'll need to mark where the wreck is. Recovery's a good possibility."

"Not in one piece," Jack said grimly.

"We'll see," the officer said encouragingly. "There are some good salvage companies around. Get warm, and one of us will be in touch."

After the cutter left the marina, the three of them stood silently for a minute.

"Well, this didn't work out the way I'd planned," Lorcas said. "I'm really sorry about your boat, Jack."

Jack shrugged. "Yeah, me too, but easy come, easy go, I guess. I got her as part of a settlement a few years back. I'll miss her, but there's nothing to be done about it now."

He frowned. "You know that water pattern wasn't natural. As I tried to climb out of the eddy it just kept getting higher and higher and steeper and steeper. It was created by Rook somehow; I'd bet on it."

"Of course it was," Lorcas said. "He could see what we were doing. I guess he didn't want me going to visit Mira and Zumar."

"He could've killed you," Jack said. "Would he go that far?"

"At this point, he might," Lorcas said. "Remember that Alan is part of the Entourage too. Rook endangered both of us. I'm sure he could have stopped us from entering the tower in other ways. Instead, he wrecked the boat violently and tossed us into the ocean. Sounds like he would have been quite happy if one or all of us didn't make it, but he could claim he didn't directly murder us."

"Me, it's not surprising," Jack said. "But I have to admit to some surprise over you two. Things have sure taken a turn quickly."

"No kidding," Lorcas said. He glanced at Alan, who stood silent, wondering what he was thinking.

"What now?" Jack asked.

Lorcas thought for a minute. "I still need to talk to Mira and Zumar. I guess I'm going to have to figure out some other way to get to them. The tower will obviously never be a route again. From what I can tell, it's gone. We can't get into the castle the normal way anymore. Maybe I can go in through the barred window, but it sounds like that's dicey at best. That's about the only thing I can think of to do right now, though."

"I'm going home and warm up," Jack said. "I was going to ask you the favor of allowing me to stop by my old office and take a look at it, but I'm not sure I want to mess around here now."

"If you decide you want to, go ahead. I had Tondra send a message out telling people to leave you alone. You'll be safe enough from the Fell Ken."

"I appreciate it. Maybe I'll take a quick swing by, then. Let me know if there's anything else I can do."

"Yes, I will," Lorcas said. "The Fell Ken will help with salvage costs and we'll replace any items you lost on the boat, too. It's the least we can do."

Lorcas and Alan headed back to the Subaru and watched while Jack pulled out and past them, his truck towing the sadly empty boat trailer. Lorcas grabbed a few towels he had in the back to pad items he'd bought and laid them over the seats. They were both still wet, although Alan didn't seem to be shaking quite as much.

Lorcas cranked up the heat inside and they sat there in silence as they warmed up.

"You sure you're okay?" Lorcas asked.

"Yeah, I'm okay. Banged up a bit." Alan rotated his left arm. "Think I got hit by something in the back of the shoulder. Just bruised though, not broken." He stretched his fingers. "This hand never works that good when it gets cold, ever since the slice to my wrist. It'll get better, though."

"You sure you don't want to drop by a hospital?"

Alan shook his head. "I'm just not really looking forward to going back to Cliffview. I've never really felt directly threatened by Rook before. This was different. I know he caused the wreck, and he didn't care if we lived or died."

"I mean, he's kind of been that way," Lorcas said.

"Yeah, I guess," Alan admitted. "Maybe I've been kind of discounting it. It's just a little more personal this time."

They sat in silence for a few more minutes. "Tell you what," Lorcas said. "I'm not really looking forward to going back to Cliffview right now either. I mean, we need to know how the Community Meeting is going, but nothing's likely to change with us there. Let's go get something hot to drink and something to eat and find a way to call Tondra. I should've asked to use Jack's phone, but I didn't think about it before he left, and I'm sure my phone is trashed."

"Mine too," Alan said. He had placed it on the dashboard when he got into the car, and a small puddle of water was forming around it.

"Maybe we can buy a couple of prepaid phones in Lafayette. We'll call Tondra from there, tell her what happened, and then head for the new chapel. I can see if I can get any more information from the monks so the day won't be a complete bust and we can put off going back to Cliffview."

Alan nodded. "Sounds like a plan."

Lorcas put the car in gear and headed out of the marina. He turned south through town, following the newly-repaved main route over the rise and past the old church. From there they trended slightly inland towards Lafayette.

They chose a restaurant on the north side, one that didn't look too formal as they were still damp and a little disheveled. It was directly across from an electronics store, and after Lorcas parked they walked over to look for cell phones. They picked up a couple of cheap, pre-paid phones and then headed back to eat.

"Hope I remember Tondra's number," Alan said as they waited for their food and set up the phones. "I never look at peoples' numbers anymore."

"Me neither," Lorcas said.

Alan punched in a number, then nodded. "Hey, it's Alan. I'm on a throwaway phone. Mine got trashed. No, Lorcas's phone got trashed too. It's a long story."

Lorcas listened as Alan described what had happened to Tondra and told her they were having some lunch in Lafayette. "We needed some food and something hot to drink," he said, omitting the discussion about not returning to Cliffview. "What's going on with the meeting?"

After listening for a while, Alan told Tondra he'd see her later and hung up. "The meeting's still going on," he told Lorcas. "Tondra said she's going to add what just happened to the discussion. People won't be happy that Rook could have drowned us, whatever they think of Jack. Rook may have made a mistake. Whether they think you're a good Lorecaster or not, people like you and they know you. I hope people like me, too. We've already lost a bunch of Fell Ken, including our elder advisers, and no one's going to be thrilled with the thought of losing more of the leadership. The last years have been pretty traumatic for everybody."

"Yes," Lorcas agreed. He ate his lunch slowly, occasionally entering a number he remembered into his new phone. He remembered Terry's off the top of his head. He hesitated about entering it, but finally did, with the justification that he might need to call her in regards to some Fell Ken business for some reason that he couldn't think of at the moment.

Drier, calmer, and refreshed, they returned to Lorcas's car and headed for the new chapel.

Lorcas was now getting familiar enough with the road up the hill that he could anticipate and avoid some of the worst rocks and ruts. He parked in his usual spot and they got out. As before, it was sunny, if a bit breezy, and Lorcas was reminded again of the ever-present fog at Cliffview. It hadn't been that way when he'd stayed there as a child. It was Rook's atmosphere, gloomy, damp, and shrouded.

They walked to a spot near the door of the chapel, sunny but with shade available along the side of the building if they ended up standing there for a while. Lorcas tested the door, but it was locked.

"Now what?" Alan asked.

"We wait," Lorcas said. "The monks will know we're here. I think they will, anyway. Although before I've usually gone inside. But I can't, now. I don't have the Key."

"What is it you want to ask them?" Alan asked.

"I'd like some more information about the Key in particular, but I'd also like to find out if they know anything about the other Objects of Power. Anything they can tell me will help. At least, I hope it will."

"They did say they could help you," Alan said. "I suspect they meant they can do more than provide information, if you'll let them. I understand why you might not want them to get too involved, though. They did murder your ancestors. But maybe they can tell you how to get to Mira and Zumar, too, now that the tower's out of the question."

"That's an idea," Lorcas said. He walked to the side of the chapel and peered behind it, impatient. He couldn't remember exactly how long it had taken for the monk to arrive, but he thought maybe twenty minutes.

"Meanwhile, you can tell me why my Key fits in the door of a building created without my help," he said as he returned to Alan.

Alan laughed. "Easy. The Katzbalgers bought a door hardware set at that antiques market in Lafayette where you found other Fell Ken stuff. It came with one key, just a normal key, though. We didn't know your Key would open it."

"It did seem to unlock whatever I needed open at the time," Lorcas admitted. He crossed his arms and stared at the new cornerstone.

Suddenly the top of it seemed to ripple. He felt a charge of adrenalin. Something was certainly happening.

As he watched, a figure rose slowly up through the stone until it was standing on top. It appeared to be made of rock, but in a moment it shook itself and the facade melted away.

"Fancy meeting you here!" said Zumar. "You rang?"

CHAPTER THIRTEEN

"Zumar, you scared the heck out of me!" Lorcas said. "What are you doing in that thing?"

"This?" Zumar glanced down at the cornerstone. "Oh, don't worry. The entity is still here, but it's small, like Rook was in the beginning. It can't do anything by itself. It's just waiting for a Messenger and a Lorecaster who's not going to come."

"Couldn't you, like, accidentally trigger it coming up through there like that?" Lorcas asked nervously.

"Oh, no, it takes a lot more work than that. But if it makes you feel better, I'll leave a different way."

"How did you get here, anyway?" Lorcas asked.

"Mira showed me her routes. They're easy enough for me to follow. It's the kind of thing I used to do. Unfortunately, I can't remain in this world for long anymore. My attachment to it is very thin now. Besides,

I don't want to be here long enough to attract attention, if you know what I mean."

He looked over at Alan. "Hello, Alan. I'm glad to see the two of you together. I thought things might not be working out so well."

Alan glanced at Lorcas. "We've come to an agreement."

"Which is?" Zumar asked. He stepped down off the cornerstone.

"Which is, we do things his way," Alan said with a chuckle. "But I'm in complete agreement."

"Very good," Zumar replied. "Mira told me what went on here. I assume that now we're looking for a way to limit Rook's development, if not get rid of him altogether."

"We are," Lorcas said. "Hang on a minute."

He went back to the Subaru, where he had some folding chairs in the back. He had thrown them in there a couple of years before, anticipating sitting around on the cliffs having a glass of wine with Terry, but had never used them. He pulled them out, handed one to Alan, and set one up for Zumar to encourage him to not sit on the cornerstone, which made him nervous. Instead, though, Zumar remained standing, pacing a bit before them.

"Now that you're here, Zumar, Alan needs to hear the truth about Rook's future plans from you," Lorcas said.

"I don't need to, but I wouldn't mind knowing the details," Alan said. "And I can tell Zumar exactly why I am the way I am. He only knows part of it."

"You first," Zumar said.

Lorcas sat back and listened as Alan told Zumar his story. He kept an eye on the chapel, checking for the monk, but it only took Alan a few minutes, and when he was done the monk had not yet appeared.

"I've been to your world," Zumar said. "They allowed me to leave. I didn't know I was in danger."

"It's mainly humans and a few others they don't allow to leave," Alan said. "They must have seen you for what you are. It was long before my time, of course. I'm only as old as I am in human years."

"Did you know any of that?" Lorcas asked Zumar.

Zumar hesitated. "Yes, and no. I always knew Alan had walked in other worlds. I didn't find it worth mentioning to anyone else. There were certain things we could talk about that others would not understand. He knew what it was like to see this world as just one of many. I couldn't talk to you openly because I was concerned about leading you down Rook's path, and that meant I had to be very careful what I said, always."

That was true, Lorcas conceded. The two of them had not always been on the best terms, as Lorcas often felt Zumar was being unnecessarily bratty and he held him partly responsible for Raine's death. Still, he felt a small twinge of envy; it was good to have someone you could talk to, a buddy who understood you, and although he and Tomash had at one time been good friends, in the last year or so he had not had anyone he felt he could share his concerns or even his daily life with. The new policy of honesty was actually a relief, although sometimes it could sting a bit.

"What I didn't tell you, Alan, were the details of Rook's plan," Zumar continued. "I couldn't risk the reality getting out. I know Lorcas has told you, but let me repeat it and fill in any details he might have missed."

Lorcas listened as Zumar reviewed what he had told them in the borderlands. Alan leaned forward in the lawn chair, elbows on knees, studying the ground and sometimes looking up at Zumar. When Zumar was done, he leaned back in the chair, his expression sober.

"I understand what Rook promised you and how tempting it was," Zumar concluded. "You and I are in the same boat, kind of."

"Don't mention boats, please," Alan replied. "Although I didn't understand the depth and breadth of it, this isn't something that is a surprise to me," he admitted. "I chose to ignore what I knew and push it to the back of my mind. Now, of course, I don't want what Rook promised me, but even if I did, these plans can't be allowed to continue. And Rook has shown today that he cares nothing for us and only uses us for his own convenience."

Together, Alan and Lorcas filled Zumar in on their attempt to reach Mira's realm earlier, and Lorcas described what had happened at the chapel with Dirk after Mira had left, as well as his meeting with Rook.

"Tondra and Tomash are running an emergency Fell Ken congregational meeting today," Lorcas told him. "Alan talked to Tondra earlier and it seemed to be going okay. They seemed to be accepting the possibility of allying with the Knights, as well."

Zumar grimaced. "If you think I'm going to start playing nice with Jack, think again."

"We'll do the negotiating," Lorcas assured him. "Just don't actively sabotage him."

"Fine," Zumar replied grumpily. "I'm surprised the rest of the Fell Ken are coming along so easily."

"I'm not that surprised. It's been brewing for a while. The Fell Ken in general would be fine without Rook. Most of them have normal jobs in town and very few of them do nothing but Fell Ken business. It would be hardest for Tondra, Alan, and Tomash, because pretty much all they've ever done is Fell Ken-related. But there are plenty of gold coins left to us by Perry as well as other funds, and there's the Cliffview Estates corporation."

"I think careers are the least of our worries," Alan said. "The earth is not like it was when Rook last knew it. Things have changed, and the Fell Ken are modern people with modern needs and wants. Living in a shadow-land with no modern amenities isn't going to be very attractive to them. I think we need to concentrate on what we, the Entourage, want to do about Rook, and trust that the rest of the Fell Ken will come along."

"Getting rid of Rook is going to be a problem," Zumar mused. He paced in front of the cornerstone. "Unfortunately, I let it go on too long."

"Rook talked about being ripped apart stone-by-stone last time, and how that wouldn't be possible anymore," Lorcas said. "He's too much a part of them now. We're going to have to do something else. I don't suppose he would simply return to the Cornerstone at our request."

Zumar laughed abruptly. "No. You can try, but at this point Rook's not going to listen to what the Fell Ken want, and you're not even a Lorecaster anymore."

"Have I ever been one?" Lorcas asked cynically. "If so, I haven't been a good one. Frankly, I don't even know what a 'Lorecaster' is, although obviously my dad named me 'Lorcas' because of it."

"'Lorecaster' is kind of a mistranslation into English," Zumar said, pacing more slowly as he pieced together the words. "You know the definitions of the parts of the word better than I do, but I believe 'lore' means a body of traditional knowledge. Those who first translated the term took it to mean something closer to 'mythology'. And 'caster', well, to 'cast' means to throw, but it can also mean something akin to 'create', as in 'cast a spell'. The title was meant to denote the one who spun the mythology or stories around the Arukak, or Rook, cult. The Lorecaster was to be the person who served as the conduit between the world of Rook and the world of humans, who interpreted Rook's wants and needs and spun those desires and plans into a legible story."

"Huh," Lorcas said. He hadn't heard the Fell Ken described as a cult before, nor had he heard the name 'Arukak' applied to Rook. "I haven't been spinning much of a legible story."

"Not exactly your fault. I admit it: I was getting impatient. We tried with your father, but that didn't work out. We figured we'd try again with the son and see if we could improve things."

"Didn't work out? He died! A slow, lingering death that nobody could figure out," Lorcas pointed out.

"Well, yes, but you have to understand that, first of all, what he did wasn't our suggestion, and second, we thought we'd be able to handle it even so. He took Paracel's potions from the vials inside the Staff without consulting us first. So did Paracel, actually he created them, and he died, too. That was part of the plan, though: he died and Rook resurrected him with part of his own energy. Paracel became Rook's familiar, so to speak, even though people saw it the other way around. We assumed the same would happen with your father, but it didn't. Rook couldn't reach him. Of course, your father had no real Entourage and very little support, but personally I think he was too strong, rather than not strong enough. He resisted Rook's intrusion, which ironically would have saved him, and unfortunately the poison got him in the end."

That explained a few things, Lorcas thought. Zumar had once told him that Paracel died young, but he knew that Paracel had actually lived for several generations. Paracel had been even stronger than he thought: dependent on Rook for his existence, but willing and able to stand against him in the end, despite knowing it would be his death.

Zumar went on. "As I said, I was getting impatient, and it looked like there was a pretty good group of Fell Ken growing in the area to support you. And then you drank the poison too, and we expected it to go like Paracel. Rook would give you a piece of his energy and resurrect you, and all would be well. He'd been priming you, supporting your Air nature by allowing you to fly and such, and he knew what to look for to make the bond stronger and avoid Paracel's eventual betrayal."

"But it didn't happen," Lorcas said, "at least, I don't think it did."

"No," Zumar agreed, "pretty much nothing happened. That was a surprise, and it foiled Rook's bonding plan. You were obviously much stronger, more independent, than we gave you credit for, and Rook began trying other things to increase the bond between you two. None of them worked that well, I have to say. But at least you weren't going to simply die like your dad, pardon me, no insult intended, destroying all our hard work. And now that strength is going to be a good thing. A bad Lorecaster equals a good opponent for Rook."

"You gave me the Key," Lorcas said. "It wasn't a Rook thing, it was a Fell Ken thing, an Object of Power. Yet you made sure I had it early and that I kept it with me all the time."

Zumar glanced at him. "Yes, and in the end, I have no regrets," he said cryptically. "But we can discuss the Objects of Power later. We need to begin to form a plan."

"According to Mira, you and I basically created him," Lorcas said. "What did she say, you formed the idea and I gave him direction? Can't you and I un-make him somehow?"

Zumar shook his head and took a few more paces. "Once made manifest, a being is as real as any other. You can only change its form," he said, repeating what Rook had told Lorcas earlier. "Possibly we could squeeze him back into the Cornerstone and contain him, like a balloon under pressure. But it would be difficult and dangerous."

"Wouldn't it be simpler to somehow make him go back to where he came from?" Alan asked.

"No, he can't do that," Zumar said. "He and his kin have already left their world behind. They exist in a kind of borderland now. Their own world has been damaged beyond redemption and made unsuitable for them, much as they are trying to do to ours."

Lorcas stared at him. "You mean Rook is basically homeless? He literally has nowhere to go?"

"That's right," Zumar said. "It almost makes you feel sorry for him, doesn't it? But that doesn't mean it's okay for him to destroy this world. Anyway, that option is out of the question: there's no place to send him back to. We have to either contain him or kill him. And we know that he's aware that we're unhappy with him. He knows about your attempt to get to Mira and he certainly knows about the meeting of the Fell Ken that's going on now. He isn't naive or unaware. He is sly and old, with many plans and likely many steps ahead of us. He will fight it. He will not go happily."

"We won't be able to sneak up on him, that's for sure," Lorcas said. "It will have to be a face-to-face confrontation."

"Yes, and we'll need to use everything we have. All the Objects of Power and all the Allies."

"Do you still have the Sazh?" Lorcas asked.

"Yes," Zumar said. "I can't seem to get rid of it."

"I thought you were enjoying it, at least a little," Lorcas said. "Doesn't it give you more power?"

"Oh, yes, it opens up more worlds to me and a few other things. But I'm getting a bit tired of it. It interferes with my normal thinking processes."

"Could someone take the Sazh voluntarily?" Lorcas asked.

"I guess so, but who would want to?" Zumar replied skeptically.

"Suppose someone did. Would it be possible?"

Zumar mused for a minute. "It depends. It won't go into certain people at all. It doesn't like water spirits or water-adjacents, so it wouldn't go into someone like Mira, or, say, Raine, if she could even contain it. Or Alan."

"What about a fire-related person, like Tomash?"

"It would, temporarily. But it couldn't really do much within another fire spirit. Most fire people are pretty honest anyway, and adding fire to fire just makes more fire, basically. While it might go into one, it would be looking to leave if it could."

"You're an Earth entity," Lorcas said. "It seems to like it in there with you. How about another earth person, like Tondra?"

"Tondra's not an earth person," Zumar said.

Lorcas was puzzled. "But Raine positioned her at the Earth position in the Wheel-turning ceremony."

"She had to have someone to stand in for the North. I'm the only Earth spirit I know of in the Entourage, and I wasn't available. Tondra's a fire person, like Tomash, although I'd say she does have some earth-like qualities. The Sazh might like her better than Tomash, but marginally."

"And how about an air-adjacent?" Lorcas asked.

"You mean you?" Zumar grinned. "The Sazh would probably be very happy with you. Air plus fire equals an increase in fire's strength. Plus, you have a strong connection to other worlds and borderlands, which it prefers. Unfortunately, it wouldn't be great for you. The heat it creates would probably burn you up very quickly and leave you an empty shell. It's hard to say how quickly. You interested?"

"Not right now," Lorcas said, returning the grin. "But maybe in the future. We'll see."

"You're thinking about sharing the Sazh to increase our power against Rook," Zumar said. "It's not a bad idea."

"You said we'll need all the Allies," Lorcas said. "Will Mira help us?"

Zumar considered. "I think so. She doesn't spend a lot of time here anymore, not like she used to. But she likes having this world available. She doesn't want it to be sealed off completely from her people and her borderlands; it's always been connected, as far back as anyone knows, and there's always been traffic back and forth. It would be a first for the two worlds to be disconnected. I'm sure she'll help in some way. She's not called an 'Ally' for nothing."

"But there are two others," Alan pointed out. "You said we would need them all. We don't even know who, or what, the Air Ally and the Earth Ally are."

"Do you even know?" Lorcas asked. "You told me before you didn't know much about the Allies. Was that the truth?"

"Basically," Zumar said. "The allies are Fell Ken allies, not Rook allies, and Paracel didn't tell me things he wanted to keep from Rook. He certainly wouldn't have told me anything having to do with an eventual betrayal of Rook; he considered me an evil familiar by that point. Same with most of the Objects of Power: anything I know about them I've found out by listening and sneaking around. I knew something about the Wellspring and that Paracel had contacted her, but that was early in his career, so he had little reason to keep it from me. That's about it. I had to deduce the rest. Of course, now I know about the Fire Ally. But I have limited information about the other two, although I do know some few things, and I have guessed more."

"Let's start with the Air Ally, then," Lorcas said. "What do you know about it? How would we call it?"

Zumar nodded. "As for that, you can call the Air Ally at any time. You've done it before; you just didn't realize it. The Air Ally is very subtle."

"When have I done it?" Lorcas asked, surprised.

"You called it first using the Smokeweed," Zumar said. "It's much more like the Sazh than like Mira, something that can only exist within another person, but it only stays there for a short period of time, although some have learned to keep it longer through practice. It increases awareness and clears or opens the mind, and you can learn to channel it with the Staff. You practiced using it when you flew as your shadow form. Yes, Rook gave you that shadow form, but the Air Ally supported it."

"You mean I've been infected with an Ally and didn't even know it?" Lorcas asked.

Zumar grinned at Lorcas's indignation. "It was to my advantage to allow you to believe that it was Rook who supported you when you flew, because we were trying to bind you to him. We were looking for something that would be interesting and useful to you. The Air Ally doesn't directly oppose Rook, although it doesn't support him either. It's there for the support of the Fell Ken, like all the Allies. But it's not very noticeable to someone who isn't aware that it exists."

"Then I'll need to smoke some Smokeweed before we do whatever we do?" Lorcas asked.

"You can probably channel it with the Staff at this point, but it wouldn't hurt to have some Smokeweed available. Since you're already an Air person, it will support and strengthen you. It's too bad we don't have time to practice channeling it again. We were working on it until you stopped flying."

Zumar turned towards the chapel and frowned a bit.

"That leaves just the Earth Ally. What do you know about it? Have we already met it as well?"

"Er, no, not really," Zumar said a bit uncomfortably. "I think the Monk will arrive soon."

"Okay, then let's have it," Lorcas pressed. "Why haven't we encountered it and how do we meet it?"

Zumar turned hesitantly to him, almost as though he was being compelled to do so. "You haven't met it because I haven't summoned it," he said.

"You?" Lorcas asked.

"Yes. In fact, I'm the only one who can summon it. Like I said, I'm the only Earth-connected person in the Entourage. But I haven't seen a reason to call upon it, although I've seen its influence a few times. It knows we're here and it knows about Rook. It's no friend of his, but it won't react without specific direction. It doesn't understand things the same way, say, Mira does, or even the Sazh."

"Does it need a body to enter?" Lorcas asked.

"That would be extremely dangerous," Zumar said. "It's very powerful, although very loyal to any group it's connected to."

"Could you handle it or direct it?" Lorcas asked.

Zumar hesitated. "Not with the Sazh within me. Even for me, it would be too much. Even immortals can be killed in certain ways, you know. And if Rook realized we had summoned it, he would kill all of you very quickly and very violently. It would have to be a last-minute thing and Rook would have to be distracted and not suspicious. Even then..."

He peered again at the chapel, leaning as though to see around it.

"What are you looking for?" Lorcas asked. "The Monk? He'll probably be here soon."

"And I should be gone when he arrives," Zumar said. "The Monks have no love for me."

"Then you should go," Lorcas said. "I still need to know more about the Objects of Power, and I still will need to talk to Mira before we put any kind of plan into action. But I have one more question: we've agreed that the Fell Ken in general will be okay without Rook. But what about those of us who have had more direct contact with him?"

"Of course, there will be consequences," Zumar said. He clasped his hands behind his back and studied the cornerstone. "Your connection to him now is strong; while we were unsuccessful at binding you completely to him, there remains a string or strand connecting the two of you and supporting you in much of what you do here. Whether you would be able to cut that string and still retain your vital force and remain in this world, I do not know. You, too, are now a creature of the borderlands, not fully human and not fully one of us."

"And what about you?" Lorcas asked.

"I am safe enough in the borderlands. There I can survive for the long term, even without a homeland. But of course, I would have to return to this world to banish Rook. You cannot do it without me. That was

Paracel's mistake. But in your world, I am chiefly sustained only by Rook's power, and currently by the Sazh, which may leave me at any time. With Rook gone and the Sazh gone, I would fade away or perhaps simply disappear. I might not have the time or strength to return to the borderlands, especially if I summoned the Earth Ally. Raine certainly could not continue at all, as she no longer exists in any world in any real way. She was an experiment, created by me after her own desire to become part of the shadow world, and I had only the experience of Bishop the Cat to go on."

He looked up again. "I must go. I'll tell Mira about your attempt to get to her and what happened, and I'll pass on our plans and see if she has any suggestions. You may be able to summon her to come here in the future, or even to a place closer to Cliffview; there are many passageways."

He made a move as though to step up on the cornerstone, but then grinned and glanced sideways at Lorcas. "Oh, that's right. It makes you nervous when I pass through this stone. I'll go another way then."

He snapped a cocky salute and sank slowly into the ground next to the stone itself. Lorcas watched him go, his final words still fresh in his mind. Banishing Rook would be the end of Raine. And as for himself and Zumar, the consequences were unknown, but unapt to be good. And yet this seemed to be the only way forward.

He turned as the Monk appeared, as suddenly as ever. He and Alan rose and went to meet him.

"Ah," the monk said. "The demon's Familiar was here."

"If you mean Zumar, yes, but he left," Lorcas said. "He knows you're not fond of him."

"We consider him a lost soul," the monk said, "unreachable. On the other hand, there is still hope for you and your kin. We believe that if you vanquish the demon, your soul will be returned to your body."

"That's cool," Lorcas said. He not only didn't believe in demons, although he was hard-pressed to define Rook, he didn't believe in a soul the way the monks did.

He had the feeling the monk was looking him up and down, although he could see nothing beneath the heavy cowl. He glanced down at himself and then over at Alan. They were both disheveled, Alan's now-dry clothing wrinkled and crusty with sea-water salt around the shirt-sleeves and trouser-hems, his dark hair, usually kept tidy and combed, a tousled mess. Lorcas ran a hand over his own hair, which was much longer than Alan's. He usually kept it tied back at the nape of his neck, but somewhere he had lost the tie, and it was now tangled and wind-blown. He could feel a few bruises coming up, too, including one on his cheek.

"You have been in some altercation," the monk said. "I suspect it is the demon's doing."

"You suspect right," Lorcas said, "but you'll be happy to know that it's cemented our resolve to get rid of him, or at least contain him. I need to know a few things from you, if you'll answer. First, tell me how the Katzbalgers are doing."

The monk bowed his head a bit and stepped closer. "They rest. The boy sleeps deeply while we turn time back for him. They will all awaken together, and be returned to you should your mission succeed."

Lorcas nodded. He didn't have time to worry about the Katzbalgers at the moment, but he felt duty-bound to inquire about them. "Okay. Then the next thing I need to know is anything you can tell me about the Objects of Power."

"Unfortunately, I know little about them, with the exception of the Key," the monk said. "I am aware of only a few of them: the Sword, given your ancestors long ago by the Lake Lady, the Staff, which I believe to be a construction of Paracel himself, and the Ring, constructed by Paracel using some dark magic with which we would have no familiarity. Of their powers, I know nothing."

"At least tell me about the Key, then," Lorcas said.

The monk's sleeves split suddenly apart, and the withered hand Lorcas had seen before appeared. The Key still dangled from the fingers, as if caught there.

"If you are truly set on returning the demon to its place and freeing yourself and your kin from its devouring evil, then I will return the Key to you. Take it, and we will see the truth of your words."

Lorcas hesitated. That sounded a bit ominous. But after a moment he stepped forward, reached out his hand, and grasped the Key. He unwound the chain and removed it from the monk's fingers. The monk withdrew his hand slowly into the sleeve again.

"Well?" Lorcas demanded.

"Your words are true and your resolve is steady," the monk said. "Otherwise, you would have been struck down when you took the Key. Now I will tell you this: the Key was stolen by the Familiar, Zumar, many centuries ago."

"From whom? You?" Lorcas asked.

"Yes. The Key was constructed by us, using certain techniques, to ensnare the Lorecaster's soul. We believed, should we be able to catch his soul in this way, we would be able to stop the demon from growing."

"What kind of magic is that?" Lorcas asked with a touch of sarcasm. "It doesn't sound very Christian."

The monk seemed to hesitate. "It is not," he said, "but the ends sometimes justify the means. The creation of the Key used the powers of the old Earth Magic, that of witches and druids. The forces of the earth are greater than those of the demon who intrudes upon it. Those powers are of the Earth itself, and he is not. It would have worked, had we gifted it to the Lorecaster ourselves. But unfortunately, the Key was stolen, and Zumar turned it to his own devices. He was not able to change it completely; each turn of the Key ensnared a bit more of your soul, but we believe in the end it kept you apart from the demon, your soul secured within it. It is possible Zumar always intended this, a bit of rebellion against Rook, but it would be against his own best interests, so we have doubts. But in order for you to vanquish the demon, it was necessary for us to regain it."

"And yet you've returned it to me," Lorcas said suspiciously, fingering the Key on its chain.

"We have restored its original purpose and added an element of control for you," said the monk. "You have the power to use it to bring the forces you will need to yourself and gather them there; they will come to you, as the Key is a centering and gathering device. Your soul is locked inside it, protected and away from the demon. Use it well. If you fail and the Key is taken by Rook or his cohorts, your soul will be forfeit for all time, beyond our reach. If you succeed, and live, you will be free, and your path will be your own to walk."

The monk bowed deeply, turned, and disappeared rapidly behind the chapel. Lorcas glanced at Alan, then carefully slipped the Key beneath his shirt.

"I don't know how much of that to believe and I don't understand how to use it," Lorcas said, "but at least I've got it back, and the monk seems to think it has some sort of protective quality. Whatever, we probably need to get back to Cliffview now."

"I suppose," Alan said. "We need to find out how the meeting went. And I guess you'll need to talk to Jack to find out more about the Objects of Power. But I have a feeling we need to hurry. Rook isn't going to sit on that hill allowing us to gather our forces and information for very long."

"No," Lorcas said, "that is one thing I know for sure."

CHAPTER FOURTEEN

They packed up the chairs and threw the towels in the back, now that they were generally dry. As soon as they were settled in the car, Alan brought out his phone and dialed Tondra.

"Not picking up," he said. "At least it's not going straight to voice mail or saying it's out of range."

Lorcas negotiated the rocky driveway down to the narrow forest road and turned north. "Try Tomash."

Alan held the phone to his ear for another minute, but then shook his head. "Nope."

Lorcas felt a jolt of adrenalin and pressed down harder on the gas. They were probably just involved in the meeting, he told himself.

"We should have gone straight back," he said.

"No," Alan said. "I didn't want to. Besides, we learned something here, we met Zumar, and you got the Key back. That's valuable."

He reached over and took Lorcas's new phone off the seat and brought up the screen.

"I don't think Tondra or Tomash will answer my phone if they're not answering yours," Lorcas said.

"I'm not calling them," Alan said, "but I don't know this number off the top of my head."

Lorcas glanced over at him. "Who are you calling?"

"Jack," Alan replied. "You don't need to meet him in person to get information on the Objects, and we might not have time anyway. We need that info now."

He put the phone on speaker and set it on the dashboard as Jack answered.

"Hello?" Jack said. He sounded wary. Lorcas realized that the new phone wasn't coming up with his name.

"It's Alan, but Lorcas is listening," Alan said, leaning a bit towards the phone. He steadied it with a finger as Lorcas drove over a rough patch in the two-lane road. "We need to know everything you know about the Fell Ken Objects of Power."

"Feel free to drop by my office and browse through the stacks of books, and I can tell you what I know, but I'm not going to start hauling car-loads of random volumes up to Cliffview unless you can be more specific about which ones you're looking for. Or, of course, you're planning on giving me my building back. Then we could meet in Seaside Heights."

"As for that, you can have the building," Lorcas said, "but we don't have time to zip over to Lafayette and browse. We need what you know now, and if it's incomplete, it'll have to suffice."

"Hmm. I see," Jack replied. "When is this thing going down?"

"Now, probably," Alan told him. "We're heading to Cliffview from the new chapel, and we're probably going to have to deal with it when we get there."

"So it's curtains for Rook?" Jack asked.

"I guess," Lorcas said. "I don't have a plan yet, only some ideas."

There was a pause. "You know this is dangerous for you," Jack finally said. "Really dangerous."

"Do you care?" Lorcas asked caustically.

"Yes, Lorcas, I do care," Jack said. "You're a human being and you belong on this earth, and Rook doesn't. This isn't your fault. It's the culmination of generations of mistakes. I don't want you to sacrifice your life to take Rook down. I do want Rook gone, but I dread the actual conflict."

Lorcas took a deep breath, but he deliberately forced down his fear. He needed to concentrate on driving as well as listening, and there was only so much room in his brain. "Then tell us what you know about the Objects, because I need all the information I can get, and Zumar had to leave before I could get it from him."

"Unfortunately, I don't know a lot," Jack admitted. "There isn't much mention of them in the documentation I have, and the Knights never found out much about them. I know almost nothing about the Key, for example, other than it's used as a 'centering' object in rituals."

"Never mind the Key," Lorcas said. "I got it back, and I understand it to some degree."

"Okay, then there's the Sword. You know it was a gift from Mira to an ancient King who was her earth-side lover and through whom she gained power to pass through the veil and interact with humans, and he gained the power to go to her and use her powers and advice to manage his kingdom. After his death she passed it on to our people when she saw fit, because she wanted to maintain that connection with our world. It has the ability to touch the other realms, the shadow-lands and borderlands, and to pierce through the boundaries between our world and the others."

"I know that, too," Lorcas said, although he hadn't heard it put quite so succinctly.

"The goblets I know nothing about," Jack continued quickly. "They're water symbols used in ritual, but I think Raine's scrying Mirror and the Needle are more powerful. They were also probably a gift from Mira, or at least she directed their creation. The Needle, as you know, stands in for the Sword and summons her. I didn't know anything about those objects until I saw them in action, but when I did, I was able to make a few deductions. But you probably know that, too."

Lorcas nodded, forgetting that Jack couldn't see him. He'd forgotten about the Mirror and the Needle. If he couldn't get to Mira any other way, perhaps he, or Raine, could summon her that way.

"That leaves the Staff and caduceus and the Ring."

"The Staff was personally created by Paracel to channel the energy of the wind," Jack said. "The caduceus is just a smaller, more portable version. Of course, it has compartments in it. I'm sure you know that. I have no further information about how to use it. It has traditionally been the symbol of the Lorecaster himself, as the Sword has been the symbol of the King. I'm sorry I can't tell you more about that Object. Its powers were a closely-guarded secret. They might not even be written down."

"Then there's the Ring. It's the one thing we know the least about," Lorcas said. "It's obviously part of the mechanism in the window, but what else is it?"

"The mentions I've seen of it treat it as an object to be avoided or handled very carefully. It may be the most powerful of the Objects, but I don't know why. It's an Earth symbol, but also a symbol of protection, death, and permanence. It's associated with time somehow, too. It's apt to be important, but I can't tell you how to use it."

"Great," Lorcas said. "Thanks for the information you do have. I guess you'll be able to figure out soon enough what's happened. Oh, and in case things go well, but I don't get a chance to tell you because maybe they didn't go well for me personally, the key to the front door of your old office in Seaside Heights is hidden around the right side in the first window frame. If things don't go well overall, I'd advise you to leave the area."

"Hmm, yes," Jack said. "I did tell you I'd support you and that the Knights will stand with you in this effort. Now it appears the time has come for me to make good on that promise. I'll be there driving time from my home, and I'll see if I can round up a few friends and encourage them to come along as well."

Lorcas hesitated. "Jack, this is our problem. You don't have to endanger yourself. We're going to do this with or without you, and if things go wrong, the leadership of the Knights may be very important. You'll be the only ones left who understand what's happening and what's going to happen in the future and the only ones with the knowledge to oppose Rook. Besides, I don't know what you can do to help."

Jack laughed shortly. "You underestimate the power of a show of strength, Lorcas. There is strength in dedication to what's right and in the support of friends. I'll be there, and I'll stand with you in the face of this thing. I'm not afraid. Or rather, I am afraid, but I'll do it anyway."

"Thank you," Lorcas said humbly. "I guess we'll see you there, then."

Alan set the phone back down on the seat. He didn't say anything. Lorcas drove on as fast as he dared to, feeling the pounding in his chest and the tightness in his jaw. His hands began to cramp on the wheel and he stretched his fingers. An odd thought that this could be the last time he ever drove his Subaru flashed across his mind.

He hadn't felt apprehension like this for a very long time. He realized that Rook was undoubtedly withdrawing some of the protection he'd conferred, which included the dulling of the human emotions. Or maybe he was purposefully channeling fear to Lorcas. Perhaps he was hoping Lorcas would be overwhelmed by the onslaught of emotion that he had been spared over the past few years. But Lorcas had experienced that withdrawal before, if only briefly, and he felt he was prepared for it now. He even welcomed it. The grief he had not truly felt over the deaths of Perry and Delva, the others of the Fell Ken, his mother, the horror of the attack by Don Bright at Perry's shop, the weight of Raine's cold body in his arms, the confusion and betrayal he'd been subjected to many times, all served, at full force, to fuel his anger and resolve. Would it last when he was face-to-face with Rook?

Seaside Heights was strangely silent, almost deserted, as they passed through. Many of the residents were Fell Ken, and Lorcas suspected they had either headed to Cliffview to answer Tondra's call, or they were hunkered down waiting for the outcome. He dared to push his speed; it was unlikely anyone would stop him now. Alan sat tensely, staring out the front window, one hand braced on the dashboard. Lorcas hoped he wasn't prone to car-sickness as they entered the winding section of road that rose through the forest.

They were barely out of Seaside Heights when the sun seemed to fade, obscured by smoke-colored clouds. Ahead, only a short stretch of road was visible. Here and there, tendrils of mist rose from clearings in the forest, as though escaping from boiling underground springs.

He slowed as they reached the final hill and passed through the firs and spruces that obscured the sight of Cliffview. Cars were parked bumper-to-bumper along the side of the road, leaving only a single lane, but since no one was driving down it, there was no particular danger. He didn't recognize any of the cars, but he was sure many of them were Fell Ken from Seaside Heights and beyond. The sight of so many of them willing to come and face whatever might happen brought a glimmer of hope. It was possible, he mused, that if Jack had managed to rally the Knights, some of those cars belonged to them as well.

They reached the spot where the road continued as a gravel two-track into the forest, with a sharp turn-off to Cliffview. Rook still crouched upon the hill, but the smog that had descended upon the area made him hard to distinguish. Here the fog was lit from below by the fires from the chasm, so that the whole of Cliffview Estates was awash in a deep, misty, blood-red hue.

As they neared the stone wall that surrounded the houses, Lorcas saw Jason's car, still parked near his own house. Beside it was Jack's black truck, and Jack himself leaned on the side. And there was yet another truck that he recognized: a big red Ford. Terry was here, somewhere, and she knew what it was they faced.

Lorcas stopped and rolled down the passenger-side window. Jack walked over and bent down to look in.

"You'd better stay outside the wall," Lorcas said. "You're none too popular with the Fell Ken, and despite our agreement, some of them might not take kindly to you. Same with Terry, wherever she is."

Jack nodded. "I'll tell her. I'll do what I can from out here, but it's possible you might need me, and if I feel you do, I'm coming in."

"At that point, it probably won't matter if you jump over the wall," Lorcas said grimly. "I'll let you know what I find out from Tondra."

He began to move forward again, but then stopped and leaned to look out the window past Alan. "And Jack. Thanks. I don't know how many of the Knights are here, but it means something."

Jack nodded curtly and stood back from the car. Lorcas followed the wall down to the gate and keyed the code in manually, since it wasn't stored in his new phone. He drove straight to the Community Center; there was no point in going to his house.

As they got out of the car, Lorcas saw Tondra approaching. She glanced behind at the crowd of people milling around inside and outside of the Community Center and Lorcas saw her head bob briefly to the side, as though she was resisting the urge to look up the hill at Rook. She was carrying his Staff.

She motioned the two of them towards the back of the car, out of earshot of the rest of the people.

"I'm glad you made it back safe," she said, looking them up and down. "Alan, you're going to get a black eye from that cut on your nose."

Alan gingerly touched his face. "Least of my worries right now."

"I wish you had time to rest, but there are some things you need to know," she said. She handed Lorcas his Staff. "I took the liberty of getting this from your house. I wanted to keep it safe and I wasn't sure how things would be going when you got back."

Lorcas took the Staff. The feeling of the hard wood and metal rings was comforting. "We weren't able to get you on the phone on the way back."

"I think Rook is jamming all phone signals in the area," Tondra said. "It started after a bunch of the Knights began to arrive. Probably trying to interfere with calling any more to our side."

"Let's have it," Lorcas said. "What's going on with the meeting?"

"We've taken a vote, and the Fell Ken have made their decision," Tondra said. Her expression was blank, her tone dead. Lorcas felt a lurch in his chest.

"What's the verdict?"

Tondra took a deep breath. "A motion was put forth by Alex Blazh. It passed on the vote by a pretty large margin. The motion orders us to put Rook back in the Cornerstone, but not kill him outright, unless it happens by accident during the confrontation, or procedure, or whatever it is."

Lorcas shook his head and looked down, gathering his thoughts and his temper. "This is what happened last time. He was shoved back into the Cornerstone, but he lurked there for hundreds of years and look what happened. He came out again, stronger than ever."

"I know," Tondra said. "I'm sorry if we didn't succeed in conveying the seriousness of all this to the congregation, but it's newer to them than it is to us. They haven't been privy to the information we have, to our doubts, and we've purposefully concealed our own confusion from them to seem like strong leaders. Now suddenly we're telling them we've been wrong all along. It was hard to even get them to trust us; some of them thought we'd been corrupted by the Knights or enchanted or something. What convinced most people in the end, I think, was just the idea of living in a medieval-style world, probably without Internet, TV, or any modern conveniences. It's pretty easy to understand that idea and accept it when you look at the castle and the other traditions surrounding Rook. Couple that with what they've been seeing has happened to Rook over the last few days and the changes to Cliffview, and the majority came down on the side of stopping him and at least curbing his influence."

"I understand," Lorcas said. "At least the mandate is to not let him continue the way he's been going. But I don't think they realize how difficult this is apt to be, and if we do succeed in somehow stuffing him back in the Cornerstone, but he's still in there in some form, what's to say he won't escape in the future?"

"The motion specified that the Fell Ken would convert to an organization dedicated to keeping him inside the stone and never let him out again," Tondra explained. "They didn't feel that killing an alien being we don't understand was the right thing to do."

"And if we can't do that? If we go too easy our effort may fail altogether, and then what? Rook will be loose in the world without us to rein him in. Most of us will probably be dead, really dead."

Tondra hesitated, then lowered her voice. "Don't let that happen, Lorcas. If we have to, we'll kill him by 'accident'. Only the Entourage will know the truth."

"More lies." Lorcas sighed. "I don't even know what to do. I don't know if we'll kill him, hurt him, cause him to revert to the Cornerstone, let him loose, or what. I really have no idea. We're winging it."

"We don't have any more time to prepare," Tondra said. "We go with what we know and what we feel. I believe we can do it. We'll be there together, to succeed or to fail."

"At least I know more about the Allies and the Objects," Lorcas said, looking the Staff up and down. He didn't actually know much more about that one, or the Ring, but he was trying to sound optimistic to make himself feel that way, as well as encourage others. "There are just a few more things I need to do. Is Raine around?"

"Yes," Tondra said with a questioning tone.

"Can we use your place? We'll need some quiet, I think. Do you know what happened to the scrying Mirror and the Needle and other objects that go with it? And any of Mira's leftover water?"

"I have them, but I don't know if we got the Needle back," Tondra said.

"I think it will be there," Lorcas said. "Bring Tomash, too."

He and Alan headed quickly for Tondra's place and Alan let them in the door. Lorcas looked around for a minute. "Let's move this table into the middle and bring the seating around," he said, pointing to a round coffee table. Together they created a circle with the table in the middle. Lorcas leaned his Staff against one of the chairs and the Sword, which was standing in the corner, against another.

"Will we need the goblets?" Alan asked. "Last I knew they were in the castle."

Lorcas shook his head. "I don't think so. The Mirror will work for this."

He stood back and thought for a moment. "I wonder if we can get Jack in here quietly? He was here last time they did this, and he might remember things."

"I can do it," Alan said. "I'll run out in my truck and get him, then bring him around your house and Tomash's house instead of along the main road. Probably no one will see us."

Alan grabbed his keys and ran out, leaving Lorcas to pace in the living room. He had a few minutes to collect his thoughts: he needed to summon Mira and get Zumar there somehow, and he would need the rest of the Smokeweed and his father's pipe from his own house. He wasn't sure how he was going to accomplish that without attracting attention from Rook.

"You looking for this?"

Lorcas spun around. Zumar stood in the doorway, pipe and packet of Smokeweed in one hand.

"Zumar!" Lorcas said. "How did you know?"

"Probably a combination of still being able to feel your needs as the Lorecaster and a good guess," Zumar said. "I checked for the Staff, but it looks like you have it here already. Anyway, I'm recharged and as ready as I'm going to be."

A minute later Tondra, Tomash, and Raine came in, followed by Alan and Jack. Alan closed the door after them and locked it.

"We left Jason with the rest of the Fell Ken," Tondra said. "He wants to stay, but technically he shouldn't be here. I told him to leave any time he wants to, that there's very little he can do. He just shrugged and said he had thrown in his lot with us."

"All right," Lorcas said. "I hope he stays safe."

"Raine," Jack said with a nod. "Good to see you again. You have my everlasting gratitude."

"You can drop the sarcasm," Lorcas said shortly. "Now is not the time."

Jack sobered. "Just a habit born of nerves," he said with a shrug.

Raine, after acknowledging Jack briefly, locked eyes with Zumar. The moment between them was long, and fleeting expressions passed over both of their faces.

Finally, they broke eye contact, and Raine turned her gaze to Lorcas as all of them settled around the table.

"Raine..." Lorcas began painfully. Someone was going to have to tell her what an end to Rook would mean for her.

"I know, Lorcas," Raine interrupted with a little smile. "It's all good. I know I can't leave here, not even to go to the borderlands. There's not enough of me to survive there. And I won't be able to stay here, either, if Rook goes away completely. Or probably even if he goes away mostly. It's okay; I don't want to end up some true haunt, a little scrap of bits of consciousness floating around aimlessly. It's better for things to end completely, like they should have four years ago. I believe I'll be with Delva and Perry and my other relatives, in one way or another."

"If Rook is only put back in the Cornerstone, there is still some hope," Lorcas said lamely.

Raine shook her head. "No, not really. He's none too fond of me. He's not going to expend energy supporting me. And I like to do things my own way, on my own terms; he knows that. But right now, I think we have a task to perform. And of course, you need my help, and of course I'll give it. You need me to use the Mirror to summon Mira again, because we need as many of the Allies with us as we can get."

"Yes," Lorcas said. "Technically the Sword, and the Needle that represents it, is supposed to be used by the King, so that leaves either Tomash or Jack to help you."

Raine nodded and looked at Jack. "You remember?"

"Yes, I do," Jack said. "I'm at your disposal."

"Alan can help too," Raine said. "He's a Water spirit. I may need his support."

Alan placed the Mirror and other items, including the Needle, which he took out of a small leather bag, on the central coffee table. Everyone settled around it in a circle, arrayed, as Lorcas and Alan had arranged it, with each one sitting at his or her respective cardinal direction. Alan, Raine, and Jack crowded together on the west side of the table, Lorcas on the east, Tomash and Tondra on the south. Zumar sat down carefully on the north side. He looked more sober and nervous than Lorcas had seen him since the time when Rook had threatened to eat him.

"I can't tell if I'm Fire or Earth at the moment," he said with a nervous laugh.

"Well, you have to be Earth, because we don't have anyone else to represent that," Lorcas said. "Tell the Sazh to chill."

"Here, this will help," Tomash said. "I reclaimed it after the Turning Ceremony." He pulled out the Ring on its chain from under his shirt, looped it over his head, and tossed it to Zumar, who caught it with an expression of apprehension. He unclipped the chain and slid it back to Tomash, then cautiously rotated the engraved outer ring around the smooth inner band. It moved freely; it had been repaired after saving Lorcas's hand from being crushed in the floor of the chapel. Lorcas remembered how strong the Ring was - it had barely been deformed by the sliding stones. After reshaping, it fit smoothly into the gears of the Control Window, a kind of gear itself, part of the mechanism that had moved the castle forward in its development, and with it Rook.

After a moment, Zumar set it down on the table.

"Not yet," he muttered. "I can't do both."

"All right, we've got business to attend to," Raine said briskly. "Everything's laid out. I see that what I need is here. Jack will need a bandage."

Tondra glanced at her questioningly, but she got up and fetched a box of bandages from the bathroom and set them on the table near Jack.

"Close the blinds and curtains and turn off the light while you're up," Raine said. "And bring that little reading lamp over."

Tondra followed Raine's instructions, setting the lamp so it shone at the correct angle onto the Mirror before re-seating herself. Silence fell on the room. Raine bent over the Mirror, one hand slightly raised towards Jack as though asking him to wait.

It was several minutes before she lowered her hand, sweeping it towards the Mirror. Jack poured a number of deep-green marbles into his hand and then carefully rolled them onto the glass with a muffled clicking sound.

Lorcas watched in fascination as Raine moved her hand over the Mirror and the marbles responded, rolling around in a mesmerizing pattern until suddenly they flew apart and slid to the outside edges of the Mirror. Raine glanced up, and Jack brought his hand over the Mirror again. Lorcas hadn't noticed him do it, but apparently he'd pricked himself with the Needle, because he squeezed a drop of blood from one finger into a cavity in the frame before sitting back and unwrapping a bandage from the box.

"The water," Raine whispered. Alan unscrewed the top of one of the two water bottles they'd brought to collect Mira's water the year before and poured a stream onto the Mirror. Lorcas watched as a curl of steam rose and the surface of the water turned smooth and black. He felt the familiar pressure in his ears, the muffling of sound that he always felt when he entered Mira's realm.

The water began to swirl by itself, rising a little around the edges. Lorcas felt a prickle at the back of his neck; it reminded him uncomfortably of another whirlpool he'd seen just that morning. He could barely take his eyes off it, but he saw that Jack held the Needle over the center.

He forced himself to look up. Jack was looking expectantly at Raine, waiting for her signal. Raine, however, was looking at Zumar, eyes wide.

"I really do love you, Andelko," she said, using his proper name.

Zumar, startled, replied, "I love you too."

A smile spread slowly over Raine's face, the most genuine expression of joy Lorcas had seen her express since the first few times he met her. She turned to Jack.

"Now, Jack," she whispered. "I'm ready."

Jack obediently slid the Needle into the center of the miniature eddy on the Mirror, where it disappeared from view. The water began to settle slowly. Raine drew a deep, audible breath.

In a moment she wavered, like the mist that rose from the Mirror. It seemed to Lorcas that she was drawn forward, that she was no longer seated in the room, but hovered over the table, mixing and merging with the steam.

"No!"

Lorcas jerked as Alan shouted and lunged forward. Alan made a grasping motion with his arms, but there was nothing there. Raine and the mist disappeared into the center of the Mirror. The water settled immediately, the muffling of sound eased, and the ambient light in the room, which had seemed to dim, rose again.

"What happened?" Lorcas demanded, jumping to his feet. He turned to Jack.

"That didn't happen last time," Jack replied. He bent forward with a frown, staring into the water.

"She's gone," Alan whispered.

"I can see that, but where did she go?" Lorcas demanded. "To Mira's world?"

"I doubt it," Alan said. He sat back down heavily, staring at the Mirror. "There wasn't enough of her to travel that far. She has gone into the water. On her own terms, she said."

There was a stunned silence. No one seemed to know what to do or say. It was Jack who finally broke it.

"Last time she had me drain the water from the Mirror," he said quietly. "Perhaps we'd better do that."

Tondra got up and brought back a travel coffee cup with a lid and handed it to Jack silently.

Jack carefully drained the water from the Mirror through a little opening in the bottom of the frame. He held it suspended for a moment over the cup, letting the last drops fall. Then he set the Mirror down and put the lid on the cup.

"Last time I drank the water," he said. "I don't think I'll do that this time."

Tondra took the cup. "Is Raine in here?" she asked Alan.

Alan shook his head. "Not really," he said. "A water spirit returns to water when they go, but the Mirror was connected to all the water in the borderlands at the time she chose to leave."

"Is she really gone for good, then?" Tondra asked, her voice betraying disbelief.

Alan turned to Zumar. "I think so," he said. "What do you think, Zumar?"

Zumar shrugged briefly. He had sunk back in his chair, his hands gripping the armrests. He stared blankly at the coffee table and the Mirror upon it, but he said nothing.

Lorcas felt the reality creeping in. There was more disbelief than anything. Real or imagined, it also seemed there was an absence at the edge of his consciousness: a place Raine had occupied in his thoughts and feelings where she no longer stood.

"Is there nothing we can do to find out exactly where she went and what happened to her?" he asked Alan, who seemed to understand Raine's action the most thoroughly.

"Maybe we can ask Mira if she felt Raine passing by when she comes," Alan said.

Lorcas stood up. He'd almost forgotten the purpose of the ritual, but there was no time to mourn Raine at the moment. They could not let this event distract or weaken them.

"I have no idea how Mira will come or when she'll come," he said, "but we need to be prepared by then. She won't be able to be here long."

CHAPTER FIFTEEN

Reluctantly, everyone rose from their chairs. Alan, Tondra, and Tomash rearranged the living room and opened the blinds, although Tondra then re-closed several of them since the only light the windows let in was ruddy and weak. In silence they gathered jackets and other items each one felt he or she needed to be prepared. Alan wiped down the Mirror and marbles, but left them unpacked and sitting on the round coffee table, as if in the hopes that Raine might re-materialize. The Needle, of course, was gone to Mira's world, at least temporarily.

Lorcas grabbed his Staff and jacket, and as he turned, he came face-to-face with Zumar. For an instant he saw through the facade Zumar was putting up and he had an impression of grief, fear, and desperation mixed together. A second later Zumar's face appeared more neutral, but Lorcas knew what he had seen. He felt the same things himself, but at that moment he also knew that everyone was counting on him to lead this foray. No one else knew any better than he did how to proceed, and they were looking to him for guidance. So he smiled and clapped Zumar encouragingly on the shoulder.

"Don't forget this," Zumar said, holding up the packet of Smokeweed and the pipe.

Lorcas took it from him and hesitated a moment. Then he set the pipe carefully on top of a desk in the entryway, although he pocketed the packet. He certainly wasn't going to sit there in front of Rook and smoke a bowl. He could hardly imagine a more ridiculous end than puffing desperately away while Rook destroyed Cliffview, and while he was trying not to imagine his own end at all, if he was going to go, he was going to do it marshaling every resource he had, with dignity.

It occurred to him that there were other ways to ignite things, anyway. Originally, smoking had allowed him to become more in touch with Rook's needs as they were building the castle, but he had used it since for other things, such as waking Zumar. And in a way it belonged to him, just as the Staff did. The smoke was a symbol of wind and of the ephemeral, but also of clarity of mind, of beginnings, and of soul and breath. His soul, his breath, he thought.

His nerves were jangling so strongly that he could feel the adrenalin down to his fingertips. He unlocked the door and walked out of the house a few steps. The red-tinged fog was thick, almost palpable. It smelled of smoke, of mold, of the damp earth from deep underground. It was unpleasant to breathe, and he heard someone coughing gently behind him. It had settled even further around the neighborhood so that the houses were only discernible by their porch lights. Ahead of him, he knew, was the hill and, he assumed,

Rook. Behind him, though he sensed that hundreds of Fell Ken and Knights were arrayed, it was eerily silent.

He turned a bit as Tomash joined him on one side, Sword in hand, his chin raised, his eyes sharp. The Sword crackled slightly, and Lorcas saw tiny tendrils of flame run along the blade. Tondra followed, slinging her bow behind her. He could see the resolve in her face, and the two of them there beside him gave him a sense of pride. He was proud that they were his friends and that they stood by him in what could be their final hour. He was much prouder of his relationship with the Entourage than anything he'd done with Rook. In fact, he realized, he no longer felt any pride at all in those Rook-related things he'd constructed or supported.

Zumar bumped his elbow as he stepped closer, with Alan and Jack just behind him. Zumar peered up towards the hill wide-eyed, and Lorcas could see he clutched the Ring in one hand, although he did not wear it. In Zumar's eyes he saw the reflection of the red fog, but also a spark from within. The Sazh was there, at least one of their Allies accounted for.

He heard, or felt, a fluttering from the west. The mist swirled and parted, obedient to the silver raven that passed through it. Mira materialized, transforming as her feet came in contact with the ground.

"I have come at your bidding," she said brusquely to Jack. Then she addressed the group more broadly. "The tower is gone. That channel between your world and mine is closed and will not be reopened. But there are many other ways for me to access your world, and the closing of one tunnel does little to disrupt me. I was able to come swiftly at Raine's call, for I was anticipating it."

"Raine is gone," Lorcas said numbly.

"I know," Mira answered more softly. "I felt her pass through, though there was no way to contain her scattered spirit. I am sorry for your loss, but I myself do not grieve such a passing. She is part of the universe, as will we all be at some point, even me. Now go forward into this task without fear, as she did. I will be with you as your Ally in some form, although it will not be this one. I hope you will be successful."

She reached into her garment and then stretched out a hand to Alan. "While the rest of the Entourage carry some symbolic Object or at least share one, you have nothing. Take this; although it is a symbol of Fire, it was created to call me, and it responds to the spirit of water. At the end, if it is necessary, it will bear your spirit to your own people beyond this world."

Alan took the Needle from her hand and held it up, examining the tiny blade. He hesitated, but then turned to Tondra. "I have no need for my spirit to return to the water or to the people from whom I was born. Whatever may be left of me after today, it will stay here with you. You take this; perhaps it's not a real sword, but it's connected to the real one. I don't need a symbol or any object. Whatever I can do against Rook, I can do just the same without one. What we accomplish will rely on our cooperation, our resolve, and our unity, and those will be the most powerful things we carry."

Tondra took the Needle carefully from Alan's hand. As she touched it, tiny flames crackled along its blade in imitation of the one Tomash wielded. She watched them for a moment, then clipped the Needle onto the outside of a vest pocket with a small clasp secured there, threaded through the open eye in the Needle's hilt.

"Perhaps it will give me some kind of luck, as sincere gifts often do," she said to Alan with a brief smile.

Mira nodded and crossed her arms over her chest. The mist seemed to close around her as though she was receding, although she took no step backwards. Her features began to fade, her clothing became one with the fog, although paler.

Lorcas stepped towards her. "Mira!"

She paused, but did not come further forward.

He lowered his voice, although he knew the others could still hear him. "Will I ever see you again?"

Mira smiled slightly. "It's doubtful. Once you are disconnected from Rook your connection to other worlds will fade, although you'll always retain some small piece of that special knowledge. But after you have mourned, as you will, for your lost comrades and lost future, I think you will find new interest in the people of your own time and experience. You are still young and resilient. You have many friends and colleagues. Even the danger you have been in from the Knights will be no more. You and I have known each other, and that is enough. I wish you success."

She raised a hand, and then she was gone. Lorcas stared at the spot for a long moment, wondering how and where she would support them. She had said she would, and he could do nothing now but trust that it was true.

He turned to the rest of the group. "Are we ready? Tondra? Tomash?"

"Ready," Tomash said, waggling the Sword. Tondra shrugged, then nodded.

"Alan? Jack?"

"Let's go," Jack said. "I don't get an Object either, Alan, but we're okay on our own, isn't that right?"

"Yep," Alan agreed, although he sounded less than enthusiastic.

"Zumar?" Lorcas turned to the Messenger. "I know you're ready. You're immortal, right?"

"Even immortals can be killed in certain ways," Zumar replied, "which might be preferable to other things Rook might be able to do to me. But there's no use stalling."

Lorcas nodded, took a deep breath, and started slowly off away from the house in the general direction of the hill. The rest of the group followed step-for-step, closely gathered together.

"I wish we could get rid of this damn fog," Tondra said. "I just have this vision of him rushing down the hill at us, suddenly emerging."

Zumar stopped short, and Alan ran into the back of him.

Lorcas paused and set the end of the Staff down. "Have you ever known Rook to rush anywhere?" he asked. "The Rising was fast, but only because it was triggered by the Control Window. Rook can't use that right now because we have the Ring, as well as the other Objects it required. And besides that event, he's generally moved slowly, almost incrementally."

"That's right," Tondra said uncertainly. "He works by taking over rocks, one piece at a time."

"Sometimes he can change them fast," Tomash said. "He used to re-arrange the tunnels."

"But only after they were already built," Lorcas said.

"I dunno," Jack put in. "He closed one up behind me pretty quickly one time. And then there was that time when, you know, he tore up the road behind us at the fastest speed we were able to drive. That was moving pretty quick, I'd say."

"Okay," Lorcas said, exasperated by the sudden ebb of confidence, "he's torn up the road in the past, he's moved tunnels, he's destroyed the tower, but he's never damaged Cliffview itself. In fact, he's gone out of his way to protect it."

"Yes," Zumar agreed hesitantly, "and those times when he moved quickly were underground. He doesn't like the light or the air. He's a creature of the earth. He hides in rocks and stones. That's why he's caused this steam to cover Cliffview in the past, and now that he is out upon the hill in the open and anticipating dealing with us, he's made it thicker to give himself an advantage."

"Of course," Lorcas agreed. "In the past he's told me himself that he dislikes our air and prefers moving through water instead, but likes moving through rock and stone the most."

"He's only out on the hill because that's where we built the castle," Zumar said more confidently. "People build castles on top of the earth, not in it, so that's what he has to deal with. Eventually he'll move back underground, out of the light, if we don't stop him. But Lorcas is right: he probably can't move as fast out in the open. I don't think."

"Still wish we could get rid of the fog," Tondra muttered as the little group moved forward hesitantly once again.

"I have an idea," Lorcas said, "but we need to at least get out of the neighborhood to do it."

They trudged slowly forward in silence, the fog impeding their view of what lay ahead. With his vision limited to just a few yards, Lorcas wasn't sure what changes might have come over the landscape, if perhaps they might encounter new chasms, pits, boulders, or other objects. The hill, as they started to climb the lower reaches, seemed steeper and longer than he remembered.

He found the pathway that ran at an angle along the side of the slope towards the bridge and led them along it with more confidence than he felt, keeping the Staff between himself and the unseen entity he could feel lurking above them. Finally, they came to the edge of the chasm. The red light that lit the fog seemed to emanate from there. Indeed, the fog itself, here more akin to thick smoke, streamed forth from the gap.

Lorcas strode up to the edge. This was the first test. Did he have any power at all against Rook? Were the Objects and the Allies just superstition, just items and ideas to give one confidence, or was there something there to back them up? If the Allies were allies of the Fell Ken rather than Rook, and the Objects directly connected to them, he would soon know.

He reached into the pocket of his windbreaker and opened the packet of Smokeweed with his fingers, leaving it in the pocket since his other hand was occupied with the Staff, and he wasn't going to put that down. He took a large pinch and drew it out. Then he extended his hand over the chasm and stepped as close to the edge as he dared.

"The air here belongs to me!" he said, raising the Staff. "As the Lorecaster, I reclaim it with the power of wind and breath!"

He tossed the handful of dry vegetation into the chasm and moved back apprehensively. At first nothing happened. He felt a bit ridiculous having made such a proclamation, especially since he had renounced his role as the Lorecaster and thus had no idea if the Fell Ken Objects assigned to him would still respond to him, but this was a time to be bold. There was nothing to lose now.

Then, slowly, the color of the fog began to change. It was as if the light from the ravine no longer tinted it as strongly, and it turned from red to a golden hue. The smoke, as it issued from the chasm, began to roil lazily instead of stream. Lorcas squinted. He could see further. The railings of the bridge began to emerge, first on the side closest to them, then farther along to the opposite side, like a zipper opening a rift in the mist.

With a final swirl, the fog halted and then disappeared, sliding back down into the chasm from which it emanated, leaving only a few tendrils drifting across the grass. It was, in fact, a bright late afternoon, with the sun reflecting crisply off the water below the cliff, the sky a bright blue, and the long shadows of the firs in the forest beyond the hill sharp and dark. It was almost shocking. He had not seen Cliffview in such bright light, he realized, for several years. The mist had been pervasive, sneaking in slowly until it was an ever-present part of life there. With it gone the colors seemed sharper, the sunlight almost too strong.

"Nice job," Tondra said from near his shoulder. "At least we can see him now."

Lorcas let his gaze travel up the hill, past the bridge, up the final stretch of pathway, along the stone steps that had once led to the chapel, and beyond. What had once been the castle was now a monumental being, half stone, half something living, the outlines of carved blocks only faded lines, with archways, flying buttresses, and balconies incorporated into his form. All of it was recognizable to some degree, and yet very different, smoothed and distorted, and with the addition and incorporation of what Lorcas had come to know as Rook, as though two entities had merged and melded.

Behind the mists, Rook had been continuing this transformation, and now he trained his eyes, each the height of a doorway, down upon the little group. The eyes now graded through deep yellow to fiery red around the slit-like pupil, narrowed against the sun.

Lorcas felt himself mesmerized by the sight of Rook in the clear of the day. Rook was, indeed, awe-inspiring. A wave of doubt washed over him, doubt not only about whether he could ever accomplish standing against this being, but also whether or not he wanted to. The realization that this was an incredibly unique relationship experienced by very few throughout history struck him strongly. He had spent the last few years speaking casually to a being that would strike fear into the heart of almost anyone, and while he had not known Rook in this form before, he had certainly seen his strength. He could continue to be a part of that. All it would take would be for him to walk up to Rook, tell him that he wanted to be in on whatever world the future would bring, and Rook would grant him power and a life that verged on immortality. The choice was that, or almost certain death for himself and his companions.

He moved forward slowly, dimly aware of the rest of the group behind him. He set foot upon the bridge reluctantly, unsure if it would buckle and throw him into the chasm below. But he felt a breeze move with him as he went, stirring the tops of the trees. He felt a familiar lifting sensation and recognized it as the one he used to feel when he flew his shadow. At that point he had believed Rook was in control; now he knew that it was the Air Ally that lifted him. He allowed the feeling to bring him across the bridge, knowing that if it crumbled, he would not fall. At the same time, he felt his mind clear, like the dissipating fog. Clarity of mind, he thought, the gift of the Air Ally. He even caught a whiff of the Smokeweed, borne to him from the chasm below. The Key vibrated against his chest and the sharp salty ocean air filled his nostrils with a breeze coming over the crest of the cliff. He allowed it to flow into him, enjoying what could be his last few breaths. He savored it; it was normal and natural, such a minor thing, but a thing he did not want to lose.

On the far side he paused for a moment and looked up again, his momentary lapse forgotten. They were now more directly under Rook, at the base of the steepest part of the hill. The path led around the depression that had once been the gated entrance they had taken the van through and then up along a set of stone stairs. The steps terminated at what had been the sidewalk around the chapel, when it had been at ground level. The chapel's spire had become the highest point of the risen castle the year before, the walkway obliterated by the broader lower walls. Now the steeple, where Lorcas's office had been, was visible as a spike on Rook's head.

Taking that route would only lead them to what appeared to be Rook's side at this point. Lorcas abandoned the trail and led the group up to the west, towards the cliff's edge. The cliff-side wall around the neighborhood ended at the edge of the chasm and the sheer drop to the sea was exposed past that point, but somehow Lorcas preferred that to being encircled by some construction of Rook's. This route was also somewhat less steep, and he didn't want to arrive completely out of breath. Besides, Rook seemed to be facing west, and he wanted to approach head-on.

Rook's head followed them slowly as they made their way to the top. It was the only thing that moved, and for Lorcas Rook's stillness added to the sense of tension. The eyes were half-closed against the sun and Rook blinked languidly. Zumar was right; Rook didn't like the sun and the clear air, and at the moment it was inhibiting him, or at least disturbing his vision.

As the hill began to level out Lorcas paused for a moment and turned to Cliffview, laid out below them. It was very changed from the random collection of summer homes he had known as a child. Yet it was still his, a place he belonged. Ranged below he could now

271

see the Fell Ken, several hundred of them, and outside
the wall a row of Knights, most of them wearing some
symbolic piece of clothing or hat with the logo of the
Koen, standing at attention. All of them were turned to
the hilltop, silent, ready to act when he asked it of them.

Lorcas felt the Key vibrating against his chest
again. It reminded him of its purpose: to hold his soul,
but also as a centering and gathering symbol. He saw
now that it had done its job without him realizing it.

The collection of Fell Ken and the success with
the Smokeweed buoyed Lorcas's confidence and
resolve. He turned back to face Rook and pulled the
Key out from under his shirt. He wanted Rook to see it
and know he had regained it, and his spirit, from the
Monks.

He watched, standing his ground, as the part of
the castle that had been the chapel, now incorporated
into Rook's head, lowered itself to meet him face-to-
face.

"So it is," Rook said. "You are here to kill me. I
do not understand why you want me dead after all I
have done for you, but it seems to be thus with you
humans."

Lorcas took a deep breath. In a way he felt sorry
for Rook, an alien creature with no home, no place to
go, and little understanding of the people he had to deal
with to survive. "I don't actually want you dead, Rook."

"You would prefer to imprison me and study
me, a curiosity, a specimen. You forget, I have been in
such a state before. Yes, time runs differently for me,
but that does not mean I don't feel its passage. Many
long years I lay trapped and immobile, suffering. I
reject such a fate. Death is preferable. Although which
of us shall die in the end remains to be seen."

Lorcas looked up at him. For a moment he
wondered if their plans for Rook were, indeed, a fate

worse than death. Nevertheless, he would try. At a later time, if they were successful in containing him, that final spark could be extinguished as an act of mercy.

"There is still time," Rook continued. "I would prefer not to destroy that which I have labored hard to create. I do not actually want you dead, either, Lorecaster."

"You tried to kill me just this morning," he reminded Rook.

"I only tried to stop you from entering the tower," Rook said casually. "I intended to destroy it, as I have no further use for it, and had you been within, or in a place far from me down in the tunnels, you would have been trapped or injured."

Lorcas nodded thoughtfully. Of course, that was ridiculous. There had been no need for Rook to destroy the tower and the connection between his world and the borderlands. He had been trying to keep Lorcas from further contact with Mira. Rook was deceitful even to the end, but this time Lorcas would not be swayed. Perhaps the tower had been Rook's to destroy; Lorcas was not positive it had actually been created by Rook, but in any event, he had obviously taken advantage of the possibility of getting rid of Lorcas, Jack, and Alan all at the same time. He had certainly not done anything to save them after the fact, although he surely could have.

"It doesn't matter," Lorcas said, determined not to be side-tracked. "The Fell Ken have voted. You will return to the Cornerstone. This is our will."

Rook sighed, and a breeze of damp, earthy air ruffled Lorcas's hair. "I suspected as much. But I am under no obligation to obey the will of the Fell Ken, and I will not go easily. You have called forth your Allies and brought along your Objects, but they have little power over me now."

Lorcas glanced down at the Key and then around at the group behind him.

"Yes, yes," Rook said. "I see the Key, the gift the Messenger insisted I give you as a way to cement our bond. A most inconvenient subterfuge on his part. And yes, I can tell that your spirit has been returned to you in whole. No matter. It is your choice, and truly it affects nothing. It will make you only a little bit harder to kill. Before, I might have simply cut our bond. Now, you are bound to none but yourself and your own miserable life. But of course, if you truly mean to oppose me, I can smash you flat in a matter of seconds, and I have noticed that humans do not survive such flattening."

That was likely true, Lorcas thought, although he still wasn't sure Rook would be able to move fast enough, given the current impressive bulk of his body, to squash any of them before they ran away. He was gratified to know that he was no longer bound to Rook, or for that matter, apparently, to Mira. Despite the earlier temptation, now that he was face-to-face with Rook, he knew he could never again support such a thing, and he would never betray the confidence of the Entourage and the rest of the Fell Ken. He felt the breeze from the cliff again, and readjusted his grasp on the Staff.

"Like the Sword, your Staff has little influence on me," Rook continued, catching the motion. "I do not like your wind, but I can withstand it. You can do nothing important with the Staff and might as well discard it as the twig it is."

"I managed to clear that nasty fog away," Lorcas replied.

"Yes," Rook said thoughtfully. "Certainly, I could have disagreed with that, but I decided to give you the advantage of allowing you to see me clearly.

You prefer it this way, don't you? And such a consideration is minor to me. I simply thought that perhaps, seeing what I have become, you would agree that continuing our relationship is for the best for all of us."

The implication that the Entourage would be so awe-struck that they would change their minds was not lost on Lorcas, but as usual, Rook really had little idea of how humans functioned, and without Zumar's translation, it was more obvious than ever.

"It's not my decision to make. I'm at the service of the Fell Ken, not of you. And you have heard what the Fell Ken want. The ball's in your court. You return to the Cornerstone voluntarily, or we will do what we can to make it happen," Lorcas replied.

Rook sneered and snorted. "How do you propose to do that? I have already noted and dismissed the Key and your Staff. As for the rest of the Objects, the puny bow will do nothing at all. Your arrows will simply bounce off me."

Tondra raised her chin defiantly, but she didn't do anything with the bow. Rook was undoubtedly right on that point; the bow was simply a normal object, and not an Object of Power.

"The Sword, yes, it can reach my world and do damage," Rook continued, moving his head just slightly towards Tomash. "What do you intend to do with it? Chop off tiny pieces until you whittle me down to size? I'm unlikely to tolerate that, although I can certainly ignore it for a rather long time if I am distracted by other things. It is hardly bigger, to me, than the tiny little sword on your pocket, Steward."

Tomash had planted the point of the Sword in the ground in front of him and stood with his hands crossed on top of the hilt. He stared placidly at Rook and did not move. But a few flames crackled along the blade, and those were mirrored by sparks from the Needle.

Rook studied Zumar for a long moment, but then he turned back to Lorcas, making no mention of the Ring. Zumar stared bravely back and stood his ground.

"We also have the Allies to help us," Lorcas pointed out.

"Their power is minor compared to mine," Rook scoffed. "Two of them cannot even exist without inhabiting a body not their own. I dismiss them. And so, the time has come, as I noted before: you wish to kill me, and I do not wish to die. You stand in opposition to me, and I to you. The conflict begins."

"What is it you plan to do to oppose us?" Lorcas asked nervously as Rook withdrew his head. He was fully prepared to run if Rook intended to stomp them, although he saw no indication that the bulk of the castle had begun to move.

But Rook said smugly, "As for that, it is already begun."

CHAPTER SIXTEEN

Lorcas frowned, puzzled. Other than withdrawing his head, Rook didn't seem to be doing anything in particular. There was no movement suggesting he was going to try to crush them. Was he just going to refuse to do anything and sit there, lurking, upon the hill? That could be awkward, Lorcas considered. They would then have to launch an attack themselves, with no real plan, knowing that most of the Objects of Power were useless against him. Either that, or stamp their feet, insist that he go back to the Cornerstone, and when he refused, retreat ineffectively to Cliffview.

Just then Tondra gave a cry. "Look!"

She pointed to the neighborhood. For a moment he didn't see anything amiss, but then some incremental movement caught his eye. In the past, Rook had caused a stone wall to form around Cliffview Estates as well as claiming the buildings themselves by moving rock partially up their walls, so that each home had a waist-high ring of stone enclosing it, except for the doors. Lorcas's house had been one of the first. Now he saw that the stone was rising slowly, enveloping every human construction in the neighborhood, encasing them. This time the rising rock did not spare the entrances. Lorcas could hear creaks and groans as the timbers of the houses and the sidings and frames were crushed in the stony embrace.

Tomash was the first to react. "Get everybody out of the houses!" he yelled. He ran several steps down the hill but then stopped, unsure what to do, waving an arm and pointing to gain attention.

Alex Blazh, who stood near the bottom of the hill with his back to the neighborhood, turned and saw what was happening. Lorcas heard his shouted orders, although he couldn't understand the words from that distance. The Fell Ken reacted rapidly. Motion ran through the crowd like a wave. He saw many of them rushing to the houses; although the adults were standing ready to act, the children had been left inside for protection. Moments later he saw people emerging, toddlers and infants in arms, young children led by teens. Dogs and cats ran from the doorways, leaping over the new sills of stone.

As they fled, the roads and sidewalks began to buckle and wrinkle. Lorcas could see people flailing and falling as the ground contorted under their feet. Nevertheless, the children were corralled quickly and led down through the neighborhood towards the southern woods by a few adults. They would be safer there anyway, Lorcas thought, in the cover of the trees, than closer to Rook in the neighborhood.

Lorcas turned back to Rook angrily. "You haven't managed to do anything. You've spent energy covering a few houses with a blanket of stone. Do you think destroying Cliffview will change anybody's mind? It will only harden their resolve. Threats and shows of force aren't a good way to gain friends here. You're certainly not convincing me to stay on your side."

Rook swung his head down incredibly quickly, considering it was made of stone, and Lorcas flinched but managed to stand his ground.

"You are a fool!" Rook spat, his anger now evident. The pupils of the great eyes narrowed to slits. "I have no need for friends. It will be my pleasure to destroy all you have made before your eyes, and then destroy you in the end for imagining you could stand against me at this point. Watch, and suffer as your ancestors made me suffer, for there is nothing you can do."

His body shuddered and for the first time Lorcas saw the entire ex-castle move as one, albeit ponderously given its huge size. He stepped back involuntarily as bits of rock fell from above. Several trees to the north came crashing down as Rook turned and the back of the castle struck them. The sound of him moving was like a combination of rockfall and the grinding of a giant gristmill, but magnified many times over to deafening volume.

Over the grinding and gnashing came a metallic rending sound louder than the rest, and Lorcas turned just in time to see the bridge crumble and tumble into the chasm, which seemed to be growing in width. There was a brief fountain of sparks, and he realized the Entourage was now cut off from the neighborhood and the rest of the Fell Ken. The only ways to escape the hill now would be to either pass in front of Rook and try to get to the State Forest road, to try to get behind him into the northern forest, or to jump off the cliff.

The earth trembled under his feet, and around them a number of boulders rose from the ground, bursting through the sod. Several car-sized rocks heaved up through the earth amid the Entourage and they were forced to scatter to avoid being thrown into the air or crushed as the stones fell one way and another. Lorcas and Zumar fled to the south, around the top of the hill just under Rook's left side. Lorcas caught a glimpse of the others running north, heading for the forest. Then the boulders cut off his view and the air once again began to darken, this time filled with the choking dust of pulverized stones and up-thrown dirt.

Almost immediately their progress was cut off by more erupting rocks. It was not going to be possible, Lorcas saw, to make it to the State Forest road, but he feared being directly under Rook's side. He turned back, but the heaving earth and the steep hillside made it impossible to return the way they'd come. Random rocks littered the landscape in that direction as well, and some of them seemed imbued with a life of their own, as they rolled unnaturally uphill or along the hillside.

Lorcas and Zumar huddled together for a moment.

"We're trapped!" Lorcas shouted.

Zumar glanced around and then pointed. "This way!" he yelled.

Lorcas scrambled after him a short distance straight up the slope, almost on hands and knees, until they came to the very edge of the top of the hill and pressed against Rook's left side in the shadow of what had been a flying buttress. There were fewer rocks there, and they took a moment to catch their breaths. There was no sign of the rest of the Entourage, although Lorcas could see Cliffview fairly well below them in between drifts of acrid dust. He craned his neck, trying to locate Rook's head somewhere above them. He hoped they were concealed from view there, so close to Rook himself, and that Rook was unable to detect them. Of course, there was also the danger that Rook would move too suddenly for them to respond. A quick vision of being crushed under an entire building crossed Lorcas's mind, but he dismissed it as best he could.

There was a sudden lull and the earth stopped belching boulders. The ominous quiet didn't last long. Again the ground trembled and the rocks began to move, this time rolling down the hill towards the chasm. More rocks rose to take their place in an endless chain. Lorcas and Zumar crouched in the shadow of Rook's flank, pelted by pebbles that broke off the larger stones and flew into the air in a constant shower. Lorcas raised his Staff horizontally over his head in a vain attempt to shield them from at least some of the onslaught. At least some of the small stones seemed to be deflected, as though an imperfect shield had been raised over them.

Below he could see the rolling boulders pick up speed as they neared the widening chasm. Instead of falling in, their momentum carried them across the gap and they continued down the other side towards the neighborhood without slowing. Panic took over, and the people who had returned to stand looking up at Rook fled down towards the southern trees and out to the eastern gate. A few of them ran west, only to be trapped by the cliff and Rook's wall, which undulated like a stone serpent. Cracks began to open throughout the housing area and smoke and licks of fire rose from them. Lorcas could see the asphalt pavement melting, flowing like a languid black river. Here and there plants burst spontaneously into flame.

He caught movement from above in the corner of his eye and turned to face it. Rook lowered his head almost to the ground and snaked it around his side to confront Lorcas and Zumar directly. Lorcas moved away reflexively, crowding Zumar behind him, but Rook's head stopped as though he could no longer bend in that direction.

"Now I will consume you all!" he hissed. "One at a time, and I will savor the return of the energy I invested in each of you!"

"If you kill the Entourage, you'll have no support in this world at all, and you'll use all your energy destroying Cliffview!" Lorcas yelled above the roar of rolling rocks, trying to keep his footing on the shuddering ground. "Then you'll be forced to retreat to the Cornerstone anyway! You're defeating yourself by trying to destroy us!"

"Perhaps," Rook replied, "but I will still have a spark left, and there will be the Messenger. Him I will not consume. He will help me rise again, as he has done twice before."

"I will not!" Zumar shouted, stepping around Lorcas's shoulder to confront Rook face on.

Rook turned his eyes to Zumar. "I know you!" he said. "I know what you are. Raine has done me a favor in the end: you cannot use the forces you may be able to muster to oppose me while you have the Sazh, because it would be fatal even to a being such as you, and the Sazh does not wish you to die. Nor do you! You have clung to your pitiful life, and in the end, you will do so again, whatever it requires."

Lorcas turned to Zumar and grabbed him by the shirt at the shoulders, the Staff falling in against his shoulder. "What do we do, Zumar? I will do whatever I have to, whatever the consequences!"

Zumar met his eyes. "I will not help Rook rise again! I will not do it! I will give my life to sever all bonds with Rook to this earth and send him back to the

Cornerstone, I swear. I have the power! But I cannot do it!"

"Why not?" Lorcas demanded. "We have to end this thing!"

"Because I have to summon the Earth Ally," Zumar replied, his eyes wide. "Rook is right: the other Allies and the Objects can counteract some of what he causes, but none of them can stand against him. Only the Earth Ally will give us a chance in the end."

"Then how do we do it?" Lorcas shouted desperately. Below, the rocks slammed into houses and cars; to the side, Rook steamed and hissed, just out of reach. Lorcas felt the wall, now Rook's side, begin to shift. Rook was turning, turning ponderously to bring his head closer to them.

"Only I can summon it!" Zumar replied. "But the Sazh will not allow it. It knows what the consequences will be!"

"Then give the Sazh to me!" Lorcas said. He could feel his heart pounding under the Key. He refused to think about what it might mean. "Hurry!"

Zumar shook his head and staggered as rocks emerged beside them on the hill. "No! You cannot withstand the Sazh! It will burn you up in a very short time!"

"Then that is what will be," Lorcas replied. "If it burns me up, it will be worth it if we can stop Rook and this destruction."

Rook's side had moved further away; the turning was slow, because Rook was occupied with other things as well as his desire to confront them, but Lorcas could feel the giant head moving closer. He let go of Zumar's shirt and rested his hands on the Messenger's shoulders. An oddly out-of-place thought passed through his mind: how solid, how human, Zumar felt, now, at the end.

"Do it now. Give me the Sazh."

Zumar met his eyes. "I'm afraid."

"So am I," Lorcas admitted, "but I'll be here beside you."

Zumar hesitated, but Lorcas maintained his eye contact. In the Messenger's eyes it seemed a flame began to grow.

Suddenly he felt a searing heat, as though boiling oil had been poured into his body. He fell involuntarily to his knees and cried out. He could see nothing but a sheet of red. His nerves jangled, his limbs jerked as though electrified. He felt himself shaking violently. It took all he had to maintain his senses and any semblance of control over himself. Desperately he groped for his Staff. His hand fell upon the shaft, and some inkling of coolness spread from his fingers up into the rest of him.

His vision cleared a bit, but what he could see was chaos and confusion. He did not know where Rook was, and Zumar had disappeared. Rocks spewed from the earth and crashed against one another all around him, the dust of their collisions thickening the air. He tried to breathe, but the grit made it nearly impossible. He could rise no further than his knees, gasping his burning breath into his lungs.

Suddenly he saw two dim figures appear in the dust. He felt a hand under each arm and was aware that Jack and Alan had grabbed him and pulled him to his feet.

"This way! To the cliff!" Jack shouted in his ear. Lorcas stumbled between them as best he could, racked with the pain of the Sazh and unsteady on the heaving ground. He remembered Zumar's words, that air fanned the flame of fire and caused it to grow. He wondered briefly how long he could continue to hold it and live; not long, he knew.

They reached the cliff and could go no further. Tomash and Tondra were there, sheltered by the Sword as Tomash struggled to hold it aloft. Like the Staff, it seemed to deflect some of the rocks, but small specks of blood dotted their dust-covered faces from where flecks and sharp pebbles struck them.

Mira was there as well, although in no form Lorcas had seen before. He knew it to be her, but she appeared neither human nor in the form of the silver raven, but as a bright glowing column of water. A continuous stream issued forth from the earth at her feet, and it flowed down the hill to cool the burning ground in Cliffview. Rook's rocks slowed and then stopped as they rolled into it. As the dust in the air shifted with the breeze from the ocean, Lorcas could see that groups of Fell Ken, emboldened by Mira's protection, had returned to the neighborhood defiantly. They were beginning to form an arc around the upper houses, a Protection in the old Earth ways, standing arms linked to arms, and members of the Koen stood interspersed with them.

Alan and Jack let him down upon the grass next to Mira. He felt some relief as though the cool of her lake's water washed over him. Still there was the burning from within, but the heat was lessened somewhat. He looked for his Staff, realizing he no longer had it. Alan, he saw, was carrying it, and threw it down on the ground next to him.

"Don't touch the Staff while you have the Sazh, it will only make things worse," Alan directed.

Tomash planted the Sword in the ground in front of the group. "Your rocks will not pass this line!" he shouted to Rook, and indeed it seemed, at least for the time being, to be true. But Lorcas could see that Rook's attention was elsewhere; the giant head had swung to the south, barely visible through the polluted air.

Lorcas felt someone shaking his shoulder. He glanced up and saw Tondra bending over him.

"Lorcas! What happened?"

"I have the Sazh," Lorcas told her through gritted teeth. "I took it from Zumar because it wouldn't let him summon the Earth Ally."

"How are you doing? Can you take it?"

"Not for long," Lorcas spat out involuntarily, unable to equivocate. "It's burning me up inside. Zumar told me it would, but it has to be done."

"Then give it to me!" Tondra urged. "Alan can't take it, it won't go to him, and we don't know about Jack. Tomash needs to be all himself right now, to do what he can with the Sword. But we know the Sazh won't hurt me as much."

Tondra fell to one knee beside him. "How do we do it?"

Lorcas shook his head. "I don't know!" But as he said it, he felt the heat rise to concentrate in his chest, and he knew the Sazh would leave him if it could. It was burning too fast, endangering itself within him. It wanted a more suitable host.

He looked briefly into Tondra's eyes, and in that moment he felt the most incredible surge of pain he had felt yet. But a moment later there was relief. Tondra gasped and fell backwards onto the grass with Alan at her side, but she pushed herself to a sitting position quickly.

"I'm okay," she said with a curt nod. "Don't worry about me. It's not so bad. If I can't take it any longer, we'll pass it on."

Lorcas's eyes were drawn back to the side of the hill. Now he could see Zumar once again, standing near where he had left him. The maelstrom of rocks had paused and the noise abated. Rook had turned completely and faced down the hill, his head just above Zumar's body. Lorcas felt a lurch in his throat; what had once been the chapel now opened into a giant maw as Rook brought his head down to destroy Zumar in a crushing blow.

But Zumar did not move. He stood upright among the rocks, arms raised over his head, palms towards Rook. Lorcas could see a bright reflection on the palm of one hand: the Ring, he supposed, although he had never seen it glow in such a way. It seemed to have become part of Zumar's hand, embedded. He watched, unable to do anything else.

"The Sazh is gone from me!" Zumar shouted. "And now I break the bond between you and this Earth! I call forth the Earth Ally!"

In an instant the upheaval started again, but this time something seemed different. No more rocks issued from the earth; instead, the ones already on the hillside began to roll around of their own accord as though pulled by a giant magnet. They rushed towards Zumar, but stopped short and began a slow eddy around him. Dust, dirt, and smoke rose again, clouding the view, but Lorcas could see what seemed to be cracks in the earth around Rook. Rook himself writhed in anger, but he seemed unable to reach Zumar within the whirlpool of rocks.

As he stared, unsure what he could do to help, he saw something odd about Zumar's appearance. He, himself, appeared to be turning to stone, petrified and immobilized as he stood.

"What's happening?" Lorcas yelled over the noise.

Jack was there at his side, squinting into the dust. "I have a feeling I understand the Earth Ally," Jack shouted. "I don't think it is what you think it is."

"No," Alan agreed from where he knelt next to Tondra. "I know it now. I have seen it before."

"What is it?" Lorcas demanded.

"It's death," Jack said. "A great ally, indeed. Peace and rest in the cool earth, relief from toils and troubles and pain. And unavoidable to any who lives."

"But Zumar is different!" Lorcas insisted. "He's not a mortal being like us!"

Jack shook his head, and Alan agreed. "There are certain things that can kill even an immortal. Most things that would kill us will not. But this is different. None can summon death and live."

"Zumar!" Lorcas shouted, struggling to his feet. "I should have given him the Staff! Or the Key! Something!" He felt weak from the effects of the Sazh, but he stumbled forward, although he had no idea what he could do.

"No," Jack replied, catching him by the arm. "The Key holds your own soul, your own life, not his. And the Staff is yours. He would not know what to do with it, anyway."

"So he dies?" Lorcas shouted desperately.

"And he takes Rook with him," Jack said grimly. "There is nothing for us to do but watch. The earth will take back what it owns. From dust he came, and to dust he'll go. He who built him up, brings him down."

The noise and dust increased and loosened rocks rolled down around them, appearing suddenly out of the new gloom so that they had to jump to the side to avoid them. The ground under their feet heaved and buckled so they could barely stand. Rents and rips opened in the soil and bursts of hot steam shot through. Behind them the cliff's edge loomed perilously near. Sod broke free along the rim and disappeared down the face, threatening to take them all with it.

Lorcas felt himself thrown to the ground, unable to avoid the errant boulders. He felt heat beneath him almost as strong as the Sazh, cooled occasionally by sudden flows of silvery water. He was desperate to do something, anything, to know what was happening, but he wasn't able to keep his feet. He groped for the Staff and used it to help himself up. He forced himself forward step by step, with no real goal. He realized he had lost sight of the rest of the Entourage again. He was alone in the dust. His Staff now seemed to do nothing to clear the air, but it did give him another point of balance, keeping him upright as he struggled to move to where he had last seen Zumar.

Suddenly there was silence. The dust fell out of the air like the last drops of rain. A few boulders finished rolling and crashed into trees or off the side of the cliff. The low western sun cast a muted glow over the side of the hill.

Lorcas blinked the dust from his eyes and looked around. He was partway up the hill, above where the bridge had been. The bridge was gone, but to his surprise, so was the chasm, now only an earthen scar across the grassy knoll.

He spun around to face the cliff where he had last seen the Entourage. They were there, scattered across the hillside, Tondra, Tomash, Alan, and Jack, picking themselves up off the ground and dusting their clothing.

Further down the cliff's edge the white glow that had been Mira was gone, along with the stream of water. Only steam remained where the flow had quenched the burning of Rook's chasms and cracks. He wasn't worried about her; he knew she would be safe.

He turned once more, his heart in his throat. The hillside was oddly smooth, void of rocks and covered with grass as though nothing had ever happened there.

Any trace of the castle or Rook was completely gone. Only the pile of windows remained, and on top of it a new window teetered: the Control Panel.

The spot where Zumar had stood was vacant. Even his body seemed to have disappeared along with everything else. Lorcas stumbled towards the spot where he had been, searching for some sign of him, slipping on the steep grassy hillside in his exhaustion. His eye caught something half-buried in the grass and he reached down and picked up the Ring. The rotating outer band was completely fused with the inner band, although the engravings remained, and it had changed from metal to stone. It seemed to vibrate very slightly. Instinctively his hand felt for the Key. It was there, but it was only an object, a key made into a necklace. The vibrations from the Ring slowly faded as it lay on his palm.

"Hey! Up here!"

Lorcas turned to face the hillside and looked to the very top, supporting himself with the Staff. The slope was pathless and empty, the way he remembered it from his childhood.

But it was not completely empty. On top he saw an object.

With the last of his energy, Lorcas scrambled up the hill. He could see the rest of the Entourage heading that way as well. As the slope decreased his pace became faster until he pulled up in front of the object, gasping for breath.

"Zumar!"

Zumar grinned as broadly as Lorcas had ever seen him. He was perched on a large, square block of stone, one leg crossed over the other, one arm supporting him as he leaned lazily in the last of the sunlight.

Tondra, Tomash, Alan, and Jack ran up and stood staring at him as well.

"I thought you were dead," Lorcas said. "Not the only time I've thought that, of course," he added. "What happened?"

"I summoned the Earth Ally," Zumar said casually. "It has a lot of control over the things of the earth, rocks, soil, that kind of thing. It took back what Rook had taken for himself at my request. That very neatly squeezed him down into a manageable size."

"It wasn't quite that simple," Lorcas said. He looked around at the dirty faces and clothing of the battered Entourage.

"Well, no," Zumar admitted. "Every one of you had a part. You stood against him, you and the rest of the Fell Ken and the Knights, with whatever you had. Rook couldn't thwart the united desire of all of us to keep him out of our world. He depended, more than you know, on your strength and support. When an evil idea is seen for what it is, that knowledge can bring it down. We all refused to be part of it, and so Rook's power waned. In the end, we needed only the extra final push that the Earth Ally could provide."

"You never told me what the Earth Ally is," Lorcas said. "Did you think I would try to stop you from using it if I knew?"

Zumar shrugged. "I thought you might, and that could have been disastrous. I knew I would have to call it in the end. And the Earth Ally brings death as one of its gifts, death for the one it opposes, but also for the one who summons it. It doesn't discriminate."

"Then how are you alive?"

"You might notice that none of you has the Sazh anymore," Zumar said.

Lorcas looked around. Jack spread his hands, and Alan and Tomash shrugged. Tondra shook her head. "It left me at some point. I don't know how."

"So it's gone?" Lorcas asked, turning back to Zumar.

"No. Remember that the Sazh and I had an agreement," Zumar replied. "We get along quite well, better than I might have expected given my history. Of course, I owe it a debt now. It saved my life for real this time."

The cocky grin faded as he looked out over the sea for a moment. "You kept it for me when I could not, and so you saved me, and vanquished Rook. But I owe my life to Raine, as well. It was she who summoned the Sazh in the first place. I hated it, but I look on it now as a gift, and one I will not forsake. I will not forget."

Lorcas looked into Zumar's eyes and thought he caught a brief spark there. He didn't want to look too long.

"What will you do with it?" he asked.

"Eventually we'll part ways, when I'm sure I'm safe and he's had enough of me," Zumar said. "But we've got time to figure that out to our mutual advantage, and there's much I would like to learn."

Lorcas looked down at the Cornerstone hesitantly. "And this?" he asked, tapping it gingerly with the Staff.

"Oh, this?" Zumar patted the rock affectionately. "It's not just a rock, it's a cornerstone." He grinned again, and Lorcas realized he was quoting Lorcas's father. Had he overheard that conversation so long ago, lurking there inside the rock?

"Is there a spark within it?" Zumar paused as though reflecting. "Maybe. If so, it's very small. But I'd keep it around if I were you. Don't lose track of it. You don't want it to go meeting new people. And besides, someday you might want to build a castle! Or…maybe not."

He stood up. "I have to go now. I can't stay here. This isn't a world for Allies, and it's no longer a world for me. I don't have a life here, and even the Sazh can't change that. And you don't need me; you've got a bit of a mess to clean up, and other things to do. Real lives to live. So I'll be going. Maybe I'll see you again someday. You never know."

He snapped a salute and allowed his eyes to roam over the five people assembled there. Lorcas waited for him to sink into the ground as he often had, but instead he took several sudden steps towards the cliff, snapped his fingers, and vanished in a wisp of flame.

Lorcas stood for a few more moments staring at the spot where he had been. Then he turned slowly to the Entourage.

"Well," he said, "it's done."

Tondra stood with an arm around Alan's waist. "I hope so," she said.

Lorcas faced the neighborhood. There was a great deal of damage, he could see, but the wall and the facades of stone were gone. A few boulders lay scattered around; he assumed they had been cast up during the chaos, but were not ones that had been inhabited by Rook, as anything associated with him seemed to have disappeared. He saw people beginning to emerge from where they had taken shelter behind the buildings and cars. His eyes roamed over them and picked out people he knew: Alex Blazh, Marek and Wyne Linden, Jason Japert, to his great relief, and Terry Bell among them. Also, off to the side, he saw a small huddled group. It was hard to make out, but he believed it was Elena and Dalibor Katzbalger and their three children, the largest no older than twelve.

"I'm exhausted," Jack said. "I vote we rustle up some dinner."

"We need to see if anyone's hurt and needs attending to," Lorcas said.

"There are others who can do that," Jack replied. "I'm sure they all feel the Entourage has done enough for today. Food, rest, and then we can begin to look at the future. It's going to be different, and that's a good thing."

They started slowly back down the hill, careful not to slip on the grassy surface. Below them the Fell Ken and the Knights, and a few others, gathered in a group to greet them. Lorcas looked over the crowd and the community. Nothing could change what they had been through together, and that bond was stronger than any he had ever had with Rook.

CHAPTER SEVENTEEN

Late afternoon sun streamed into the summerhouse through the screened-in porch and western windows. Lorcas pried the tops off two bottles of beer, poured them into glasses, and carried them carefully into the living room.

"Here you go," he said, handing one of the glasses off.

Jack took the glass and raised it a bit in thanks before he took a sip.

"It's from the new brew pub Marek and Wyne Linden opened in Seaside Heights. What do you think?" Lorcas asked.

"Pretty darn good," Jack said. He crossed one leg over the other and settled back in the armchair, balancing the glass with one hand on his knee.

Lorcas had come to know Jack's taste in drinks pretty well over the last year. The two of them saw each other regularly when Jack came to Cliffview to discuss guard rotations, the distribution of duties, and other topics with what had been the Entourage, now the Cliffview Estates Management Committee. Jack habitually stopped by Lorcas's house after the meeting for a drink. Often, he brought some small piece of Fell Ken memorabilia he'd found boxed up in his office that he thought Lorcas would appreciate, or some story he had remembered about one of Lorcas's parents. Despite old wounds, Lorcas seemed to connect with Jack on some level. Partly, he supposed, it was a shared trauma they could reveal to very few others in the world. They got along in a way he could not have imagined previously.

"Anybody else need a refill? Or just want to sample something new?" he asked before he sat down. "No?" he confirmed when no one else responded.

Lorcas gazed around his living room as he sat back with his own beer. Jack was not his only guest. Jason Japert and his wife Jennifer were there along with their two young children, a girl and a boy. The kids played on the porch with a number of objects Lorcas had set out for them, including a few gold coins. Jason looked smug and happy. He sat on the couch with his legs extended, one arm behind Jennifer's head on the backrest.

The final guest sat in the chair nearest the door. She had come up with Jack, but it wasn't the first time Lorcas had seen Terry Bell during the last year. She was working for Jack as a paralegal and sometimes accompanied him to the Committee meetings. She and Lorcas had not resumed their relationship, not yet, but they had talked. Lorcas had given her a few drawings for stained-glass pieces. They had met for lunch in a couple of restaurants around Lafayette. Lorcas was not quite trusting enough to move forward, but he felt no rush, either. It would work, or it would not.

It had been a tough year, and things, he felt, were just beginning to even out, with the good days at last starting to equal the bad days for himself and for the Fell Ken in general. About a third of the Fell Ken had moved out of Cliffview to Seaside Heights and beyond, but two-thirds had stayed, which he frankly found remarkable. The neighborhood had been heavily damaged, but they had set about cleaning up debris and repairing houses and community buildings quickly. There was now no trace of the event; even the dust on the roads had been washed away. The houses all looked like normal little homes with new repair jobs, some better than they had been before. The Community Center featured a little museum displaying the glass windows, except for the Control Panel, the suit of armor, the goblets, and a small glass case with the scrying Mirror and associated objects in it, and a tribute to Raine. The Fell Ken felt they should not forget their past, ever.

Repairing the people themselves had not proved as easy. As Tondra had put it, "We've been fighting a war that no one else knows we've been fighting, and we've all got PTSD." After some hesitation, Lorcas, like the rest of the Entourage, had accepted counseling help from a Fell Ken therapist. Some of the things he had done personally, as well as what he had seen others do, haunted him. His self-image was badly damaged; it was hard to accept that he had been led down a path towards what he now had to admit was at the best a terrible idea, and at worst pure evil. In addition, he no longer had the emotional distancing Rook had provided him, and it seemed as though rather than suffering grief, regret, guilt, and horror spread over time, he now had to experience it all packed into one chunk.

He was, of course, not alone in that. The best thing about Cliffview was that everyone there understood to some degree what he was going through, and the Entourage understood it intimately. All of them were proceeding through their own processes at their own pace, and at times it was rocky and went in fits and jerks, but whoever was feeling good at a given time tried to act as a solid post for the others to lean on.

There had been good mixed in with the bad. Tondra and Alan had rapidly re-oriented to the management of Cliffview Estates. Tondra seemed to do best when she was occupied with something important and complex, with an eye towards community-building and the future, and she also had the trust of the rest of the Fell Ken. They had taken Jack on board as an adviser; he had, after all, run a successful company prior to the events of the last few years, and his generational and institutional knowledge was lacking in the Fell Ken. It made sense, too, because Jack was already involved in managing the Knights' participation in the Cornerstone Guards.

A few months previous, Tondra and Alan, who had never been formally married, had tied the knot in a ceremony in the Community Center officiated by Alex Blazh, and Tondra had dropped the name Sivitko and become Tondra Bistry. Tomash had taken a break and a vacation away from the area, traveling to visit distant relatives in Europe for several months. He had come back refreshed if not completely repaired, and he and Lorcas regularly shared a beer, though they both preferred watching TV while they drank over reminiscing or any kind of discussion of past events. Neither of them drank wine anymore. Tomash had completely bowed out of management of Cliffview Estates, but he had yet to establish any kind of new career. No one seemed to feel it necessary to rush him.

"Well, I guess we'd better get going," Jason said, interrupting Lorcas's revery. "We promised the kids we'd take a run up through the State Forest in the new Jeep. We didn't mean to intrude on you for too long."

"I'm driving," Jennifer said. "You've had a beer."

"Just one," Jason said, but he didn't argue.

"You're not intruding," Lorcas said. "It's a nice day for a drive, though."

Lorcas got up to collect Jason's empty beer glass and Jennifer's soda glass while Jennifer rounded up the kids. He took the glasses into the kitchen and rinsed them briefly before setting them aside. As he turned to leave, he caught a glimpse of himself in the little mirrored shelf that hung near the door to the porch. He stopped abruptly. When he caught himself in a mirror or reflection nowadays, he often had the odd feeling that he hadn't really looked at himself in several years. It was as though he was looking at a self he didn't quite recognize. He ran his hand through his much shorter hair. He was still getting used to that; it was a recent thing. There were flecks of gray in it now, too. He didn't believe in trauma-related hair color changes and was sure it was due to age. Still, he didn't remember noticing it prior to the last year. He didn't care to do anything about it, though. In a way, it served to remind him of things he didn't really want to forget, or at least felt he shouldn't forget: the last four years and everything that had happened around him, to him, or because of him.

He turned his back on the mirror and returned to the living room. "How's the boat coming?" he asked Jack.

Jack shrugged. "Still a lot of work to do, but she'll be sea-worthy by next spring. The salvagers did a good job, but there will be enough new about her that I'll be re-christening her. I haven't decided on a name yet, but I was thinking of something like 'Chance of Raine'."

Lorcas stood very still for a moment, but he knew Jack well enough now to understand that it wasn't a joke. He really did want to honor Raine and the memory of how she had been willing to help him. It wasn't inappropriate, Lorcas decided. A boat on the water was as good a tribute as any.

Jack finished off his beer and set the empty glass down on a side table. "I guess we'd better go too," he said. "I've got a furniture company coming to replace stuff at the Seaside Heights office. I'd like to be all moved in by next week."

He stood and Terry followed suit. On the way out the door Jack paused and gently laid a hand on the Staff, which stood in its customary place, leaning in the corner.

"Just a nice walking stick now, eh?" he said.

Lorcas shrugged noncommittally. Jack looked at him out of the corner of his eye for a moment, but then he turned and opened the door.

"Call me," Lorcas said casually to Terry as she passed. She smiled and nodded. She would, Lorcas knew. Besides a decrease in his ability to say anything that stretched the truth since his brief experience with the Sazh, he could often tell when others were deceptive, and she was not. He hoped that ability would wear off in time, frankly. It wasn't normal, which was what he most wanted to be.

Jennifer placed the items she'd retrieved from the kids on the coffee table and took the keys to the Jeep from where Jason dangled them on one finger. Lorcas shook Jason's hand and Jennifer's briefly. She didn't like him much, he knew. She associated him with whatever had happened to Jason. He really couldn't blame her for that, but he also wanted to keep in touch with Jason. He liked the detective quite a bit and appreciated his perspective. But besides that, Jason was 'one of them' now. There was an undercurrent of connection that would never be severed, although it was a bond of shared experience rather than an unnatural tie.

After they were gone, Lorcas put on a windbreaker and stepped outside. He didn't lock the door; nobody did in Cliffview. He did take the Staff; like Jack said, it made a nice walking stick. It was useful when hiking, since some of his back problems seemed to have reoccurred. And secreted inside it, in the little compartment where he had first found it, lay the Ring, wrapped carefully to keep it from rattling.

The Objects of Power were simply objects now; none of them seemed to have any special qualities at all besides historical significance. Some of them, like the goblets, it had been easy to give up to the museum. But others he had found more difficult to part with. He knew that Tondra kept the Sword locked away in a case, and he had done the same with the Key, although he thought he might one day turn it over to the Community Center. He also kept the Control Panel carefully wrapped and boxed in his library. The power it had once held was too great to allow it to see the light of day, at least any time soon. The Staff simply felt like his, and he used it. As for the Ring, he was ambivalent.

He walked through the gate in the newly-rebuilt hand-laid stone wall and up the dirt road and hiked slowly up the back side of the hill. The chasm had closed, leaving only a rocky scar, but he didn't like to go that way. Crossing where the chasm had been was too stressful.

At the top of the hill he could see the four guards, Knights this time, although the Fell Ken rotated in to the 24-hour shifts as well. Each one stood facing one of the cardinal directions, their backs to the

Cornerstone. The uniforms they wore were ceremonial, but also weather-protective. Some of the people from the community were working on a cover more permanent than the pop-up tent they'd set up the winter before to protect the guardsmen. It was a somewhat ugly little modern composite wood construction, with no stonework.

Lorcas entered the shade along the edge of the firs and followed a narrow foot-worn path just a little further. There, in an area that had at one time been the back side of the castle, lay the little graveyard. Zumar's crypt had been moved there from where it had been tossed on top of the hill, and sat empty but closed, serving as a climbing object for neighborhood children.

Robert Dover lay somewhere in the graveyard. Lorcas had begun tentative talks with Jack about the possibility of repatriating the body to family members if they could find it, with the agreement that all law enforcement, even Jason, would be kept out of the proceedings. Korrin Bright's body lay there as well, and Lorcas intended to repatriate him eventually, too, although he had no idea what kind of condition either would be in. That would leave the little graveyard with just two bodies: Bishop the Cat, and Raine's physical remains.

Lorcas paused at Raine's marker. It was a new one; the one Rook had concocted had disappeared. He hadn't decided what to do about her yet. He knew her essence was not there, but was perhaps part of the waters that washed the shore below the cliff, as well as the waters in other lands. But in a way he didn't like to think of her lying there on that cursed hill. He had looked into the possibility of interring her near Delva and Perry. Wherever she went, he would make sure that Bishop went with her. It seemed only fitting. Bishop, as far as he knew, had ended with the end of Rook, and while the cat's essence wasn't in the waters with Raine, he somehow felt better thinking that the two sets of remains would lie near each other.

There had been other bodies to deal with, as well. Within days of Rook's disappearance, the slump of material at the base of the cliff had begun to disintegrate and slide into the ocean. This triggered another search by the county recovery team, and five sets of remains had eventually been discovered, including his mother's. Lorcas had her remains interred next to his father's in Princeton, where he'd grown up and where they had owned a home. He didn't think she would have liked being buried in the little cemetery in Seaside Heights; it was too close to Cliffview. Without Rook's interference, he felt the regret at the lack of reconciliation before her death keenly, and he had struggled for a few months.

Now some of that seemed to be lifting, or he was getting used to feeling things in a way he had not for several years. He had to be careful; sometimes emotions would come upon him more strongly than he remembered them, including resentment and anger. He had learned to walk away when he felt like that. He let others deal with the Katzbalgers, for example, and their re-integration into the Seaside Heights community. He knew Tomash was involved with that since he felt a particular bond with Dirk, but they didn't talk about it. Except for Jack, he didn't deal with the Knights either. On the other hand, when the community turned to him for guidance regarding all things Rook, including history and tradition, he found it easy enough to provide that leadership and quickly make the necessary decisions.

He had not seen Mira or Zumar since that final day. He missed Zumar a great deal at times, but Mira less, as she had told him would be the case. Yet he felt he would see Zumar again someday, at some time when he least expected it. Every time he hiked up the hill, he half-expected Zumar to pop out of his crypt, impish grin and all. He had secretly moved back the lid on occasion, just to check. So far it had not happened, and he wasn't sure what he'd say if it did. But despite his desire to be nothing but a normal human again, he enjoyed keeping that hope alive. He could stand contact with one being from another realm, he figured.

He knew, having checked several months after the confrontation, that the monastery was completely gone. Only a rough dirt road with no signs or any other development remained. The chapel was still there; it had been built by humans and was a physical part of the world. The doors stood open and it looked deserted and dusty. The property was now owned by Cliffview, having been gifted by the Katzbalgers.

Outside the chapel there was a rocky spot in the ground. It looked to Lorcas like the very top of the new cornerstone. He didn't touch it. Grass was beginning to grow in from the sides. Eventually it would be all grown over. He had not been back, but he suspected that Tondra had been there a number of times, just keeping tabs.

Zumar was not at the graveyard today, either. Lorcas spent some time there anyway, the memories spiraling through his mind. He went off under the trees and sat on the stump of one of the firs Rook had knocked over, which had been trimmed off flat. As he sat there, he unscrewed the Staff and removed and unwrapped the Ring. He held it on his palm, feeling the weight. He knew now what it could summon. He felt nothing from it, nothing more than the coolness of the stone. But it was not an object connected to Rook; it was, and always had been, a Fell Ken object, a symbol of a Fell Ken Ally. There didn't need to a be a Rook in the world for it to function.

He didn't know whether or not his contact with Rook and the borderlands had affected his lifespan, but he knew one thing for sure: he did not want to be like Zumar. He wanted only a normal life, a normal span of time. Would there come a time, some day in the far future, when he wanted what the Earth Ally could give?

He re-wrapped the Ring and stowed it away. Even if that day did come, it was doubtful he'd have the power. He was not an Earth Entity, after all. He studied Zumar's crypt. Perhaps Zumar hadn't visited because Lorcas didn't really need him, and both of them were busy learning how to be themselves, free from Rook's coercion.

After a bit he hiked back down. As he reached the bottom of the hill his phone buzzed. He pulled it out quickly; he recognized the ring-tone he'd set.

"Hello, Terry," he said as he let himself into the house.

"Hey, it's supposed to be good weather for the next few days," she said. "I was thinking about how nice a UTV ride up the coast would be."

"Good idea. Lunch?"

"I'll bring stuff from Lafayette," she said. "No wine."

"No. Tomorrow?"

"Tomorrow," Terry confirmed.

Lorcas put the phone back in his pocket and sat down on the couch. He would need to pull the UTV out and clean things up, make sure it had gas and a charged battery. He hadn't used it for quite some time. But there was no rush. There was nothing he had to do right away. He could sit there for a while on the couch, doing nothing, enjoying the quiet in the neighborhood and the quiet in his mind. He could enjoy thinking about what the next day would bring, instead of dreading it. It would be nice weather, and a very nice tomorrow.

About the author:

K.A. Krisko is the author of epic/medieval and modern/contemporary fantasy fiction novels, literary short stories, and mysteries. She grew up living in national parks, where her father worked as a ranger. Her mother, a William and Mary graduate in English Literature, encouraged her to write, read, and recite poetry competitively. Her father took her on star walks and taught her about lightning. Later she became a ranger herself, and worked in parks from Texas to California. She now lives in northern Colorado where she enjoys walking, hiking, training and competing with her dogs, reading and writing, digital art, Tai Chi, and many other activities.

Kakrisko.com

Other works by K.A. Krisko:

Novels:

Raising Rook (Book One, Cornerstone Series)
The Delving (Book Two, Cornerstone Series)
The Wellspring (Book Three, Cornerstone Series)
Stolen (Book One, Stolen Trilogy)
Crypt of Souls (Book Two, Stolen Trilogy)
Hyphanden's Box (Book Three, Stolen Trilogy)
The Stolenworld Companion
AFTERThought: A Derange Mystery

Short Stories:

The Snow Deer and Other Stories (short story
anthology)
One Wet Dog (stand-alone short story, also in Happy
Endings II)
Almost A Dog (Happy Endings I)
The Possessed RV (American Blue: Real Stories by
Real Cops)
Mother Bear (Wisdom of Our Mothers)
Finding Mandel (Of Words and Water 2013)
The Name of the Dog (Of Words and Water 2013)
The Natural Seize (Of Words and Water 2014)

www.ingramcontent.com/pod-product-compliance
Lightning Source LLC
Chambersburg PA
CBHW020912200626
46814CB00001BA/294